Eddie Hest
VS.
Suburbia

A delightful romp
through the world of Eddie Hest.

Catherine Castoro

wunderWay publishing

ISBN: 979-8-9867142-5-7 (Paperback Book in Print)
Library of Congress Control Number: 2024905085
First Printing September 2024.
Find the author at: www.catherinecastoro.com
To order in bulk, contact Wunderway Publishing at: info@catherinecastoro.com
Cover design and illustration by Catherine Castoro.
Fiction/Commercial/Women's/Adult Coming Of Age
MPAA Rating: PG for Language
Barnes & Noble Paperback Identifier 979-8-9867142-9-5
ebook Identifier 979-8-9867142-6-4
Audiobook Identifier 979-8-9867142-7-1
Hardcover Identifier 979-8-9867142-8-8
Available in:
paperback • ebook • audio • hardcover

For my mother,

who made me realize life is too short to wait.

I miss you.

Eddie Hest
VS.
Suburbia

CATHERINE CASTORO

Seeking Participants for:

VIDEO
THERAPY
Study

Video Therapy is an innovative way to achieve better mental health. Participants control their counseling by taking an active role in therapy. Video Therapy focuses on the people in your life instead of the situations you are in. Participants take a survey at the end of the yearlong study. Why Video Therapy? Because sometimes you need someone to only listen.

- Yearlong Study.
- Innovative Therapy.
- Sessions are at the Psychology Research Lab on campus.
- Completely Confidential.
- Free. No cost to you.
- A licensed therapist will guide you to further help if needed.
- Stop by Lab for more information and to sign up.

Research Study Introduction:
What if the best advice you can get for yourself is from you? When someone is listening, it gives strength to our voice, even if the person listening doesn't respond. Hearing our life out loud gives us clarity to self-heal. When listening to what is going on in your life, you often hear the solution.

Method:
Participants:
Adults living near the University Research Lab who volunteer for the study.

Materials:
Subject room with window to therapist room, vintage-style video camera, blank VCR tapes, white board/marker, stool, microphone.

Procedure:
SUBJECT enters room with a list of people in their life and writes the first name on the board. **A therapist and vintage-style video camera are visible through the glass window in the adjoining room. Therapist doesn't speak to SUBJECT, but hears SUBJECT over the microphone.** Therapist turns camera on; a red light glows, indicating recording. Therapist's room darkens. **SUBJECT** freely talks about person on the board. Everything said is confidential. Sessions are scheduled at **SUBJECT**'s convenience, with a minimum weekly attendance. During the next and subsequent sessions, **SUBJECT** discusses the next person on the list. **SUBJECT** may not talk about the same person in consecutive sessions. At the end of the yearlong study, **SUBJECT** takes a survey on the therapy received. The videotape is theirs to keep or destroy. Lab keeps no record of what is on the tape.

Subject #57: Eddie - Session 1
Topic:

Grace

So, this is weird, alone in a room, spilling my guts to no one. No one I can see, anyway. But I know you're listening, and I'll assume you're watching through that window. Even though it's dark in there, I can see a tiny red light from the video camera. You do realize no one has a way to watch a VHS tape anymore, but the vintage aspect is cool. Okay. The rules were on the flyer. Write a name on the board. Sit on the stool. Speak into the microphone. And, no one else will hear this, right? First, my name is Edwina. People call me Eddie, and I'm fine monologuing, by the way. I like to hear my voice. It's just...it's nice to see some kind of reaction, so I know how far I can take things. So here's my warning. Some things I'm going to say will be shocking. At least I'm going to try. I refuse to be seen as mundane.

I'm starting with my daughter Grace. She's the reason I'm

here. She's special, has this curiosity to soak up as much of the world as she can. I like to think I've had some influence there. She's alive because it was *my* choice to have her, even though the circumstances weren't ideal. She's *my* purpose for living, and I want to be the best mom possible, which, I'm aware, is hard for *some* people to believe, those who judge as soon as they see me. This last thing is where I'm having some difficulty. I mean I like drama, but this is too much. Our happy little world suddenly exploded, and for the first time, I don't know what to do.

Where to begin? We live just north of the university, and we're happy here. I'm in the dining room, sewing at my worktable when Grace comes home and says, "It was outside, leaning on the wall next to the door. Everyone got one." This was three days ago. She's holding a large envelope the color of caution. It can't be good news. She must know it, too. She's gone pale.

I'm a fabric artisan, fancy name for a seamstress, and was making curtains for a new client when she came in. They're a mucky blah-tone. Who chooses brown when there are marvelous colors like teal and magenta? Or a calming purple, like my hair. I should have recognized the muck to be an omen. The death knell to life as we know it presents itself as a bright yellow envelope. I blame the ugly curtains.

My friend Arjun peeks in right after, and says, "Did you hear?" His face is full distraught. I'm not sure why, but I'm suddenly anxious, and I flee the muck at my machine. Grace hands me the envelope and waits, frozen. I open it, but can't focus, so I pretend to read the top page of the small stack of paper while Arjun makes everything clear. "They're selling the building." And just like that, my mind is vacant, and so is our future.

⌘

So why should this matter? We move a lot. Always have. This happens when you're renting. Grace is on her fifth home, and next fall she'll be in fourth grade. So if you do the math, we move about once every couple of years. People question if this is good for Grace, but she transitions well, and all that moving has taught her how to make friends quickly, and that's good. Right? So, why is this time different? Because it's insulting. We're not wanted. It's being forced upon us. And it's not my choice.

I shouldn't take it so personally, but an eviction is not the image I have for myself as a good mother. I've never been kicked out of anything unless I wanted out and did something out of spite. I don't like Grace to see me as the target. It sucks because we finally found a place that's decent, one where we fit in. Arjun's singsong accent softens the blow, reminding me to force several lengthy exhales. So, I'm focusing on the tune of his voice instead of what he says. Maybe I don't want to register the words. Grace looks from Arjun back to me. Her usual smile is gone, and she's still pasty. She knows what the letter means, even though it takes me a few seconds. We're losing our home. We have to move again. And mostly, she probably thinks I'm a failure as a mother.

⌘

Our complex is a diverse mix of older students and ex-student dropouts. Plus some eclectics (me and Arjun), and a couple other weirdos I won't mention. I'm trying to be nice. Grace and I get along with everyone, almost everyone. She's very outgoing, and she's thriving here. There's sixteen apartments, and we all take care of each other.

Whenever Arjun is cooking, Grace yells, "Arjun is in the Yard." Sounds like a prison term, and that would be almost accurate because there isn't much to the Yard. It's a common area with a lot of concrete and patches of grass in the dirt. But in the middle of this nothing is a barbecue grill, erecting like a monolith. Arjun is from India, and his cooking is phenomenal. Everyone congregates there when Arjun is cooking.

"Wait," he tells Grace, and she lingers, watching with wide eyes, her curls hanging in her face. He performs his own little ceremony, spreads a towel before placing his spice case on the nearby picnic table. He carefully opens the lid, and quietly stands, looking at his spices. I'm not sure if he's taking inventory or saying a silent prayer. Maybe he thinks of his home? The case is old, like it was his grandmother's or something.

"Okay, get the garam masala," he tells her. The jars aren't labeled, but she knows which one to grab, even though the colors are almost identical.

When I ask her how she tells them apart, she says, "The texture is different. Some powders are more clumpy and some are balls or look like brown rice." I've asked him where to get the spices, but he says you can't buy them here, and he'll mix some for me. I'm still waiting. Maybe he knows I couldn't pull off a proper Indian meal with any amount of spice, and he's trying to save me, and Grace, from myself.

Later, we usually move indoors, taking turns on whose apartment, depending. We're usually up pretty late, and my Grace is right there talking with us. She sometimes has a hard time getting up for school the next morning, but she's fine. Don't get judgmental on me. She's the only kid in the complex, and gives us the kids' point of view on things, one with no filters. It's refreshing. It's good for her to be around different types of people, different lifestyles. You know, to see that there are different ways to live. "Dare to be different" is my motto. Something Granny taught me, but it's like society is yelling at me to conform. Be the mom they want me to be instead of the one I want. I want Grace to recognize that with everything, there is a choice. Except for us to stay in our apartment.

Anyway, that evening, after we get the eviction notice, the other tenants gather in my apartment and discuss what we're going to do. Everyone but Beth, which is fine with me. She kind of reminds me of my ex in the way she doesn't look you in the eyes. *I know what she's hiding.* Grace is in her usual place on the arm of our old couch, listening. No one has any answers. When there's talk of trying to fight it, I see hope in her eyes.

Darrel, the ex-law student, says, "Nope. We don't have a case to stand on. I checked. It's written in our contracts." The text about what would happen if the owner sells the building or if it's demolished is highlighted in the copy of the contract that comes with the eviction letter. They only have to give us thirty days. Seems the lawyers thought of everything. I see Grace contemplating Darrel's words, probably picturing us standing on our suitcases among boxes of belongings, the both of us defiantly claiming our ground.

Someone else suggests we rent a house together. I don't remember who. My book reading buddy Daria says, "I'm going to move to the other side of town, closer to my new job," which is sad because she always brings cake. She asked me once if it was hard on Grace being the only kid in our little village of adults, which I thought was odd. Daria isn't as sad that we're all splitting up. She doesn't seem to need these people as much as I do, as much as Grace does. Grace keeps looking at me for answers, but I got nothing.

I can't cook, so I order pizza for everyone, thinking this helps the situation. Grace doesn't eat, even though I get her favorite—pepperoni and pineapple. The crisis doesn't affect my appetite. I devour enough for the both of us. She has a piece of Daria's cake, though. Mark, who has a business degree but works as a bartender, brings beer, and I open a couple bottles of wine I have in the cupboard. A good mother's supposed to make things right, and all I can do is pick up the paper plates as people finish eating. And eat cake. A few stragglers stay late into the night. Grace stays up to hear every word we say.

After they leave, she climbs in my bed, and I hold her. I'm trying to invade her thoughts with some sort of osmosis. For the first time, I don't want to move Grace again. I don't want to put her in another new school. Moving no longer feels good. It might be a repeat of the last place, so the timing of this therapy study couldn't have been more perfect. And it's great that the research lab is so close to my apartment. Anyway, I've got one month to figure this out, and it shouldn't be this hard. Granny always said I have a superpower, but never mind that. Anyway, I need some help, so I hope this works. It has to.

Subject #57: Eddie - Session 2
Topic:

the Landlord

So when I left yesterday, the student at reception said I can come as often as I want, but at least once a week for the study. I'm back so soon because something happened since I was here that makes me question my competence as a mother, and I'm kind of freaking out. It's a comment Augustin made, the instigator of my current drama, so I'll talk about him. Augustin is the landlord, Lord of the Land. He's also the handyman, the electrician, the plumber, groundskeeper, and the entire office staff. During the next couple of days after he gives the eviction notice, he stops by everyone's apartment to check how we're taking the news. It's probably a good idea he informs us first before presenting himself. It gives the shock time to settle.

Yesterday, after the session, there's a knock at my door. When I open it, Augustin's standing there looking very sheepish.

and I say, "Augustin, it's so sad you're selling the building." I'm as nice as I can be to keep our relationship positive. It's never good to fight with your landlord.

"No. This is good," he says with his gruff voice, and he puts emphasis on the *d*, adding a hint of a *t* at the end of his last word. He's this wide man with large hands and retains much of his accent, although he's been living in the Detroit area for well over twenty years. When we moved in, he told me he was originally from Czechoslovakia, near the Polish border. His broad face and shiny head make his intense eyebrows flare. He made me nervous when we met. But since, I recognize him to be one of the nicest men I've ever known.

Then, he says, "To maintain this building is too much work. I am too old. I will go live in country three hours north. Maybe I have goats." He also switches out the *g* for a *k* on any *ing* word. I listen for that too. He looks tired. He's getting on in years, but he has always done an excellent job of keeping the old building running and looking somewhat presentable. Not luxurious, but orderly. To him, the building is a reflection of himself. No one wants the old building. It's the land that's desirable. They'll tear down our homes and new life will begin. "New owners will build bigger, more expensive. It will cost too much to live here," he says. Augustin's life will become simpler, closer to nature, and for him, this is good. (Or is it goot?)

"You must do what is in contract," he says to me. It's strange. Even though the building will become a pile of rubble, he wants each tenant to agree to the terms of their contract, which means leaving the place exactly how it was when we moved in, if we want to get our full deposit back. Augustin is a stickler for the rules. He's stern when he says, "They will deport me," fearing deportation from the tiniest infringement, even if he isn't breaking any law. He's been a citizen for years now, so I don't think that's even possible. I have to admire that in a person, even though in this instance, I can't see the logic behind it. But I'll do it. It's in the contract.

I ask him, "Will you do a quick walk-through with me and point out what I need to do to get my full refund?" I need the money. All the money, especially if I have to put a deposit on a new place. He shows me things that need to be cleaned, baseboards and tub grout. We get to Grace's room, and it's odd to see her personal space through the eyes of a man who undeniably believes there is a right and a wrong way to do anything. I watch him look at her single mattress on the floor. He's too nice to say anything. The bed, or mattress, isn't made. That isn't something we do. I'm not a drill sergeant.

For some reason, I'm a little embarrassed about the mattress on the floor thing, and say, "She had a bed, but it broke when we were moving out of the last apartment. We threw it in the dumpster," Then, he eyes the shelf I made from some old apple crates. I like those. Grace and I painted them. She picked the color, a bright fuchsia. Her clothes and stuffed animals are on these. She also has a couple of horse posters taped on her wall, so it's not like the room is bare. I think it reflects her. She likes animals. I'm proud we've done so well with the little we have.

"This move is good for Grace," he tells me. There's that *t* again where the *d* should be. "She should be in proper home with children to play. In neighborhood. A place to ride her bike. You can be normal parent."

And it's like, did I hear him right? Oh my God! Maybe he isn't so nice. I'm standing, probably with my mouth open, unable to move, and his words echo through my brain, then slap me in the face. It isn't the ideal room for a kid, but I'm doing my best. I mean, does it make a difference if a mattress is one foot off the ground? All I can think of is that one of the nicest men I've ever known has just insulted me, and I'm getting emotional. He's just shattered the good-mom image I had for myself. I'm doing my best to control my sass, but it's *really* difficult. I don't want to alienate myself from him before I get my deposit back. I tell myself he didn't mean it the way it came out, with the language barrier and all. But they say the truth can be harsh. Whoever the fuck *they* are.

Now, I'm doubting myself as a mother, and he's just standing there like he's just complimented me or something. In my mind, I proclaim I'm the cool mom. Right? Grace's friends like to hang out at our house. My face gets hot. It's like he's been talking to my cousins.

I hold myself together and lead him back to the living room, and he says, "There is dent in sheet rock." That happened when I was reconfiguring my worktable. Those curtains were extra large and heavily pleated, and I needed more space. I liked the fabric on those, Tiffany blue with an ivory damask.

"I don't know how to fix that, but I'll try to hire someone," I tell him, my voice a higher pitch than usual. I can't tell if he picks up on this or not.

Then he nods, quick and sharp, saying, "I will help you fix." I'm glad for the offer, and quickly accept, even though fixing it up to tear it down is silly. His offer eases the tension, so I know his "normal parent" comment was with good intention. He probably doesn't realize it was inappropriate.

I make a pot of herbal tea, and we stand, leaning against the counter that separates the kitchen from the living area. He tells me about his future goats, showing me a brochure of a goat farm he pulls from his pocket. It seems like quite the endeavor. "I won't keep so many," he says. I think the animals will give him a purpose to get up in the morning, like Grace is mine. Then he says, "My wife will make cheese."

I bob my head as I sip, trying to hide the fact that I didn't know he had a wife. I can't ask about her. I don't know if she's living here with him or someplace else and plans to join him. It's something I should know, and me asking will let him know I don't.

"Grace would love a place like this. I would too," I say, trying to make him feel good about his plans. But I have to live where the work is. Selling on the internet isn't for me. Color is never accurate when you're looking at a computer screen. It would mean a lot of returns, and a lot of shipping costs. Plus, I'm not computer savvy. I only have a little notebook computer. And anyway, I prefer dealing with people face to face. One of the ways I'm old school.

"You can visit," Augustin says.

"We will," I say. "Grace would love to see your goats."

His face becomes sad, and he says, "I will miss everyone. I will miss Arjun's cooking."

Me too. I feel like someone's died.

Then he asks, "Where will you go?"

My mind is blank. I only know what I don't want to do, which is move again. I'm almost afraid to decide because of his normal-parent comment. I'll likely get it wrong, but I have to decide quickly. Before I can answer, Dylan walks by. (The door is open; I leave it that way when it's nice outside.) Augustin calls and gets his attention.

"Thanks for the tea," he says and goes with Dylan, so I never answer his question. I see a chapter of my life walking away, slipping away. A good mom should take some sort of action, but I don't know what to do. That's why I'm here. I need answers. Quick.

Subject #57: Eddie - Session 3
Topic:

Me

Back again already. I walked here today, trying to think about my options. It took me about ten minutes. To walk, not the options bit. It'd be great if that's all it took. I'm a little sweaty, so it's good I'm alone. Thanks for having the AC cranked, by the way, and I'm glad you've put that small table in here so I don't have to put my purse on the floor.

Anyway, I know I'm supposed to be looking for a new place to live, but I can't shake the landlord's comment, even though he tried to make up for it by being so nice. *Now you can be normal parent.* I've been repeating it in my head using his accent. It's harsh. I know I'm not the normal parent type, but I thought I was one better. I wonder how many other people think this about me. Is this what Grace wants? For me to be normal? That's why I'm the topic for today.

It's important I be fabulous in the eyes of my daughter. A good mom equals a daughter who loves you. Right? That's the only thing that matters. A bad mom, or even a boring one, leads a daughter to look elsewhere. Not for a mom, but for life lessons. That's what I did.

I've got jelly-brain trying to understand why Augustin thinks I'm not a normal parent. My thoughts are on this when I should be focusing on moving in less than a month, with nowhere to go. Is it my tattoos? My black combat boots? It can't be my clothes. I imagine women where he's from wearing skirts long and draped like mine, but maybe without so much skin peeking through. They're comfy. And when it's hot, I can bunch up my skirt up and get air on my legs. Maybe it's the tanks? I know they're a little stretched out, but I like not having the restriction of sleeves. And my bra straps shouldn't surprise anyone. Is that even offensive anymore? At least I'm wearing one, keeping the girls contained.

Maybe where he's from only men get tattoos. I got my first tat on my back shoulder when I was in high school. It's a butterfly. The typical first girl tattoo and placement. I was alone when I got it. No peer pressure. But it hurt like hell. Like a thousand bee stings all in succession for nearly two hours. So, why do I keep getting them? Well, when I went to school the next day, wearing a tank top to show it off, everyone suddenly deemed me cool, even though it was still all red and puffy. It was an easy thing to do to change everyone's mind about me. No one would mess with me. I hid it from my mom, but she was cool when she found out. "I wish you would have told me," was all she said.

From that first tat, the artistry continues down my arms. Patterns. And, colors. It's taken me over ten years to get to this point. It's not a full sleeve, but I'm getting there. I had to go back for several sessions with some of them. I've also got several on my legs, but my favorite is the one on the back edge of my ear. No one has a tattoo there. I like them because it's like I'm wearing a beautiful fabric. I've been sewing most of my life, making my own clothes and now clothes for Grace, so it's like my own personalized print seared into my skin, like permanent jewelry.

Although, maybe it's not an appearance thing. I hope Augustin isn't referring to the way I'm raising Grace, in an apartment surrounded by adults, talking about adult things. I thought that was a good choice. It didn't work out when we were at the apartment with kids her age. And I just can't see myself living in the suburbs and driving a minivan. That's my cousins, Tiffany and Stephanie. They both have toddlers now, and slid effortlessly into this lifestyle. I'd be so miserable and bored. I'm sure that would reflect in my parenting.

Is that what a normal parent does? Make themselves miserable for the sake of their kid? Grace would be so sheltered in this type of environment. She wouldn't learn many of the lessons I'm trying to teach her. Primarily that every place is different, and different is good.

⌘

Okay. Off track. Time to focus on the dilemma at hand. Some of the other tenants are renting a house two blocks over. It used to be a frat house. I know exactly the house my friend Dylan's talking about. The houses are older in this neighborhood (maybe Victorian, but I don't know architecture) and close together. It looks as if there was a good-size yard in the front before they turned it into parking. It's got a great porch.

Dylan stops by all excited and says, "There's eight bedrooms, each with their own en suite bath!" He makes it sound fancy, but he then says the carpet smells from the toilets bubbling over too many times. Not a good salesman. And who puts carpeting in the bathroom? Even my roach apartment had linoleum. But, the owner said we could replace the carpeting, on our own dime, of course. I'm considering.

Arjun is right behind him. "I'm taking one room, and there's only one left, so you need to decide quickly." They'd gone together to view the property, taking a couple more people who live here. I was too busy working to go. And I didn't want to jump into something I'm unsure of, which is what I usually do.

"Why are there so many rooms suddenly available? What's wrong with the place, besides the smelly carpet?" I ask. I'm trying to ask questions a normal parent would ask.

"It's the end of the summer session," says Dylan. I understand *his* desire to live among college-age girls. I think it'd be interesting to be surrounded by a liberal outlook on life.

"You should take a room too," Arjun tells me, nodding with his eyes wide, trying to persuade me. When he looks at me like this, he's got a little boy quality to him that makes me laugh. "You'll be near my cooking." He makes an excellent point, but I know the real reason he wants me there.

"You're going to miss me," I tell him, and he blushes, just a little, but I'll miss him too. "I'm considering," I say. He looks satisfied with my answer. I start listing pros and cons in my head. The rent at the frat house would be cheaper, and Grace wouldn't have to change schools, so that's good. But, there isn't space for me to sew, and I need to work. I could try to get my old job back at the fabric store, the one I'd worked at after quitting college. It's a bit of a drive from here. I'd chosen that job for the discounts.

⌘

I've had a passion for sewing since my seventh-grade home economics class. Sewing, to me, is calming. The hum of the sewing needle repeatedly rising, then sinking down beneath the fabric like a bird diving in a great body of water for fish, weaving its thread and uniting two individual pieces together. It's like I'm in another world. Maybe that's what the tattoo artist feels.

It wouldn't be so bad working there again. My boss Suzanne and I always got on. She's funny. She'd get so concerned if a customer came in seeking advice about a stitching gone rogue. On went the glasses she keeps on a chain around her neck. I know it sounds cliché, like a typical old lady, but she's cool, and she changes the chain out like an accessory. She's not as old as my mother, either. The customers appreciate her, and she's such a good influence on me.

After Grace was born, I enrolled her in the daycare near the store so she'd be near me, and I kept her there when I moved back in with Mom. It wouldn't be fair to make Mom babysit every day while I worked. I'd pop over to see Grace whenever they had something going on for the parents, like the Fourth of July parade. Suzanne was great about it.

The kids decorate their bicycles or Big Wheels, then ride them back and forth in the parking lot. It was a hoot. But this probably comes across as boring. People don't enjoy hearing about other people's kids, no matter how adorable they are. I felt stupid because watching her ride her bike made me cry, which sounds like I'm overly sensitive, but that's not the case. But watching Grace is like a bubbling up of pride and love that I can't contain, kind of like Dylan's frat house toilets. No, that's a horrible comparison. Forget I said that. I'm pretty sure I hide the tears well. No one looks at me weirdly, like they notice. But they never talk to me anyway. I've never made any friends with the moms at her daycare.

Back then, the money I make at the fabric store barely pays for the daycare, but because I'm at Mom's, I manage to save. Fast forward to when Grace starts kindergarten. I quit the fabric store and start my own business, so I'm around the house if she needs me. Her school is near Mom's now. I'd worked at the store long enough to have a good rapport with the clients. So at Mom's, I make curtains, pillows, bedspreads, do some alterations, and a few dresses. Not everyone knows how to sew, and working from home, even at Mom's when there isn't much room, ends up being the perfect solution.

Suzanne is totally cool about me going out on my own. She even sends me clients and lets me put some things I make in her store. I also have an ad in her weekly newsletter. She lets me place it for free. Although working at Mom's is a good thing, I don't have my own work space. She'd never say anything to me directly, but I see it in her eyes. If she has a friend over, or even a repairman, my fabric mess is everywhere, and she's uncomfortable. She always keeps a tidy house. That's who she is. A homemaker. This space is Mom's, and I know the situation isn't fair to her. I realize I need my own place.

⌘

But this happened years ago and none of this helps me get out of my looming eviction situation. Does it? If I take the frat house room, it might be hard to run a business there. I picture my sewing stuff all over the house like it was at Mom's. I guess I should work at the store again. It's in a strip mall, but it's a pretty large store. The hours would be long, and I'd have to work more because the hourly wage isn't as good. But, I don't know if I have any other option.

Also, Grace and I would have to live in a one-room. What would I do with all my stuff? I like my setup now. Arjun put up a wall of shelves for me. He's pretty handy even when he isn't in the kitchen, only with the shelves, he doesn't want to get his button-down dirty, so he takes it off, folds it, and put it on the arm of the sofa. He's skinny, but in good shape, so this whole shirtless man, wearing trousers, while using manly tools scenario is fun to watch. He'd be a great catch if he was more my type. I tend to gravitate toward men who are disasters, which is why I rarely date. I'm not his type either; he likes men.

The shelves are perfect for storing my bolts of material. To me, it's like an art installation. In the empty shelf space, I display scrapbooks Grace and I made. I like looking at them, looking at their spines and textured covers. The scrapbooks are another bond that holds us together. We're both great storytellers and like a bit of drama. I was into drama in high school.

Anyway, I knew after a couple of months of living here that this place was good for us. But, good things never last for me. And I don't want a repeat of our last apartment, the roach apartment, which I signed on a whim, which may have been an example of irresponsible parenting, something I don't want to repeat with Dylan's frat house. Grace and I don't talk about my poor decisions.

Since living here I've started doing upholstery which pays well. It's pretty physical, turning furniture over and around, hammering tacks and forcing staples into soft wood. Not to mention getting it up to the second floor. I get Dylan or Arjun to help if the pieces are too big for me to handle by myself. It's satisfying seeing something worn come to life. I'd hate to give that up. Maybe the commune house has a garage I could work from? I'll check with Dylan. I should tell him I'll take the room before someone else does.

God, though! What would my ex's lawyers say about Grace and me sharing a room in a house with a bunch of other adults? They've started calling me out of the blue. They're asking questions, hinting that his parents want custody. I guess they don't think I'm a normal parent either, but there's no way that's happening. Ugh. Maybe the commune house is a bad idea. I'm not sure these sessions are helping. I can't figure out what to do and now I've got like three weeks. I'm going to call my friend Abby. I need someone to tell me what to do. Immediately.

Subject #57: Eddie - Session 4
Topic:

Abby

I'll bring you up to date. I call Abby after the session yesterday. She's my lifelong friend who now lives in London. I use my computer, so it's free. Here's how it went. It's in the afternoon, my time, evening for her, and she answers right away. "Dee." She calls me Dee. She's the only one who calls me this. Eddie is her cousin's name, and she doesn't like him. What is it with cousins?

"It's time you buy a place of your own so Grace can live somewhere long term," she says, coming straight to the point after my long monologue about the whole apartment eviction thing. I like that she listens. Few people do. I'm searching for apartments while on Skype talking to her. But, I've got to be careful. I've hung up on her by mistake more than once.

"Believe me," she says. "I've moved around a lot growing up, and I always envied you for staying in one place. You had a history there, and I always knew where you were." Funny. I was jealous of Abby because I never knew where she'd be next.

But now that I'm an adult, I don't stay in one place. Maybe I thought I was giving Grace the same experiences Abby had. I'm just realizing they're very different. I'm not taking Grace to the same kind of magical places Abby experienced. I feel pretty silly thinking I was.

Abby and I met in fourth grade when she moved into the school district. I never had a best friend before her. Everyone I wanted to be friends with didn't return the favor, and the girls who were kind to me, I ignored. I feel bad about that now. Sorry.

Abby stood out when she came to our school. Not that she's black, but because she's beautiful and confident. Worldly. Everyone wanted to be her friend. There's something about confidence that draws people in. She chose me as her BFF because she said I was fun and not afraid to do anything. She moved in after the year had started, so she stood out as new.

Here's how we met. I'd fallen asleep the night before while doing my homework, so I didn't finish. I'm in class, and it's hard to pay attention. I'm thinking of the TV show I'd been watching at the time I dozed off mid-sentence, creating a squiggly line across the page of what was due the next day. It was *The Monkees*. It's an old show. When you think about that show, you have to think of the theme song. So, the teacher sees me daydreaming and calls on me. I only halfway hear her question.

I respond by singing, "I get the funniest looks from everyone we meet." It just comes out, sort of reflex-like. The kids laugh, and I get sent to the principal's office. It was an honest mistake, like when a kid calls a teacher Mom. A far cry from the shy kid who talked into her armpit, I know, but since those armpit days, I learned that a bit of sass gets attention. If you're brave enough to sass a teacher, kids don't mess with you as much. Since I didn't expect to blurt this out, and was kind of embarrassed, I had to reinforce this bold choice by continuing the song as I left the room and walked down the hall.

The next day in class, Abby sits next to me and says, "I like *The Monkees* too. Want to hang out after school?" It was like, yes! Someone who I wanted as a friend wants to be my friend too. And this is before I started dying my hair. I guess she could see my superpower. Some people can see things in others that other people can't, and Abby saw me the way I wanted to see myself. That's like a superpower, too.

Granny died a year after I met Abby. I don't think I would have survived losing her without Abby. It was the hardest thing I'd ever gone through. Everything was different. I felt lost. I didn't know who I was without my Gran. Abby didn't have to say much, just sat with me and listened, then held me when I cried. I cried a lot. An incredible sadness fell over me; it was suffocating. It took a long time to climb out of it. Sometimes I think I'm still climbing.

Even though our lives eventually took us on different paths, Abby and I always kept in touch and remain the best of friends. She moved away, went to college, and now has a high-paying corporate job where she travels the world. I stayed home in

Beeville, went to community college, got bored, dropped out, got pregnant, got married, got divorced... and here we are.

We're different, Abby and me. She's focused on the end goal and I'm easygoing, ready to live in the moment, or at least I used to be. I'm not sure since the eviction. She says her job is stressful, which makes her put up a barrier. As an adult, people think she's cold and unfeeling. She's not. She just gets straight to the point. I'm relaxed and open, and Abby says I ground her, remind her of what's important in the world. She helps me too. She's levelheaded, and when things get a little too hairy, she gives me perspective, so we're good for each other. I think in the end, even with the married bit, I fared better. I have Grace.

Abby advised me not to marry my ex, but supported me when I did. I should have listened. Now and then, this mistake resurfaces to haunt me, in more ways than one, including every time I bring Grace to any kind of family function. I'm positive that either Tiffany or Stephanie have discovered my secret. Whenever I'm with the Cs, I have to prepare myself. For some reason, I can't bring my sass to a family gathering. I revert to the kid who talks into her armpit, and know they're waiting to bully me again. Why am I such a threat to them that even as adults, they feel the need to tease?

When Abby moved away after the seventh grade, my world fell apart again, almost as bad as Gran dying. Middle school is hard enough for a kid. You're not quite grown up, but not a child either, and it's difficult to know from day to day exactly where you fit in. When Abby's by my side, I'm confident. So with her suddenly gone, my insecurities multiply like a zillion times. I found myself alone, wandering the corridors. I probably looked creepy. It was just me and her for so long, I didn't want another friend to replace her; no one could. So I became a loner, and later, when I was in high school, started hanging around with what my mother calls questionable people. But I guess that's another topic.

Anyway, I always looked up to Abby. Still do. Even as a kid, she knew about things when the other kids had no clue. I was the hometown girl pretending to be like her. I fooled a lot of people because we were always together. Here's how it worked: she'd point us in a direction and I made that direction fun. Like when I helped her get extra credit in one of her classes by collecting items to donate to the women's shelter. I made a list of the cutest boys in our grade, plus the seventh and eighth graders, and we only went to their houses to ask for donations.

All the moms were into our cause, so they were happy to invite us in while they gathered things. If the boys weren't there, we'd make up some excuse to come back later, then got them involved when we did. Abby's good at convincing people to help, to where they can't say no, even the older boys. That's why everyone loves Abby; she earns their love. She was hesitant at first, but she was all in after the first house, when she saw how well it worked. If we're helping people, why can't we get a little somethin' something for ourselves, right? And we did. We both got several boyfriends out of it. Not at once. Although in sixth grade, we didn't do anything. A kiss here and there. It was more bragging rights than anything else, and junior high relationships only last only a couple of weeks, anyway. Then we'd start looking at the next boy. That's when boys were important to us. They're not so much anymore.

After she moved, I'd ask her advice on just about everything during our weekly phone call: what classes to take, who my next boyfriend should be, suggestions on my science project. She wasn't thrilled when I told her of the friends I'd made without her, so I didn't listen to everything she said. I'm still my own person. It's just nice to hear a different viewpoint. You know, checks and balances? I give her advice as well. She rarely follows it, either.

During high school, Abby's in New York City; a private prep school, so her grades are more than acceptable for college. Then, she goes to a university somewhere near Boston. At this time, we talk sparingly because she's succeeding while I'm dropping out, so I feel funny letting her know my actual situation. The truth is, I have a hard time focusing. I'm into my ex, and at the time, feel pretty bad about myself. I don't want her to be disappointed in me, so I keep contact to a minimum.

⌘

She came to visit last year. We'd been living in Augustin's apartments for about eight months. I could tell she thought I was in a good place because she didn't try to convince me to do something else. Remember, she's good at that. My work was going well. She liked my friends, and Grace was happy in school. All good.

She flirted with Dylan the entire time, and I tell her, "Go for it." Dylan's kind of a playboy himself. His confidence makes him more attractive than he is. Grace did her best to wait up for her while they were at his place, very late.

Later, I tell Dylan to forget about Abby, that she's too good for him, knowing full well he probably already had. Abby says she's glad she came. I'm happy she's got me to look after her. Otherwise, she'd be all work and no play, and we don't want her to be an ax-flailing Jack Nicholson. No, Abby would never do that. She's the type to get revenge in a more organized, professional manner. Not that she'd ever want to get revenge on people. She's not like that either. She's perfect.

⌘

So anyway, I'm mentioning the background on Abby so you understand why I need to call her. Abby doesn't bat an eye after listening to me whine about my current problem, and starts giving advice right away, like she's been thinking about it for a long time, which is what I would do. Some people call it procrastination. "Your own house means you don't have to put up with any more landlords," she says after I'm done explaining.

She didn't meet Augustin when she was here. He was away, a death in the family. She wouldn't say this if she knew him. She doesn't like the short notice he gave, after selling the property without any of us knowing. But I think he did it this way so we wouldn't worry in case the deal fell through. "Besides," she says.

"You're throwing your money away on rent. Get a place with a yard. You could have your own garden, and Grace can get a dog. You know she's always wanted one."

"We'll call the dog Abby," I tell her. She thinks I'm kidding. I google dogs with wild, dark curly hair. My free phone on the computer is voice only, so I can't see her. The dog search replaces the apartment search on my screen. I'm happy she can't see me. I'm not at my best. Anyway, the dog would also need to have gigantic eyes and be one that likes to travel. But, with my luck, it'd be always running away.

"And with a house, Dee, you'd have your own space, for your sewing and upholstery. You're so good. It's going to be great." Lovely Abby, always my cheerleader. I actually hadn't thought of this. I was just going to do what I've always done by renting. But, it hasn't worked out well for me, so why do I keep putting myself in the same situation? It's the definition of insanity, right? Hence the therapy. But, a house feels unattainable, like a dream so far away the image isn't even clear.

"It sounds like you want me to move back to the suburbs," I say. "I've been trying to escape them ever since I was a little girl."

She tells me, "It's so important Grace gets a good education, and that may be the best place to get one. Find a place with the best schools, even if Grace has to move one more time. If you find the right place, it will be the last time you move." This makes sense. I stayed in one place growing up and could have gotten a good education if I applied myself.

Things make perfect sense coming from Abby. And since it's

coming from her, I picture a cute little bungalow somewhere in a suburb that's very different than the suburbs where my cousins live. The suburbs of Detroit seem to go on forever, so there has to be more than one type, right? Grace and I could decorate it, make it ours. It could have a porch even better than Dylan's frat house. I'd make all the curtains, and it'd be nice to have a garden. Maybe we'd get that dog. I'm actually excited just thinking about it. Then reality hits me hard.

"I might be able to swing the monthly payments if they were low," I say. "But I don't have any money for a down payment. No one gives a loan without a down payment. Especially to me." In my mind, I'm back to the one room in Dylan's commune. It's cramped. It smells like poo. Grace has no space of her own. She doesn't want to invite friends over. There's no place for a sleepover. Meanwhile, I'm working at the fabric store, which is okay, but I picture Grace coming home from her same school, and I'm at work. So, she comes home to an empty house filled with other people's things, some of them strangers. She doesn't look happy. Her face is a repeat of when we were in the roach apartment. There's probably roaches at Dylan's place, too. For some reason, *this* image is perfectly clear. It's incredibly dreary, and no amount of Febreze will spray it away.

"Ask your mom for a loan, Dee," she says. "She always wants to help you, but you never let her." She's right. But, I hate asking for help, especially after Mom helped so much when Grace was a baby. How can I be an independent adult if I'm constantly running back to Mommy? Abby seems to know my "I got this" mantra, even though I've never specifically told her. Still, I don't want to be the loser adult who can't take care of herself, but somehow that's exactly where I find myself. I just hope Grace doesn't see it.

"I don't know," I say, then Abby reminds me of all the times my mother was there for us when we were young. But, I'm just realizing now that Mom waits for me to ask her, otherwise it's like she feels she's intruding. Asking is the hard part. Something I've never been good at. It makes me feel I'm incapable or admitting defeat. I'm suddenly that weak little kid in the backyard before Granny told me about my superpower. Abby then says, "With a house, you can give Grace the great childhood we had. The four years I lived in Beeville were my favorite."

I love that she says this. They were my favorite too. But somehow I never equated fond memories with my house, only with her. We'd have sleepovers almost every weekend and stay up all night talking or watching old TV shows. That's how I know about the talking horse. And *Star Trek*. And *The Monkees*.

I know Grace deserves a better childhood than I had. Isn't that how it's supposed to work? And by that I mean her focus should be on herself and school rather than pining after some boy. Abby and I grew up always in search of a prince to make us whole, like the boys on the list I made. But that was what little girls did back then, and it's funny that neither of us has a man now. Abby realized quickly that this prince image wasn't attainable. Or even desirable. She never married. It took me longer to reach this revelation, after a huge mistake with my ex. That's why it's so important for Grace to be independent. She doesn't need her other half. She is whole enough all by herself.

⌘

So, I'm torn, reluctant to make a decision about my homeless dilemma, but Abby gives me courage to approach my mother. We rehearse what I'm going to say, and before we hang up, we go over step by step what my plan will be. Then I tell her I love her.

"I love you back," she says. But I love her more. And I love that I have some sort of plan. I'll let you know what happens.

Subject #57: Eddie - Session 5
Topic:

Mom

I skipped yesterday, so I've got tons to tell. I'm excited to report that I have it all figured out. Here's what happened. I call Mom, aka *June Cleaver*, when I'm home from last session, which by the way, gave me confidence just by talking about my plan. Maybe this is working? Anyway, Mom's actually excited I'm asking her for money. Who does that? It's just like Abby says, Mom wants to help. She approves a healthy down payment on one condition: I come and get the boxes I've been storing at her house. I agree. I've been meaning to do that anyway, for years. They're full of special things I could never throw away.

"I'll pay you back as soon as I can," I tell her.

"When you're ready," she says. Dad provided for her handsomely when he passed a couple of years ago, which is why she's able to help. He died when Grace and I had been living at a fancy place for a couple of months. I think if we'd lived at the roach motel, I might have moved back in with her. But by the time we moved from the fancy apartment, she was happy by herself, finally doing things for herself. Besides, I would have been going backward. That wouldn't have been good for me or Grace.

Abby and I think she'll want to house shop with me, to make sure I make a good decision, and I prepare myself to be firm on where I want to live. But she says, "You and Grace decide. You're the ones who will have to live there. I trust you." And I'm thinking, wow. She must see how focused I am on Grace, and I know she's happy my ex is out of our lives. She doesn't know about his parents' lawyers calling.

"I want to look near where we now live, so Grace won't have to change schools," I say, and she likes the idea. "Abby suggests we look where the schools are the best, since the new house will be long term." Grace's current elementary school is good. Although I'm not so sure about the junior high. I don't tell Mom that when driving by, I've seen police cars there more than once, or that both the junior high and high school are a bit run-down.

"Abby's a smart woman. I've always liked her," Mom says. I agree.

After I hang up, I'm tempted to drive directly to her house and hug her. It's a lot of money and I couldn't do this without it, without her. But Grace will be home from school soon, so I can't leave. Maybe we'll surprise Mom this weekend? I feel like my world just got lighter, like the force of gravity is more moon-like, and I'm bouncing. So after I hang up, I do my happy dance, something close to interpretive. I'm swirling my skirt and flailing my arms, imagining Grace and me in our own home, one where I get to decide when or if we have to leave. One where I call the shots. One where I'm better than a normal parent. But then I knock over my coffee and it spills on the curtains I'm working on. I shout the f-word.

Don't worry, Grace isn't home. Luckily, the coffee only gets the edge of the material, and I've become very good at getting rid of stains. As I'm sopping it up, I'm happy. I finally have a plan that makes good sense for Grace. Maybe it makes good sense for me too. Now I just need to find a house.

⌘

I should mention my mom was a good mom, is a good mom. I kind of regret if I've indicated otherwise. It surprises people when they hear this, given my appearance, like I'm rebelling against my parents with my body art. Although I don't know why what I look like should matter. Those people treat me differently, you know, judge. That's just wrong. That's their problem, not mine.

Mom always supported me. It's just that I never wanted to be like her. That sounds cruel, I know, but I don't mean it to be. She was always home, waiting on the sidelines for anything Dad or I needed. Dad got preference.

She never complained about Dad or me being late. She was there, on the perimeter, at the ready. But I don't want to wait for anyone, or be a wallflower. I want to be where the action is. I have to be out among people. Maybe that's the reason for the tats. I want to stand out.

While Mom was always around, Dad wasn't. I know this is supposed to be about Mom, but Mom isn't Mom without Dad. He was a good provider, but only financially, never emotionally. My memory of him is either coming home or leaving the house for work. He traveled a lot and was gone days at a time. He was in sales, and salesmen are fast talkers, and everything is positive. Too positive, like on *The Brady Bunch*. Everything's hunky-dory. But it's all on the surface. They have to be hiding something, right? Hell, the Brady kids' bathroom didn't even have a toilet. Like, they're too perfect to take a dump. That's pretty fucked up. Everything can't be all good. And because Dad only wanted to acknowledge the good, I never could get close to him. I wasn't all good.

My dominant memory of my dad is him reclining in his chair, eating chips. He allowed me to watch TV with him, only if I didn't talk, which was fine most of the time. It was our weird way of bonding. Only once did he try to teach me any kind of lesson. Yeah, it didn't turn out so well. I was in fifth grade, and Mom was out bowling. She had just joined a league, and it's the only time she went out to do something for herself, but it didn't last.

So, Dad was watching TV, and I was trying to surprise Mom by cleaning up the kitchen. I accidentally drop a plate, and it shatters. The s-word comes out pretty loudly, but he's in the other room with the TV blasting; I think I'm safe until he appears in the kitchen, face red, veins sticking out on his neck. "What did you say, Potty Mouth?" he spits at me.

I don't think I've ever seen him so angry. He grabs me my arm and drags me to the bathroom. I'm thinking I'm going to get my mouth washed out with soap, but no. "A potty mouth needs to be cleaned with potty water," he says. I'm in shock.

He takes my toothbrush and dips it in the toilet, and makes me brush my teeth with it for two minutes straight. He timed me. I'm crying, and praying that this time, I remembered to flush.

Mom found out when she got home, and boy, was she angry. She actually went against him and stuck up for me, for the first time ever. She makes him apologize, and promise never to do it again. Then, after Dad leaves my room, she hugs me and tells me why he is like he is.

"He was beaten as a child, and his mother did nothing. He wasn't raised knowing what a proper punishment was, never got the affection every child needs. But it doesn't excuse what he did. It was wrong." She's not smiling when she says this, and I'm scared because she always smiles. In the morning, there's a new pink toothbrush waiting for me in the kitchen at breakfast. Dad gives it to me, making a big deal over it, but I knew who it really came from. Mom.

From then on, Mom does the punishing, but that's how it has been anyway, except for this one time. Looking back, I wonder if he'd been drinking. I know he had stopped at some point when I was young, but I never knew why. It wasn't something they talked about. We had to keep up that *Brady Bunch* image. That's why he had always kept his distance. He couldn't know when or if he had gone too far. No one in our family has talked about the toothbrush incident since.

⌘

Sorry to turn the session into such a downer, especially when I was so excited coming in, but I'm nothing like my dad. I'd rather go out than sit in front of a TV eating chips, so it's weird I chose to work from home. But working from home lets me be creative and be near Grace. The Yard, with its gathering of friends, is my social network. Even though I'm not far from home, I'm out of the apartment. That's exactly what I did in high school when I'd sneak out in the middle of the night. Get out and socialize, never went far, and Mom never knew. I'd put a lump under my covers in case she peeked in. I even bought a wig to put on my pillow so she'd see hair. The poor woman. At least, I think she never knew. What she put up with! I'd go crazy with worry if Grace did half the things I did.

The secret outings started just after that first tattoo. It was like a written pass to do whatever I wanted. And, like I said, it got me noticed. I was happy to act the part. Dyed hair and clothes from the secondhand shop instead of the mall made me anything but a wallflower. Whenever I felt like I was fading, I'd get another tattoo. They make me feel present.

In high school, my only concern is that I make it fun, which was one of the reasons I joined drama. Abby warned me about blowing off my schoolwork. And just like she said, my grades aren't at the college acceptance level when it's time to apply. Dad was pretty upset about this, but Mom was cool. He quieted down when I said I'd go to the community college, and by doing this, save him money. What else could I do? Most kids went away to college, and the ones who didn't, traveled or left to become a success someplace else. I'm one of the few who stayed, and it was kind of lonely. Maybe that's why I latched on to my then boyfriend, the same guy who eventually becomes my ex.

⌘

So yesterday, I'm getting anxious and start questioning my plan, which is why I didn't come in. Mom's helped me so much already, and I don't know if it's fair to bother her again. Plus, I have to work sometime. Also, a house sounds sort of desolate, too far away from my friends, but then I hear Abby somewhere in the back of my mind, (and Augustin) reminding me that Grace needs a proper home. Still, I feel myself slipping, wanting to do what is comfortable, what's familiar. By going through with a house, I'm forcing myself to change and it's making me anxious.

Anyway, I'll get the down payment from Mom so when Grace is home from school, we start house hunting. We don't find anything in her school district. And anything near campus is way too expensive, or it's pretty run-down. So, we search a little farther out, where schools are good and houses are within my budget. And then, we find it!

"It's in Rossville," I tell Mom on the phone as we pull away from the house. Relax. It's on speaker phone.

"Where's that?" she asks.

"Not far," I say. "A suburb of Detroit about twenty minutes north from where we are now. Grace found it. She saw the sign as we drove around looking." I catch myself shouting. I must be excited. "It's a cute little one-story in a charming neighborhood. We took a flyer and I have an appointment in two days to look at it with the real estate agent." I don't tell her it's kind of a fixer-upper. Grace takes over, giving Mom more details while I drive.

Mom's happy for us, but doesn't ask to see it. It's like she's still waiting on the sidelines for the coach to put her in. I liked this about her when I was a teenager, but sometimes I want her to be a little more involved, tell me what to do. I have to rely on Abby for that.

Anyway, in two days we'll know whether or not we've found our new home. I pray that we like it because we're running out of time. Now I'm thinking I may need a backup plan. The appointment with the agent cannot come fast enough. Eviction day is looming.

Subject #57: Eddie - Session 6
Topic:

Tracksuit Man

So it's been like almost two weeks since I'm here last, and the big news is, I bought a house! I know I'm supposed to come once a week, but I've been busy with life. Anyway, we started the paperwork and I've been packing, and working. We toured it with the realtor, and the inside is lovely! The neighbor, I quickly discover, is a little strange. But I don't intend to hang out with suburbia, so it's fine. Actually this man, the man I've written on the board, is *wacko*. He should be in here, not me.

Picture this. We're excited for the realtor to show us the house, so we arrive early. I notice more details as I drive through the neighborhood the second time. The subdivision is called Shady Hollow, which sounds both lovely and creepy at the same time. Flowers are sprouting and leaves burst everywhere, giving the neighborhood a newness even though the houses are a little dated. There are only a few large trees, which totally contradict the neighborhood's name, but they are gorgeous. The rest of the trees are on the small side. Each home looks as if it was built in a different year by various builders. The style and how well each is maintained varies as well.

There's one tree in front of every house; different sizes and species. The neighborhood resembles mismatched dinner plates like it wasn't created all in one swoop, which I love. It makes me think the food in each house is different as well. I imagine the better meals, like what Arjun would cook, in the homes with the larger, more majestic trees. Some homes have no landscaping. These homes must rely on takeout. A row of bushes adorns the front of random houses. The house I'm looking at has a small twig, which is fitting. I see myself getting takeout, but there's a lot of room for growth. Abby would approve.

As we park in front of the house, we notice there's something piled up, blocking the front door. "What's that?" asks Grace. I don't have a clue.

It wasn't there when we first saw the house. We get out. The street is quiet, vacant of other cars and people. Our realtor isn't here yet, so we go check it out. An old cattle gate draped with a weathered army blanket leans against the bushes, spanning the front walk. It prevents easy access to the front door.

"What the ...?" I leave out the last word. Remember, Grace doesn't like it when I swear. Then, we hear a screen door slam, and turn toward the sound, which comes from across the street. A tall, thin man in a burgundy tracksuit with white racing stripes down the arms and legs comes toward us at a determined, brisk pace. His reddened face continues up into his Dracula hairline.

"Can I help you?" asks the man. He looks annoyed and purses his lips.

"Um, we're waiting for our realtor to look at the house," I say.

"You don't want to live here," he sputters, shaking his head. "It's been on the market for a long time. The windows leak. So does the roof. And it needs a new septic. That can be pretty expensive." He wrings his hands. "And it's too far from any major shopping malls. Most people are moving out of here." He speaks with an authority that doesn't entirely mask several little twitches behind his left eye and at the right corner of his mouth.

"Is it your house?" I ask.

"No," says the man. "The owners live out of town." The man stands his ground, though technically it isn't his. It makes me uneasy. He reminds me of Major West, the handsome pilot on *Lost in Space*, the original series from the '60s, not the reboot, which I haven't seen. I always had a thing for Major West. The tracksuit is almost like a space uniform. But Major Don West didn't twitch and was always kind, so this man is no Major West. It doesn't matter how handsome a man is—psychotic isn't attractive.

Anyway, Grace and I go to our car to wait for the realtor. The tracksuited man straightens, then restraightens the barricade. It's as if he doesn't want anyone to live here. Or maybe he's screening people, and I'm being judged again. I don't let it dissuade me, thinking he does me a favor with his routine. He's probably the reason it's been on the market for so long. I'll be able to talk them down in price.

Kevin, the realtor, is ten minutes late and full of apologies. He's familiar with the house and verifies that everything Tracksuit Man said is untrue. He removes the cattle gate and lets us in. The interior is clean with wood floors. There's a lot of space for a bungalow, more than what appears from the street, especially after living in apartments. Grace runs to look at the bedrooms and says I can have the bigger one. When she looks out the back door, I join her. Several small lovely trees grow, and there are remnants of a vegetable garden. It's a house I can easily imagine us in. In my mind, we're happy. She has lots of friends who live close, doing well at school. And I'm the perfect mother. My business thrives. I get along with all the neighbors and moms at Grace's new school. The ladies and I even do lunch. That's a suburban thing, right? When Arjun and Abby visit, they both see that our life here is perfect.

I tell Kevin what I have for a down payment and what I can afford monthly. I'd have to offer something below asking price, but with the amount of time the house has been on the market, he thinks they'll accept. He'll make the offer and get back to us. As we leave, I see Tracksuit Man peering from behind his curtains. Maybe he's one neighbor I won't become friends with. I want to give him an Italian salute, but Grace doesn't like it when I do that either. I do it anyway, when she isn't looking.

The house is farther away than where we're at now, so once

we move, I don't think I'll come as often, but don't worry. I'll still shoot for once a week. I can talk about other things. Anyway, I'm in a good place, now. All my problems seem to be solved.

Subject #57: Eddie - Session 7
Topic:

Mom

We moved! Thanks to Mom, my eviction dilemma is over! I know I've been gone like over three weeks, but I'll come once a week now, to keep up with the study. Sorry. Anyway, everything is going great. We're able to move into the new house when our thirty days are up because the owner is renting it to us until the final paperwork goes through. Mom waits until we get the place set up before seeing it. It's weird she isn't more curious.

Grace wants me to dye my hair green to match the backyard and garden, our first one ever, but I keep it the calming purple. I'm too busy setting things up, and working, to think about what I look like. I want to keep the good vibes going from the last place we lived. It's funny how she's picked up on my change of hair color when I hadn't realized I was doing the new home, new hair thing.

In the short time we're in the new house, we've had the old neighbors, now the frat-house gang, over a handful of times already. Everyone comes but Daria, my book friend, and Beth. It turns out my house is a good party house. One night, I walk them out when they're leaving, and Tracksuit Man is just getting home from somewhere and heading to his door. "Is that your weird neighbor?" Dylan says too loudly, and I shush him. They've heard the story about the cattle gate. Tracksuit Man either doesn't hear or pretends to ignore us.

Mom finally comes yesterday. I'm thankful Tracksuit Man isn't around. As she walks in, she says, "I like the two dormer windows in the attic. They remind me of my house when I was a child."

"What I like is that there's an actual laundry room instead of a machine in a closet, or worse, a machine in another building you have to share with God knows who," I say.

She almost tiptoes as I show her around, as if she might be disturbing someone in her flats, nodding with a tight smile at each room. She forces out several "Oohs" during the tour, and comments on how nice it is to have the extra half bath.

"Guests won't be able to snoop through your personal items." She whispers that last part.

Mom brings a house plant for me and a bejeweled mirror for Grace's room as a housewarming. Grace's gift is perfect. It's girly yet grown-up at the same time. I hope I don't kill mine. She should know better, but the woman seems to have faith in me now that I'm a responsible homeowner.

We head back to the kitchen and I make tea while Mom sits at the table. "How do you like sleeping in your new room?" she asks Grace. Mom knows Grace usually sleeps with me, and this is her way of asking if this is still the case. She thinks it's unusual, but never parent-shames me for it.

"I love my new room," Grace says, with a vigor that erupts from pure honesty. She was excited for her grandmother to see it and even made her bed, all on her own. Mom doesn't mention that Grace still has a mattress on the floor, but we've painted the walls, so that's something. Instead of little-girl pink like her old room, Grace chose a more sophisticated purple; it's more of a lavender. Grace's new mirror has stones in both colors. It's funny how Mom knows. The paint actually kind of matches my hair. Maybe that's why Grace wanted me to change it. She wants the color all to herself.

Mom looks relaxed here, especially compared to my old apartment, even though I basically have the same furniture. Maybe she'll come over more often. She hugs and kisses Grace nearly the entire time she's here, and Grace takes it in. She did that with me until I didn't let her. I wish I'd inherited this trait. I'm more like Dad, put up a barrier. But, Grace wants to please others just like Mom, and I'm not surprised she fibs and tells her grandmother what she wants to hear about the sleeping arrangements. Grace inherited that from me. The fibbing part, not the people-pleaser bit.

The truth is, if Grace isn't already in my bed, she tiptoes into my room in the morning. She's in her pink nightgown and her hair is usually tangled in a bed-slumbered nest. She curls her hands in front of her, like a squirrel or a prowler. It's delightful. I hug her in, snuggling her under my chin so I can inhale the sweet kid sweat of her hair nest. Maybe I am a little touchy-feely. I hope so.

"Where are you keeping your scrapbooks?" Mom asks as she looks around the kitchen. Grace is on her lap. She's referring to the books Grace and I have been making since Grace was able to hold a crayon. Before then, Grace used to entertain herself by playing on the floor with my leftover fabric scraps while I worked. I used the prettiest scraps to make our book covers.

"I haven't unpacked them yet," I say. "I'm trying to figure out the perfect place to put them." My mother nods and sits a little straighter, which tells me she approves of my answer. She and I had made a version of these scrapbooks when I was little, and she's happy to see the tradition passed down.

"These are more authentic," I'd told her back when Grace and I first started making them. "We use scraps for *our* scrapbooks." The covers on Mom's version are decorated with crayons or markers. I can still visualize her sitting in her favorite armchair holding the first book Grace and I made, caressing the cover. We were living at her house then. She smiles and nods as I stand over her, as if daring her to disagree that my scrapbooks with Grace are somehow better. I'm such an idiot. This isn't a good memory I have for myself. I don't know why I'm so adamant that our books are different, like I don't want to admit that the books were her idea.

⌘

"Grace, do you have any new friends that live nearby?" Mom asks.

"We haven't seen any girls Grace's age in the neighborhood," I say, before Grace can respond. Mom slumps, just a little, and tilts her head, but the way she holds her mouth doesn't change. There's still a perceivable smile.

"Don't worry, honey," she tells Grace, kissing her head. "When school starts, you'll make lots of friends. Everyone likes you."

"She joined a girls' soccer team, so she's already made some friends," I say, even though Grace has just joined and hasn't yet had her first practice. Mom acts as if a heavy burden has been lifted from her shoulders. Her posture is back, and she smooths her hair before wrapping her arms around Grace again. She doesn't ask to go to the games or when they are, and I know why. She'd feel like she was in the way.

We don't talk about the money she's lent me. I can't decide if I should bring it up and when, or if I should wait for her to ask. It bothers me I couldn't do this on my own, so if I feel the conversation heading in that direction, I switch it to something fun. I can't be strapped for cash right now. The good mother in me says Grace needs a bed.

Subject #57: Eddie - Session 8
Topic:

Grace

We've been in the new house for almost two weeks, and now that things are settled, I want to explain why this whole thing was so devastating for me and how Grace and I ended up in Augustin's apartment. When she was born, I lived with Grace's dad in a one bedroom near the Natural Foods store where he worked. I moved in officially just before we got married. The apartment was run-down, but back then it didn't matter. I was finally independent and living on my own. Well, living with Grace's dad and not at Mom and Dad's.

I wasn't ready to have a baby when I had her. I couldn't see any image of myself as a mother, so when I left the hospital, I couldn't believe the nurses were entrusting me with this precious little life. She was so tiny. I can still picture the nurse bouncing into the hospital room, swinging something. From the way she carried the package in her arms, then passed it to me, I thought she was handing me a football. It took me a moment to realize the nurse had just handed me my new daughter. She was early and a c-section baby, so she didn't have that weird-shaped head some babies have. She was perfect.

I'd never taken care of a baby before, let alone a newborn. I was having trouble making my own life work: I didn't make much money and the marriage I was in was obviously not ideal to everyone but me. No, I guess I knew, but I chose to hide that fact from myself. So why, I kept wondering, were they trusting me to properly care for this baby? So I take her home and I just wing it, much like everything else I do.

I'm good at figuring out things as they come. Anyway, we're managing. I don't know where we get the money for all the diapers and baby stuff, let alone where I get the energy to get up every morning to take care of her when I had been up all night. I remember hallucinating from lack of sleep. It was hard for me to lose the baby weight because I kept trying to get some quick energy from junk food. I gained way too much weight, still trying to lose it.

I don't remember her dad ever offering to help, aside from bringing home diapers. But I'd tell myself, "I got this." Hours and days blurred into each other. Daytime and nighttime were the same. Then one day, like right out of the blue, I fell in love with her and I'm forever hooked.

This happens suddenly. A tightness somewhere in the depths

of my being gradually flourishes, and completely engulfs me. It wraps around my heart so hard that it throbs. I feel an undying love for something that, at this point, can't give me anything in return, nothing. Yet, it's a love so great that I'd happily do anything for this tiny person. A love so great it aches. So, I sit alone in the quiet room and cry. It's at this point I commit to Grace that I will be a good mother. So clearly, something needs to change.

⌘

I move after the divorce, when Grace starts walking. She's already been crawling and started getting into things, his things. I'm not sure if she remembers this first apartment or her dad being around. I don't want to ask. So then, I'm back at Mom and Dad's, in my old bedroom, which helps me get back on my feet. I dye my hair black again. The same color it was when before I moved out.

Mom's such a help. Dad just stays out of our way. Or maybe we're out of his. Grace spends her toddler years bonding with her grandmom which is great. It reminds me of me and Granny. It's tough, though, for me because at my mom's house I'm like a child again, only now I have a child. My cousins come over and it's the same old routine. Everyone reverts to their childhood roles, only now there's Grace. They hear me calling her my little football, and the teasing begins again, saying she's the cartoon genius baby with the football-shaped head when that's totally not where the name comes from. I stop calling her that.

I worry what will happen when she learns to talk, and what

she'll think of me when she hears the cousins tease. I start to see myself from a spectator's viewpoint and I realize I need some independence, so Grace and I move to an apartment several years later, just before she starts the first grade. This is how long it takes me to save money. It's a long time; I know, but during this time, I start a business. I buy an almost vintage sewing machine. It's an industrial Singer. I was using Mom's before then, a Singer too, but it's a basic home model. I think I'm making enough to live in this new place I found, especially if I use my savings. It's nice. Really nice. There's a park close by and it's gated.

We move into the fancy place where there's new carpeting, nice appliances, and stone countertops in the kitchen. I don't know if they're real. The large windows bring in a lot of light, so it feels like a happy place to live, so happy I dye my hair pink. It's a big change, but it fits, and Grace likes it. She switches schools and lives near kids in her new class, which is good. I join a mother's group through the complex. Weird, I know, me in a mother's group. The mothers remind me of the girls I wanted to be friends with before Abby moved in. Grace has a lot of little friends, and she's invited to a lot of kid parties, ones where the parents tag along. It's like we're living the life of happy TV mini-series.

We only invite a few kids to our apartment to play because I don't have a lot of furniture yet. The kids don't mind, but Hailey's mom seemed puzzled when she came by because the only surfaces to eat on are the kitchen counter and the makeshift coffee table I made out of boxes.

Her mom must have said something about our lack of proper

furniture to the other moms because for some reason Grace stops getting invitations. So do I. That's okay. These parents are overly involved, something I'm not used to. We don't belong here. What was I thinking? Anyway, this new place is too nice for my budget, especially with the monthly resort fee, which covers trash, parking, landscape, and mandatory access to the clubhouse.

It's stupid they call it a resort fee. You'd think they're walking around serving martinis. So then, I try to work my way back in with them by extending my own invitations for coffee with the women and pizza for the kids, and it helps a little, but I let my business slide trying to be an overly-involved parent. I quickly go through my savings trying to buy our way into this social clique. When the yearlong lease is up, we have to move to something cheaper. Unfortunately, this means moving to a different area of town, and by this I mean worse. And a different school for Grace.

I criticize the old place to make our new one seem like we're here by choice. "I'm glad we don't have a gate anymore. It makes it hard for friends to visit," I tell Grace. "Here, we have free parking and free trash pickup." Grace nods at the first thing I say, but doesn't respond to the second. Kids don't care about trash pickup.

The not so nice apartment has a heavy cigarette stench, so I'm constantly spraying air freshener. The stink must be embedded into the walls and carpeting, although they've assured me both have been thoroughly cleaned. But the walls aren't exactly white, or even a consistent color, and the rugs are frayed to where there's a bit of the padding exposed. It's not a consistent color either. I used to be a smoker, but quit when I got pregnant. (See? I'm a Good Mom.) It wasn't until later I realized how much cigarette smoke makes everything reek. The smoker has no clue. The smell now makes me gag, so I'm spraying a nice, clean scent every time I walk into the room. Mom could probably smell smoke whenever I walked in the door back when I was in high school. She never said anything.

I dye my hair blue. It's more like a faded azul. The color even stains bits of the bathroom sink, whatever it's made of, but I don't think the landlord will notice.

This apartment also has cockroaches. Tons! I don't like spraying pesticides with Grace around, so I grab whatever's close, which happens to be the air freshener, so I Febreze the hell out of them. I'm not sure this kills them. They run back under the floor molding and hopefully die, so now there's a ton of fresh-smelling dead roaches in my walls.

There isn't a mother's group to join in the new place, and Grace's school isn't very inspiring, hardly any extra activities. I'm trying to build my business again, but the whole situation is depressing and I'm seriously lacking motivation.

After a year, it's clear that this neighborhood and school aren't a good place for Grace, or anyone for that matter, to grow up in. There's crime, and strange people walk around at night, either drunk or on drugs. I've even heard gunshots. The only good thing about living there is that when tenants move out, many leave behind unwanted belongings. This is how I get my dining room table.

The tipping point is when a man comes pounding on our door in the middle of the night, yelling for me to open it. Grace was so scared. This all happens close to when our lease is up, and for me, it's the last straw. I can't be a good mother if we live in a place like this. Even before this near break-in, Grace is quieter than she used to be, not smiling or laughing like before, and is more agitated. But now she's worse. It breaks my heart to see her this way, and I know I've chosen poorly just by looking at her. This is the motivation I need.

That's when we move to Augustin's, where we're happy, and I'm sure we'll be as happy in our new home. It's not hoity-toity like the fancy apartment. It feels honest, real.

Subject #57: Eddie - Session 9
Topic:

Me

Back for my weekly. Grace is good. She started soccer practice, and there's no drama to report. Anyway, you need to know some backstory, especially after I let the superpower comment slip the first time I was here. I didn't forget. It's what people do in movies, right? Lay on a couch and talk about their childhood. Although, I'm sitting on a not so comfortable stool. I guess the theory is that problems stem from deep-rooted past experiences and all that crap. And it'd be nice to understand why I was so freaked out by the eviction, more than anyone at the complex, when a solution should have been so easy. But, I *am* the only one that has a kid to consider.

Anyway, the secrets of my past. I have two, and they're silly. I'm mentioning them here because it's easier to say things to people you don't know than it is to those closest to you, especially if you can't see them. Am I right?

My grandmom knew my superpower secret. She's dead now, and no, I didn't kill her, nor does her death have anything to do with anything. She was just old. I'll unveil that later, the secret, not the details of her death. That's not your business.

You have to understand the first secret to fully appreciate the second. The first, the one my grandmom never knew, is that my name is Mrs. Horse, and it was my choice. I am literally Mrs. Ed Horse, as in the lady-version of Mr. Ed, the talking horse in the old sitcom. Never heard of him? Look it up on YouTube.

I'll explain. My married name is Hest. It surprised people I didn't keep my maiden name, but if I did, I'd be doing what they expected. Right? I don't want to be predictable. I've made my mind up about that long ago.

People don't know that Hest means "horse" in Danish. Thankfully, nobody around here speaks Danish. Tiffany and Stephanie, my cousins, are the main reason I keep the translation quiet. "Horse face!" they'd say if they knew. I can hear it now. They made fun of my first name when we were young, saying I had a boy's or an old lady name, while they have names the popular girls have. Kids can be so mean. Adults can too. My first name is Edwina, Eddie's the short version, and joking about my name was only the beginning.

"Your clothes are ugly," Tiffany would say, which makes me self-conscious. And of course, they're out of the earshot of any adults.

"You talk into your armpit," Stephanie would tease. I spoke softly back then, head down and to the side. This comment hurts. Something about being closely tied to an armpit, I think.

I was large for my age, not fat, but big and clumsy, like a puppy. "You're a big oaf and you act like a baby, so it's even more weird," Stephanie would laugh. I can hear it now.

"Ya, we're more mature," Tiffany would add. They're a couple of years older, so back then, I looked up to them even though they were cruel. Now I see it isn't mature to tease, so something's wrong with that logic, but I took it, hoping one day they'd include me. They didn't, and they told me why. "You're not cool."

Sorry. I'm whining. Anyway, Edwina was my grandmom's name. I miss her. In retrospect, I like to believe the Cousins, or the Cs, as I call them, only teased me because they were jealous. And yes, there is an intentional double meaning there. I'm just too much of a lady to say it. Anyway, I was closer to Gran than they were. And I like my name. It's like a special bond to an amazing lady. My name stood out, even if, back then, I didn't, but I always imagined it in a good way, not like the "abnormally large child" way.

Tiffany and Stephanie are the sort who make you gag, always in the spotlight, do everything right. They make sure everyone's aware of it, too. It's all I heard growing up. "Tiffany made the honor role." "Stephanie is class president." They're sisters, and they try to outdo each other with their wit, but one of them is definitely funnier.

I won't say which one. I like the continuing banter. It sometimes veers toward ugly, and that's when it's most fun. Not like it'd matter what I thought about who'd win the wit competition. The other sister wins on another trait, and if I had my choice, I'd rather be funny.

Anyway, if they knew about the horse name, I'd never hear the end of it. They'd remind me I was big, big as a horse, and my teeth were large when I was little, but I've grown into a nearly perfect smile. The other kids eventually caught up to me, too, so I'm no longer huge. Then, there's that time I ate grass and threw up. Not a good choice, but I was a kid, and it was a dare from the Cs. I thought if I listened to them, they'd think I was cool. But throwing up green doesn't exactly make others think highly of you, unless you're that little girl in *The Exorcist*.

This is probably why, as an adult, I've stopped spending so much time around my extended family. They don't take me seriously, treat me like that child. But on a positive note, maybe all that teasing is why I became the rebel.

I acquired the name Hest from my idiot husband, who is now my ex. His ancestors supposedly came from Denmark, and I *knew* the translation before we got married, but it wasn't important to me because I was expecting. Gran died well before then. I would have told her, because she would have loved the joke. I keep the name Hest because it is also Grace's last name. And I want to keep everything that links me to her. Grace is my life.

My superpower secret? I'm not ready to share; it feels too weird. Even though I like to imagine myself as a superhero mom with a cape flapping in the wind, that's not my superpower. It's something I've had a long time, way before ever becoming a mother. It should have helped me figure out my homeless predicament.

But since things are going so well, maybe it kicked in after all.

Subject #57: Eddie - Session 10
Topic:

Coach

I'm back. Why does it smell like Mexican food in here? Now I'm hungry. Anyway, I'm feeling a little uneasy about Grace's soccer coach.

Grace and I first meet Coach when we enroll her in the new school. They have sort of a "before the beginning of the year fair" with information on clubs and activities. It's in the gym, and it's noisy. Kids running around. Mothers congregating in small private circles, whispering. I don't know these people yet, and on first impression, it's hard for me to imagine me in one of those circles. The whole experience is a little overwhelming.

However, there's one person I know and it's creepy she's there. It's Beth. The only person who didn't gather at my apartment when we tried to figure out what to do after getting the eviction notice. The only person at the old complex I didn't get along with. She's helping to register students, and I'm shocked she works at a school. I wouldn't think they hired people like that.

Grace doesn't seem to recognize her. Luckily, there's another woman also enrolling. I go to her table, pretending I don't see Beth. She must be pretending not to see me, either. The woman takes Grace's information, and I find out that most, if not all, the kids are returning students; the families are permanent structures in the district. Grace stands out because she's new, like Abby did. I think back to what Tracksuit Man said about people moving out of the neighborhood. I'm beginning to wonder if I should have paid more attention to that comment.

A poster catches Grace's attention. Girls in uniform are smiling, their arms flung over each other. The one in the middle holds a soccer ball. Grace has never played soccer. We go over and talk to the coach, who has some equipment on display at his table. Grace likes the idea of wearing the leg armor and shoes with the big nubbies on the bottom. We sign her up. Practice starts later that week, which is good. It gives Grace a chance to make friends before school starts.

When I bring Grace to practice, what surprises me most is that parents drop off their kids and leave. I was also hoping to meet some parents, but no one's here, only the coach. Maybe they figure since they're in fourth grade, the girls are old enough to be left in the coach's care? Or maybe since they've been living in the same neighborhood forever, they're comfortable doing this? But I stay. I don't know these people and I want to make sure Grace is okay. I get some weird looks as parents come and go. I don't look like them. They know I'm the new mom. Grace and I are new to this whole organized sports thing, so I don't know what protocol is yet, but I don't want Grace to feel all alone.

Augustin's comment still haunts me, so by the fourth practice, which was yesterday, I try to do what the normal parents do and drop Grace off. You learn things by watching people. Right? And she wants me to do this because it's what all the other moms do. But dropping her off is hard. I mean, she used to walk around the apartment neighborhood by herself, even walk home from her bus stop, and I never even gave it a thought. Why is this so different?

I'm nervous but force myself to leave. All the while, I'm imagining the ugly things happening precisely because I'm not there: Grace breaks her leg, there's a mass shooter, she gets struck by lightning. Like me standing on the sideline is going to prevent any of this. Anyway, Grace is happy about this independence. Me? I have to keep reassuring myself that Coach is there and she'll be fine.

I pick up some burgers for dinner. Not knowing the area well, I get turned around when driving back to the field. I'm in a panic because I'm three minutes late from the time practice is supposed to end. I don't want to start a new school by being that parent who forgets to pick up her kid, and I'm nervously shoveling fries in my mouth as I drive. I pull into the lot so fast that I park at an angle, taking up two spaces.

There's no time to straighten. I run to the opening in the fence, down a dirt path, then through the small cluster of trees that shelter the practice field. It's like I'm late for a flight, and I'm dodging anything in my way. My heart pounds the entire way and fries jostle in my stomach. I just know Grace is alone with an angry coach, and they'll both be glaring at me upon my tardy arrival. I feel I'm going to throw up because of all the jostling.

When I get to the field, I stop and catch my breath. My anxiety dissolves, because the girls are running around, carefree, in the adjacent playground. Unfortunately the queasiness from running after engorging on fries remains. Grace is running with them. I take a moment to slow the pounding in my chest as I look for Coach, but don't see him anywhere.

One befuddled parent lingers at the end of the practice field, the opposite end of where I usually stand. I recognize the man to be one of the satellite parents from the game, so I walk over to him and ask where Coach is.

He says, "I don't know. I just got here. The girls were just running around by themselves." Satellite Dad stands tall, with his hands in his pockets, watching the girls. Grace waves and continues running around the playground, shouting something at a teammate. I start to think that maybe the horrible things I'd imagined might happen to Grace weren't so far off, especially without any adult around to watch them.

I ask, "Was someone hurt? Maybe that's why Coach had to leave quickly?" I know the girls aren't supposed to be left unsupervised, so it's weird.

He says, "I asked. The girls said Coach left as usual." This dad's expression is just as baffled as I feel. We're both like in the twilight zone, like all the rules to what's appropriate when watching a bunch of kids suddenly change.

"If you need to leave, I'll stay here with the rest of the girls until their parents come," I say. But he says no; his daughter Lucy is having fun. So we both wait. Me and Satellite Dad supervise until each parent picks up their kid.

As the parents come and go, no one mentions the coach's absence. To me, this makes it more strange. It would be my first question. But then again, I'm not afraid to ask questions. Is this what Augustin means? Is a normal parent afraid to ask questions? When I'm back home, I email the coach to find out what had happened. His reply comes this morning:

> *Hello Mrs. Hest,*
> *I had an appointment yesterday, so I left*
> *15 minutes early, and my wife stayed with the*
> *girls until the parents came. Grace is a joy to*
> *have on the team. See you at the next game.*
> *Coach Davis*

So. The coach knew he'd have to leave early but neglected to tell the parents they should pick up their child early. That's wrong, isn't it? He's also unaware his wife didn't stay. That's really wrong. I can't hold back. My fingers click hard on the keys with my reply:

Hello Coach,

When I picked up Grace, your wife was not there. (I was actually three minutes late.) If I had known you had to leave, I would have gladly picked her up early. The girls were left unsupervised. In the future, could you please let us know if you have to leave early so we can make other arrangements? I wouldn't want anything to happen to any of the girls while there isn't an adult around. Thank you.

Eddie Hest (Grace's mom)

Coach hasn't yet replied to my second email, but then I just sent it. There isn't a game this Saturday or practice, some sort of schedule conflict, so I'll wait for his reply or I'll see him at the next practice. If he's there.

Subject #57: Eddie - Session 11
Topic:

Psycho Soccer Mom

Okay. Grace's school started last week. We're easing into our new schedule. But, things got weird since last time I'm here. Really weird. The whole thing leaves me asking a lot of questions. Here's how it went. Grace had her first game the Saturday before school starts. I go, and sit with the rest of the team parents then instantly regret it.

"KILL HER!" a woman shouts at the young girls. I'd seen this woman before at practice. At that time, she hadn't come across as being violent. She's wrapped in fleece and sits by a large blue cooler, using it as a side table to hold what appears to be a three-course meal. Her shouting spews between bites, and bits of her food burst outward with each guttural yell. No one else acts like this behavior is odd.

I begin scheming a way to move my lawn chair away from the caterwaul. I'll have to do this delicately; I don't want to be obvious, or rude, especially since I'm new, but I have to get away from these people. It would have been nice to sit with the other parents, get to know them, but I'm here to watch Grace, and this woman proves to be too much of a distraction.

It's half-time when I finally move my chair. I find sanctuary at the end of the field, away from the fans. I'm getting settled in my new spot when Grace comes running to me for water, her hair in two braids bobbing at her shoulders. Her shin guards create great bulges at the bottom of her birdlike legs. It's hilarious. Each bounce toward me adds a spoonful of pride, and they're mounting inside me. I feel full, but would never decline another helping. "Great job, kiddo!" I tell her.

Grace shrugs and scrunches her face. "I want to be goalie next half so I don't have to run so much." Sweat gathers at her hairline and she takes a long swig of water. With a toothy smile, she breathes heavily while gazing toward her teammates, her new friends. I'm happy for her. This is exactly what I want for us.

"Why don't you ask the coach?" I say.

"Okay." Grace hands me the bottle and runs to her coach where the team gathers. She joins the flaming red mass created by their uniforms, and they begin their firecracker chant, stacking their hands in the center of the formed circle. On cue, all hands launch skyward, as they shout their mantra, "Boom, boom, firecrackers, go, go, go!" Grace runs to the team's goal and stands ready. She's convinced her coach. She's an excellent persuader.

I admire the crisp morning air of the Michigan suburbs, thankful the move has turned out so well, and laugh at myself when I realize I'm a soccer mom. And I'm a good mom who comes to the game and cheers on her daughter. I relish the solitude where I've dragged my chair, then look to the woman who continues to shout. What a friggin' psycho.

Other parents surround her, each with their own chair and water for their daughter. They all have clear plastic bags full of orange slices. I didn't get that memo. Some have a blanket spread underneath their chair. Even from afar, this area bubbles with tension. I notice a few satellite parents, ones like me, preferring to watch from a distance. Grace loses interest in the game soon after the second half begins. The Psycho Soccer Mom yells at her to be ready.

The battle continues opposite of Grace's end of the field. She probably doesn't hear Psycho Soccer Mom. She's thrown herself on the ground and picks through wide blades of grass. That's my girl! She looks as if she's singing. Psycho Soccer Mom stands and moves toward Grace yelling, "Get up, girl! What's wrong with you?" Her tone and movements are aggressive.

I may have to intervene. I sit up in my chair, but as the girls on both teams run to Grace's end of the field, she gets into position. Psycho Soccer Mom retreats. I would never talk to a child like that. I wonder if she is what Augustin means by a normal parent?

⌘

Grace's team won that first game, by the way. Anyway, yesterday, I'm on my phone standing on the sidelines in the shade at the far end of the field, waiting for Grace's coach to dismiss the team. I'm talking to my ex's lawyer, well his parents' lawyer, and she's asking me questions. I'm not liking where this conversation is going, but it would behoove me to be polite. Right?

While I'm on the phone, I'm also watching the girls run through drills, so it takes me a while to notice a woman walking toward me. She's too far away to recognize, and I don't know that many people yet to recognize anyway. So, I'm not paying attention until I see her swishing her straight arms by her portly body, walking with an undisputed determination. At the same time, tiny flying insects begin to swarm in smoke-like clusters in the air around me, each seemingly afraid to fly too far from the pack. It's annoying. At first, I'm glad at least one other parent has come. A good mother should be involved in their daughter's life, not overly but involved.

The coach is still working with the girls, and they're eager to please him. The girls work as a team and the coach is patient and kind when running drills, good qualities for coaching fourth-graders, which makes it weird that he did what he did. As the woman moves past the team, I presume we've come for the same reason—to ask Coach why he left the last practice early. And more importantly, why did he leave the girls alone on the field, unattended. I thought he'd respond more quickly to the second email I'd sent, but I got nothing from him. Surely, leaving the girls alone isn't standard procedure. Surely, someone else had complained.

When the woman is closer, I recognize that she's the loud lady at Grace's game, one of the moms. With her apparent lack of inhibitions, I may not need to say anything to the coach at all. She'll most likely do it, and do it loudly. I have an ally. It's what good moms do, work together for the sake of their kids. But, I'd sure hate to be on the receiving end of that one.

The woman contorts her face as she comes near; I'm not sure if it's from the sun in her eyes or from the seriousness of the situation. I stand, eager to greet her, swatting away tiny flies. The woman holds a piece of paper, and when she's close, she begins to flick it at me.

"How dare you!" says the woman, and I'm immediately dumbfounded.

"Excuse me?" I say after asking the lawyer to hold. My mind goes blank. I have no idea what this woman is talking about. Did she think I was rude by moving my chair away from her at the game? Surely, she can't be that sensitive.

"I said, how dare you! You are not allowed to question the actions of my husband!" I can see she's holding the email I'd sent the coach, and I'm connecting the dots. She's his wife.

"What are you talking about?" I say, still lost.

"My husband is graciously volunteering his time to teach your daughter. You should be more appreciative!" The woman screaming at me is so surreal, it's hard for me to respond. So I partially tune her out and instead focus on her appearance while trying to make sense of what she says. She wears way too much makeup, and the hairstyle isn't her best look. She's like one of those women who may have been attractive at one time, maybe in high school, but is trying to hold on to that look, never changing their style or appearance. She isn't a good match for the coach, who is athletic and sort of good looking in his own way. I try to interject. "He shouldn't have..."

"Never! Ever! Question what he does. Or you'll have to answer to me! And..." She pauses and gets right up in my face so I have to reel back my head. I can smell her breath. She's been eating bologna. "Don't even think about mentioning to him or anyone else that I talked to you. If you say anything to the soccer league, you'll be sorry! I will do anything to protect him!" The woman pivots and walks away. The sun shines hard upon her like a spotlight. She stops momentarily, turning to give me one more message. "I'll be watching you."

I'm standing there like I'm frozen or my feet are encased in cement blocks as she struts away, using her hips and shoulders to maneuver her body forward, swaying them almost mechanically. Oddly, an entirely different walk than when she approached me. The whole thing is laughable, thrashing the email in my face, forbidding me to tell anyone what happened. Who does this woman think she is? But then it dawns on me; this woman just threatened me. What a friggin' psycho. I'm still finding it hard to move.

My stomach twitches, and I try to control my breathing. I feel hot, even in the shade, and the gnats gravitated toward the warmth. Watching her leave, I start to pry my feet loose from the earth's hold, moving them from side to side as if I'm weighing the possibility of her threat being real. Maybe it's nerves. The ground is hard and unforgiving. I wonder if this is how things work around here? Is this my new normal? Or is this lady the local loonie who screams at everyone?

The lovely image I have for me and Grace in our new home shatters.

"Hello?" I hear a faint voice. I forgot I'm on the phone, and the voice jars me back to the moment.

"Sorry," I say as I watch the woman waddle to the other side of the field. She disappears as the lawyer continues, but I'm having a hard time focusing. Luckily, the call doesn't last too much longer. All the while, the girls and the coach keep practicing. It's like the entire world kept moving forward while I was stagnant in time. I don't think anyone on the field noticed the outburst. For them, everything is normal. For me, it's far from it. The only thing I think is that my role as a mother has changed. I now have to protect Grace from this Psycho.

After the Psycho Soccer Mom incident, I know why Coach never responded to my second email. He never got my letter. Psycho Soccer Mom evidently screens her husband's inbox. I wonder if she saw my email by chance or does she routinely check up on him? And why? Was she checking to protect herself because she didn't stay when she should have? Or was she trying to protect him from me? And what did she think I was going to do besides what I said in the letter? Steal him away from her?

Subject #57: Eddie - Session 12
Topic:

Abby

After I'm back home from the session yesterday, I text Abby to get her take on Psycho Soccer Mom. But by the time I send it, it's in the middle of the night for her and she's probably sleeping. So early yesterday morning, when she's at work, she gives me a thumbs-up, and I call her on her mobile, through my computer. She's in some meeting, but I hear her excuse herself, saying it's an important call and she needs to take it.

She whispers as she brings me down the hall, back to her office. I know what it looks like because she FaceTimed me when she first started working there. A long neutral-colored corridor, suits walking around, foggy view outside large windows. God! I can't imagine her life. I hear her office door close, then she speaks at full volume.

"You've got such good timing," she says. "It's like you knew I needed rescuing. They're droning on, repeating themselves. They think if they say the same thing more than once, it becomes more important." She rarely rants like this, so she must be having a bad day. It's good I bothered her at work.

I'm on my bed with my notebook open as I tell her what happened with Coach and his psychotic wife. There isn't video, so I stare at her phone number on the screen like it's her face. She's in London, but knows Grace's soccer is what the English call football, or whatever.

"I can't imagine why she would threaten you for your email. She sounds unstable." Abby sounds worried, which is unusual. I flip through my perception of unstable, and fittingly, Norman Bates comes to mind. "Have you told anyone who knows her? Maybe they'd have some insight."

"I haven't really met anyone yet, aside from Coach, and I can't tell him," I say. "The only other people I've met live in my neighborhood, and I don't think they have kids." Then I mention Tracksuit Man and his weirdo antics. "There's no way I'd talk to him about this. I've been avoiding him since I looked at the house." Then I remember Satellite Dad. "There's this one guy."

"Be careful who you speak to," she says. "She may be in tight with some of them, and not like you asking questions. Get to know them, then find out who to talk to before you say anything." I think this would take far too long, and the other parents seem to avoid me. God, why is this woman so upset about my email? Abby's right. She'd also be weird about me asking questions about her.

But why? What's the big deal? I shift on my bed, making my computer and Abby's phone number sway like she's on a boat in turbulent waters, when it's actually me that's wavering.

I'm quiet because I don't really like her advice. I need to do something now. "Maybe Grace should quit soccer," Abby finally says.

Right away I think Grace is *not* going to like that, and this mental image of the great mom I thought I was being evaporates. "Maybe I can go to all the practices and watch over her?" I say.

"Didn't you tell me Grace doesn't want you watching her at practice because no other parent does that?" Abby asks, and she's right. Grace won't like that either. I'd embarrass her with my hovering. Maybe I should hide in the bushes and watch? Psycho Soccer Mom would probably see me and yell that I'm spying on her or her husband. But seriously, I can't put Grace in a situation where there's a psychotic mother and an irresponsible coach. I'm suddenly ill, with a burning feeling deep in my stomach. Grace won't like it, but quitting is the only way because I don't have a support system here yet. I wonder if there'll be a scene or if she'll quietly hate me for days, or weeks on end.

⌘

Abby takes this threat seriously. She doesn't say why, but I know. Someone had gone psycho on her when she'd gotten a promotion they thought should have been theirs. The man was plotting to— and notice I'm doing air quotes here—*get her out of the way*. But the idiot wrote a long email to another employee using his company email, detailing his plan to either run her over with his car or shoot her. He didn't have a gun, and was trying to get one they couldn't trace back to him. Instead of sending the letter to his friend, the idiot mistakenly sends it to the entire company. It's funny, but it's not. Fortunately for Abby, he's an idiot. The police came and took him away, and his friend was reprimanded for not bringing the matter straight to Human Resources. The friend thought the guy wouldn't actually do it, but how could he know? "Some people are unstable," Abby said after it happened. She was stoic about the whole thing. And I get what she's saying. Some people can't handle pressure and go wacko. But, what kind of pressure can a suburban housewife have?

Abby hasn't been herself since this happened. It's probably only me who notices. She's overly cautious, but who can blame her? She wants me to be extra safe with Grace. I do too, but I pulled Grace from her last school and friends. Is it fair to do it again?

"Dee," says Abby. "You can't tell her why. It'll frighten her." Abby's adamant about this, but I'm not ready to commit. I can't decide if she's overly cautious or normal cautious. We both know that when you give someone a reason for doing something, and if it's a good reason, it simplifies whatever point you're trying to make. That's what a good mother does, explain things.

"I can't tell Grace to do something because I said so. That's what my mother used to say, and it pissed me off," I say. When my mom said this, I felt like she considered me a child, like she thought I wasn't able to understand the truth, or worse, was unworthy of it. Abby knows this.

"Okay, tell her the almost truth; leave out who and *exactly* what they did." Then she adds I should do something to make up for it, like get a dog. She really wants me to get this dog.

I ask, "How do I tell Grace the almost truth?" It's sort of like saying to just halfway jump off a cliff.

There's a knock at her end. I hear a door open and someone speaks. "You'll think of something," Abby says, then tells me she has to go. "Let me know how it goes."

I tell her I love her, and don't hang up because then I'll have to face what I've been avoiding. Abby ends the call. I have no clue about how much to reveal to Grace, but I need to figure it out before her game on Saturday.

⌘

Last night, after I talk with Grace, I want to fill Abby in on the drama that went down. But it's like the middle of the night in London, and I'm too anxious to wait for her morning, so I write an email, and send it flying. It'll be waiting for her in the morning while I'm still sleeping.

So, I'm in the kitchen with a glass of wine when I start clicking away. I tell Abby I talked to Grace and it did not go well. I'd been convincing myself all day that Grace wouldn't really care because of how she preferred playing in the grass instead of watching the game. For some stupid reason, I thought I'd simply tell her she didn't have to stay on the team if she didn't want to, and she'd be happy to quit. I'm such an idiot. Abby, my fingers click, you should have been here to save me from myself. Here's how it went. (I take a large sip of wine before continuing.)

During dinner—

Me: So, do you like playing soccer?

Grace: Yeah, it's fun. (She's bouncing, swinging her legs back and forth underneath the table. And right away it's not going like I planned because I thought she'd say no.)

Me: But you sit down a lot when you're on the field and don't pay attention to the game.

Grace: I like my new friends. (She's smiling. And happy!)

Me (starting to panic): It seems like you don't like playing. Don't you want to quit and do something else? (I mean, who am I to tell her if she's having fun or not?? When did I become so controlling!!)

Grace: No, I like it. (Here's where Grace starts to look worried, and she stops bouncing. And, I see this, but I keep going!)

Me: We can do something else on Saturday mornings, just you and me. (I clearly didn't think this through. I probably should have opened with that, or said something about how much I missed her.)

Grace: No! I want to play soccer! (Now she's tearing up and her face is red, and I feel like I'm in a corner. I don't know what to say.)

Me: (So, wait for it. Here's where I totally mess up.) Well, you're going to have to quit. (Oh my God! I sound just like my mother! The whole "Because I said so" thing. What the hell is wrong with me?? What happened to the explaining?)

Then, I type to Abby: Grace lets out a yell. "No," she screams in horror. "Wwwhhhhyyy??" There's chewed up food still in her mouth. Abby, I really fucked up. And I'm just sitting there all stern-like when my baby is crumbling.

But then! It takes me a little while, but wait till you hear my reaction! (You are going to love this!) The way I *choose* to react to her meltdown affirms that I am *not* my mother. (Yay!! Even though I love the old woman dearly, especially since she gave me the money for the house!) I do a complete 180. I don't shrink or become quiet. I go to Grace, crouch down beside her chair, and take her hand.

Me: Grace, I want to tell you the truth. It may be confusing. (Grace's eyes are wide, like she's trying hard to focus on my words. She's calmer, but tears still roll down her cheeks. A rust-colored drool slides down her chin. It's from the spaghetti, but it looks like blood.)

Still Me: One of the parents on your team did something uncool. I'm afraid they may do it again. My job as your mother, besides loving you forever, is to keep you safe. I don't know if I can do that if you're still on the team.

⌘

I tell Abby I have no idea where this reasoning comes from, but I have to admit, it's pretty damn good. That's what a good mother does. I take a break from typing and raise my glass, giving myself a toast, then finish its contents. I refill the glass.

At this point, I'm convinced the worst of it is over. But then, it's not. I continue typing.

Grace: I want to play soccer with my friends. (She's trying not to cry, but her chin still quivers. It's sort of like she's thinking about something, or remembering it. My thoughts dart to the time the guy tried to break into our apartment, and I hid her in the closet. So, I think she understands.)

Then something weird happens. Just when I'm expertly handling this, things start to turn. Her face morphs into something horrific as she contemplates what I said. She pushes herself away from the table and shoots me the saddest look ever. Oh my God, Abby! It broke my heart. It's still breaking my heart. I can't believe what I've done to her, and I thought I was doing so well! All of the sudden, there's this remorse that falls deep within me, and it keeps going, feeling like it never quite hits the bottom of anything.

Grace runs to her room, and as she does, lets out this great wail. I watch her go, feeling helpless. It's hard for me to breathe as if I'm locked inside a small box for too long. I'm supposed to be this great mother, but I took away her home, and now her new friends. I tell myself it has to be done, for her own safety. Abby, my head goes wobbly. Grace's sadness, which I caused, rips from me a weld that has always held the two of us together. As she stomps away, it's like she's pulling a piece of my heart carelessly over the ground on a tattered string behind her. It bounces with each step and bleeds from betrayal. My betrayal. I'm clueless on what to do. I want to call to her, reach out and pull her in under the covers to keep her safe. But I sit helplessly and doing nothing. Why do I do nothing? Abby, I write, maybe I am my mother after all.

I finish the email by telling Abby that while Grace is crying in her room; I come up with an idea that will help her forget soccer. It's a good one, if I do say so myself. Good Mom is back! I think Grace has cried herself to sleep, but she's going to love me for it.

So, I send Abby the email and start planning. I take my wine to my room, crawl under the covers, and fall asleep going over the details in my head. I'll give details on my idea another time, since this is Abby's session. We implement my plan the next Saturday morning, purposefully during the game, and at night, Grace and I have a blast.

Subject #57: Eddie - Session 13
Topic:

Psycho Soccer Mom

Today's about Psycho Soccer Mom 'cause it just keeps getting weirder. So, Abby knows my plan to make Grace not hate me for making her quit soccer. Remember, I told her in that middle-of-the-night email I sent? Last Saturday, I throw Grace a dance party. It's just me and her, with flashing lights and loud music.

Anyway, backtrack. Grace and I head to the rental store Saturday morning when I know Grace's soccer team has a game. It's the first game since she quit the team. She's happy about the party, but she's a little quiet, probably thinking about what she's missing. I tell myself at least she's safe, that I've made a good choice, one a good mom would make. I just hope this plan doesn't bite me in the end. The timing of this excursion coincides with everyone being at the soccer game, or at least they should be.

I blast the radio and sing, trying to get this party started. Grace joins in, but only half-heartedly even though it's her favorite station instead of mine. She doesn't perk up until we reach the rental store. It's in a warehouse on the outskirts of the town where my old fabric store is. I turn in the lot, and scruffy-looking young men take large black boxes and collapsible tubular things out of a van, most likely returning what they rented for their gig the night before. Grace sits tall in her seat, watching them as I park. Everyone wears black and their hair is black. Grace, I can tell, is curious.

Inside, the checkout counter sits straight back in the middle of the store. It's a dull Formica and old handwritten flyers are plastered on the front. As soon as we walk in, Grace points out the array of disco balls and strobe lights hanging from the ceiling. Her eyes are big, which makes me think my plan is good. We walk to the two employees standing behind the counter. They're in their mid-twenties, slightly younger than me, but somehow they make me feel old. The posters on the front of the counter look older than they do.

I tell the men what we're looking for and the more pierced of the two brings us to the lighting section in the back of the store. Metal shelves hold lights identical to the ones Grace saw hanging near the front. Shelves tower over us on either side of the aisle, full of equipment. The man explains the different lights available. As he talks, I notice his facial hair is sparse. Maybe he's trying to grow a beard, or maybe shaving isn't a part of his daily routine. His stubble matches the condition of the equipment. It's like how an owner resembles his dog. Equipment for rent lies in wait. Dust collects on the cords. The metal boxes are scratched and battered from use. The man is older than I initially thought, maybe older than me? Grace hops from one foot to the next from excitement. She listens carefully to the man as she bounces, but his attention remains on me, ignoring her altogether, but he shouldn't because she's paying more attention to what he's saying a hell of a lot more than I am. He obviously doesn't have kids, but knows who is making the decision on how much money we'll spend at his store.

I refocus on the man and the lights he's giving way too much detail on, but then a large flash of pink makes me look in the vicinity of the checkout counter. I'm like, what is pink doing here among all the black? Grace is wearing pink, but she's a kid, so the color is low and compact. This pink is higher, more expansive. Maybe someone else is having a dance party for their kid. I turn to the bold color and my neck tightens so much that it constricts my flow of air. It's Psycho Soccer Mom.

Why is she here and not at the game? She's ruining my plan. Psycho Soccer Mom turns and heads toward the exit, but her face still points in my direction. I see her big round eyes poking out of her big round head. Her short blonde curls wrap around this globe. The face has no expression. It's spine-chilling, like a horror movie. The woman gives no sign of recognition, nor does she make any kind of gesture toward me. But then Grace notices me looking, and follows my gaze. Grace sees her, and smiles and waves. I freeze. Psycho Soccer Mom remains stone-faced and doesn't wave back. What the fuck? She doesn't return a hello to my daughter. Who does she think she is?

Then, I worry she'll come over and say something about soccer and Grace will know she was the reason I made her quit. But she doesn't. She just stares and continues toward the door, gliding as if her feet aren't even touching the ground. I try to keep my expression unchanged as well, pretending I don't know who she is or that she's affecting me in any way. Grace can't know this is the soccer parent who did something bad. I hold my breath. I need air. And just in time, right before I become too lightheaded, she leaves the store and the door seals her departure.

The man has been talking the entire time and doesn't notice we've been distracted. Maybe he doesn't care and just needs to get through his spiel. I choose the least expensive light, and we head to the counter.

After completing the paperwork for the rental, I abruptly stop at the glass door. Psycho Soccer Mom hasn't left the parking lot. She's standing outside. Maybe she's waiting for me. A scenario runs through my mind in a matter of milliseconds; she's screaming at me like she did when she flicked the email, while Grace and the black-clothed musicians stand around watching.

"Let's look at the percussions," I say to Grace. They're in the aisle closest to the door. I explain to her what percussions are. We move away from the glass, and I put the opened Chewy's box holding our strobe light down on the floor. Grace picks up an egg-shaped rattle and shakes it while she dances. I dance with her, swishing my skirt like I'm a flamenco dancer. Her mood has lightened since the car ride here, and she wants to play with all the gadgets. I'd be having as much fun as Grace if there wasn't a psycho lady waiting for me outside, but I'm hiding my angst pretty well, though I'm angry Psycho Soccer Mom has ruined this for me too.

We meander through the store. I pretend to be interested in the various things for rent, and Grace, I can tell, is planning for her next party, one where she can invite friends. I'm hoping I didn't open a Pandora's box by bringing her here. Going to the other side of the store, we pass the glass door, and I casually look outside, making sure that Grace doesn't notice. Confirmed. Psycho Soccer Mom is still there. Why is she waiting for me? Does she want to gloat? Throw it in my face that she's successfully gotten us off the team? That her threat worked and made me do something we didn't want to do? We go to the keyboard aisle and play with the different settings. We're getting stares from the man who explained the lights. He's irritated.

Light Man comes over. "Is there something else you need?" he asks. He's not real subtle about wanting us to leave. My guess is he wants to get back to his conversation with the younger dude who hasn't left the protection of the Formica counter.

"Just this," I say. In my fluster, I buy Grace the egg-shaped maraca she's still holding, which is fine. We'll use it at the party. After paying, as I go to pick up my light box, I see that Psycho Soccer Mom is gone, so I've succeeded in saving Grace from at least one detrimental encounter. I don't think I'll mention that we saw Psycho Soccer Mom to Abby. I want her to think I have everything under control.

Subject #57: Eddie - Session 14
Topic:

Gladys

Things are happening so fast, and to understand what motivates this craziness, I need to mention Leigh, aka Gladys Kravitz. She's the proverbial nosy neighbor. Anyway, sometimes I forget I'm supposed to set an example for my daughter. That's what a good mom does. Right? I kind of blow it when it comes to this woman.

Soon after we move in, I'm bringing the trash out to the curb, thinking how nice it is to have a can on wheels where I don't have to lug bags down a flight of stairs and throw them over my head into a smelly dumpster. I've had the bag break on me several times when hoisting it over the side. So, I'm wheeling the cart, looking across the street to see if Tracksuit Man is watching me, and I don't notice there's a woman standing on my sidewalk, staring at me until after I turn back to my house. I nearly bump into her.

"Hello, I'm Leigh. You're new to the neighborhood," she says. I'm kinda creeped that she just sort of appears out of nowhere. She keeps talking, doesn't give me a chance to respond. It's too early to be bombarded like this. I haven't had my coffee. "I live with my husband Steve, two houses down from Philippe across the street. And right next door to Bonnie," she says.

She pauses for a second, barely giving me an opportunity to tell her my name. Then before I have a chance to say anything about Grace, she cuts me off, flying through details of who lives where and what they do. It's making me dizzy. It's like she hasn't spoken to anyone in years, and I'm the first chance she has. I can't keep up.

And I don't. Instead, I revisit what she led with. Philippe across the street. So Tracksuit Man's name is Philippe. He doesn't look like a Philippe. It sounds French, almost exotic. But, with the barricade, the light bulbs, and the almost encounter at the grocery store, the last thing anyone would call this man is exotic. Eccentric, maybe. Although his eyes are a little exotic, but I'll stick with Tracksuit Man. It suits him better.

As Leigh continues telling me the personal details of people I don't know or care to know, I begin to liken her to the neighborhood busybody in *Bewitched*.

"Okay. Well, I have to get Grace to school. See you later." I abruptly end the conversation, cutting her off mid-sentence. I go inside and tell Grace about my bizarre encounter with Leigh. Grace is eating breakfast. And this is my mistake, where I set a bad example. I tell Grace that Leigh's a nosy busybody.

"Like Gladys Kravitz?" she says. She knows. We've watched the show.

"Exactly," I say. Sealing the nickname that becomes her alias. We're making fun of the woman and I shouldn't, but I kind of like it.

When Grace gets home from school, I fill her in on "The Return of Gladys." Twice in one day! This time I'm in the backyard, trying to figure out what the previous owners were growing in the garden, and suddenly she's just there. It's like she has a superpower to teleport. I tell Grace.

"I let myself in through the gate," says Gladys. "I saw you as I walked by."

I'm thinking her walking by and seeing me is deliberate. Anyway, she's going on again about people in the hood, and I remind myself not tell her anything personal because then, everyone will know. I continue digging in the garden, and discover tons of these florescent, almost translucent little bugs gathered under the leaves of whatever plant this is. There are literally hundreds of them.

She breaks her own monologue mid-sentences and says, "Those are blueberry aphids." Then, she continues right where she left off, like she flipped a switch, then switched it back again. I stand and make a mental note so I can get rid of them. It turns out it's actually helpful she's here. But, I don't want it to be a daily thing.

I say, "Well, I have to go meet a client about their curtains." It's the downside to working at home. Your neighbors always know exactly where you are, and assume you're available at their whim.

So when we go to bed that night, Grace flickers the lights on and off. She says she has to let the busybody know what time we're going to bed. I can't hold back a laugh. It's funny. So as I pass the switch I give it a couple of flips myself, telling Grace it's our Morse code to say good night to Gladys. Not a good example, but she laughs, so it's a point for team Mom. Grace asks me what Morse code is.

⌘

Saturday, she's outside again when I'm unloading my car. Then she's back again yesterday. "You had a party this weekend," she says.

It's like, how does she know this? She's chomping on something. Her chin moves side to side instead of up and down. I have to assume she's telling the neighbors my intimate details and wonder what she has said about me to Tracksuit Man. Then I wonder why I care what she says to him.

"How do you know about the party?" I try to sound polite, keeping my sass under control. It's hard, let me tell you, but I pull it off.

Then, get this, she rubs my arm and speaks as if I were a small child, "I saw the flashing lights, and notice what time you turn your lights out." And I think, Grace was right. I pull back from her touch and hold my breath while listening, a reflex, I guess, to someone invading my personal bubble. I try to remain pleasant, but it's hard. I still don't know what she's chewing. Okay, that's it for this session.

Subject #57: Eddie - Session 15
Topic:

Tracksuit Man

I'm here so often lately, the students at reception know me. It's like when I came more than required when trying to figure out where to move. Now, it's been so crazy since Coach abandoned the girls at practice and Psycho Soccer Mom's threat that the eviction dilemma I had when I started seems like a piece of cake. So I'll get to it. If, chronologically, Psycho Soccer Mom's is the second Blackball List I find myself on since moving here, the first would be Tracksuit Man's. But ever since Gladys told me his name, for some reason, he's been on my mind.

I'm sure he hasn't forgiven me for not heeding his warning and buying this house against his advice. I don't expect him to come over with a housewarming gift. Truth be told, I'm avoiding him. Abby thinks he's harmless, and in the past she's been a good judge of character. Even so, I'd rather keep my distance. What do you say to someone who clearly doesn't want you as their neighbor? Every time I see him, our first encounter comes to mind. Who does he think he is? Judging me?

So, in my house, my sewing workroom is in the main living area where I'm told the TV should be. I have it this way so things won't be tight. I don't want to dent the sheet rock like I did at the last place; it's mine, and Augustin isn't around to fix it. Remember I have my own sewing business? I make pretty good money because there aren't many people who sew and a lot of people with money who want something custom made. I get jobs through interior designers and alterations through dry cleaners and wedding dress shops. Plus, I've got a couple of small ads out there.

Anyway, I took my shelves from the last apartment and my friend Arjun put them up in the dining room. I'm reserving the garage for upholstery. The TV is in my bedroom. Grace and I like to watch under the covers, with popcorn. I'm doing my best to educate her on my favorite old TV shows, when I can find them, just like me and Abby had watched. I like my arrangement. There's a lot of light coming in from the front window, which is great when I'm trying to match fabric patterns as I seam them together. They need to be precise. I'm pretty particular. I'm mentioning all this because you need to know the layout to understand this next bit.

The old sofa's against the wall in the living room where it should be. It gets used, but mainly for works in progress, a staging area. This work setup happens to give me a good vantage point to the house across the street, Tracksuit Man's house. I get to see all the weird things he does. It's not like I'm spying on him or anything. He's just there in plain sight.

In the short time I've been here, and that I am actually in the front room, I've witnessed a couple of peculiar things that reinforce my choice to stay the hell away from him. The camo-covered cattle gate he'd set up was only the beginning.

When we first moved in, I saw him on his hands and knees scooting along the curb to trim his lawn with scissors, big sewing ones like I have. How anal! I can't even begin to imagine what goes on when I don't just happen to be looking. I kind of enjoy letting my yard get a little wild before Arjun helps me mow. It must bug the hell out of him.

Then a couple weeks ago, it's a beautiful day and I'm working. Front curtains are open, windows open, even my front door is propped like I'd do at our last apartment, although I'm not expecting anyone to drop by. The difference is that this house has a screen door. It's my first screen door. Apartments don't have them, and I can't decide if I love it or hate it, but suddenly, I hear the sound of continuous broken glass, ribboned with a monologue of swearing. I hear it over the sound of my sewing machine and it's one of those industrial models, so it's pretty loud.

I look up, and Tracksuit Man is breaking light bulbs, one after another, on his porch. The regular kind that screw into a table lamp. He's throwing them hard on the ground so they shatter. Then, he stomps on the larger pieces. I go and stand in my doorway because I'm like—what the fuck? He catches me standing there. For some reason, I'm thinking the screen door obscures me, and anything in the house. But maybe it doesn't because he looks over like he can see me watching him. I don't want him to come over and start yelling, all twitchy and everything, so I close my door and curtains, and turn on the stereo pretty loud just in case. If I can't hear him knock, I don't have to answer the door. Right?

A couple of days after the great light bulb incident, I see Tracksuit Man on a ladder installing some kind of globe-shaped thing that hangs down from the overhang of his roof. He looks in my direction. I'm like, why does he keep looking over here? I don't think he sees me, because I'm standing back inside my house this time, not at the door. But then, he repeatedly looks back over his shoulder, as if he's checking to see if I'm watching. It gives me the heebie-jeebies. I almost feel like he's putting on a show for me, making me aware that he's manly and handy all in one go.

Then, he's back on the ground, looking up to assess his work, before going inside. The globe-looking thing begins to move, like it's scanning the area in front of his house. He comes back out, watches it rotate, then looks over at my house as he picks up his ladder and takes it in his garage. I'm enraged, because I'm sure the hanging thing is a security camera. It's like he's encroaching, just as he did with the cattle gate. Kevin, my realtor, said there wasn't much crime in this neighborhood, so I wonder why he's installing one. It's focused on everything in front of his house, which is *my* house. I am now the target of his observation 24/7. Is that even legal?

He's as strange as Psycho Soccer Mom. Maybe there's some

sort of connection there? Now I'm on defense. I have to be extra vigilant with Grace and who she comes in contact with. But I haven't seen any kids at his house, so it's unlikely he'd be at the school or any of its events. I tell myself I'm just being paranoid about the camera, but I'm not convinced. In my defense, it messes with your head when somebody threatens you.

I make sure I know where Grace is every minute she's not with me. And I continue to avoid Tracksuit Man, so if he happens to be outside when I'm coming or going, I hurry to the car or my front door without looking around. I've started making a game of it. It doesn't occur to me that I may run in to him elsewhere. Elsewhere happens to be at the grocery store.

This happens a couple days ago. So my new town has the greatest grocery store. I'm surprised when I first walk in. The entire entrance is filled with flowers. It's like flower stands you'd see walking down the streets of New York or London where they wrap your bouquet in a brown paper and tie it with string, so when you're walking down the sidewalk, you look like you've just won the Miss American Pageant. At least that's what I imagine. I've never been to either of those cities.

There's also a beautiful selection of local delicacies: organic fresh fruit and veg, goat cheese, craft beers, local honey. And it's set up like a farmers' market. I like to wander through the aisles, weaving back and forth almost like I'm a needle and thread, recreating the embroidered flower on my seventh-grade book bag, and pretending I'm visiting Abby in London. There aren't many people when I walk in, and I don't need anything. Just need to get out of the house. That happens sometimes when you work at home.

So I'm walking aimlessly, casually picking up items and reading labels, putting things in my cart. Then I remember what my mother always said, "If you can't afford two, you can't afford one." I put them back on the shelf. I'm not looking where I'm going and neither are the two young men who work there because they walk right into me. They're focused on something in a different part of the store, and they're laughing.

"Psycho," says one, and I'm thinking Psycho Soccer Mom is here. And they say nothing to me about our collision. I'm curious, so I turn the corner to see, and it's Tracksuit Man. He's in the water aisle holding a large plastic bottle he's taken from the shelf. It looks as if he's going through the same monologue he gave to the broken light bulbs. Swear words included. I find myself staring in a curious sort of way. Why is he so upset? It's like I want to peer into his life to make some sense of his actions.

He moves over a few steps to some empty shelves, then slams the bottle down and starts heading toward me. I panic and quickly turn down another aisle. I worry he's coming after me, so I hurry to the ladies' aisle, pick up a large package of feminine pads, and shield my face, pretending to read. Best way I can think of to get a man not to talk to you, or even come near. Lucky for me, it works. He leaves me alone.

So strange. I can't imagine what his ranting is all about, but this time, I know I don't have anything to do with it. He's just odd, or has something odd going on in his life. Either way, I'll take cover behind the pads whenever I see him. I don't want anything to do with odd. I may be different, but not odd like that. I leave. The only thing I buy is flowers. For myself. Mom always has flowers in the house. Flowers feel like home. Mom also says, "The most important person you can ever buy flowers for is you." Every so often, I listen to her advice.

Abby brushes Tracksuit Man off as harmless, and she may be right. But, with people like Psycho Soccer Mom around, and my obligation to protect Grace, I can't be too careful.

Subject #57: Eddie - Session 16
Topic:

Grace

So I'll continue with what happened at our dance party, which is supposed to make up for me demanding my daughter quit soccer. I can't wait to run the idea by Grace, so after I send Abby the middle-of-the-night email, even though it's late, I wake Grace up. I tell her we're having a pop-up dance party. I make sure to throw in "pop-up" because that's all the rage. She'll be more excited. The girls on the soccer team aren't invited. It's only me and Grace.

"We'll transform the living room into a dance club with loud music, and we can rent flashing lights. We'll even set up a makeshift bar, and you can be bartender," I say, and she's delighted, even though she's half asleep. And relax, she's only mixing juices and pop, but I'll be having wine, which I'll bring from the kitchen. The flashing strobe lights make this party extra special. I have a couple of days to find a place that rents the equipment, and on Saturday morning, Grace is ready to go. She's a little quiet, but at least she doesn't mention soccer. I already mentioned what happened there.

We used to have a lot of dance parties, but it's been a while. At our old apartment, the music drew in the neighbors, our friends. We'd switch off the lights, open the curtains, and dance by moonlight. Grace would fall asleep on the couch after wearing herself out. I'd leave her on the sofa, afraid to wake her. She'd later sneak into my room in the middle of the night. We didn't have flashing lights at the old parties, so this is what she looks forward to the most.

When Grace waves to Psycho Soccer Mom at the store, I'm surprised Grace is smiling. I didn't know Grace knew her. Grace seems quiet with her greeting, as if she's trying to hide their acquaintance from me. She can't possibly know that this was the parent I told her about. Can she? But I'm still wondering, why is she here and not at the game?

So, when I go to put the lights in the back of my SUV (I need a large car for my business), I ask her, "Do you know that lady you waved to in the store?"

"Ya. She's Coach's wife. She helps out sometimes." Or pretends to, I think. When I open the back, I realize I'd forgotten to take the boxes out, the ones I promised Mom I'd pick up, which took me weeks to pick up after we'd moved. Grace sees the labeling. They've got "Baby Grace's favorite things" written all over them. They're my favorite things too.

"What's in here?" Grace asks, and pulls a box toward her. She starts going through the contents right there in the parking lot. It's a fortunate change of subject. She's excited to reunite with her baby toys, and clothes, and the other things that have been at my mother's for a while. Things I don't have the heart to throw away.

"Let's wait until we get home. We don't want everyone seeing our stuff." I cringe when I hear myself saying this. It's something my father would say, worried about what other people think. I'm not supposed to be my parents. The boxes are such a wonderful distraction from soccer, as if I planned it this way. "We can go through them when we're home. We've got hours before it gets dark, and can use the lights." Truth be told, I'm just as excited as Grace to reunite with these treasures.

When we're home, Gladys is there. It's like the third time I've ever seen the woman, and it's as if she's waiting for me in my driveway, like we have an appointment or something. This is before she asks if we had a party, which I mentioned a couple sessions ago. I'm jumping around in time so I can talk about the one person written on the board. Sometimes it's hard to remember what I said already, and keep everything straight.

So, when I get out of the car, she grabs my arm. I'm like, why does she keep touching me? "Philippe got a security system," she says. "It takes a video of the neighborhood. It's that thing hanging down in the front of his house. It's more sophisticated than the ones you find at the big box stores. Look, you can even see the camera moving." She come out with this stream of intel about Tracksuit Man, and all I can think of is why? Why is she here?

Why is she telling me? Why does she think I care? She's excited about it, like someone famous has just moved in across the street. In her mind, the entire street is now safe. I'm wondering how long she's been waiting in my driveway to tell me.

"Oh, yeah?" I say. I was right when I saw him on his ladder. And Gladys mistakes my engagement as interest when it's me congratulating myself on my nearly expert inference. But again, why is she telling me? Does she think I'm some weak woman relying on Tracksuit Man to keep me and my house safe? Grace, I notice, listens, and looks a little disturbed. Gladys has put a seed in her mind that this neighborhood is as bad as the place we lived before Augustin's. Oh my God, can this woman be any more annoying?

"Smile! You're on camera!" Gladys says. "It's focused on your house." And it's like, I guess she can. It's like she's egging me on, begging me to react in some dramatic way, but I'm not sure if she thinks I should be happy or upset about this camera thing. Then I think, I wonder if she's right about the camera's position and Tracksuit Man's motive. Is she trying to warn me? My mind flashes to Psycho Soccer Mom. Is she behind it? Does she really think I'm out to get her or her husband? Am I being overly paranoid? Can you be overly paranoid?

"Okay, we're busy. We've got a lot of unpacking to do," I say. When I open the back of my car, she sees the moving boxes that conveniently reinforce my statement. The rental lights are back there too. That must be one reason she was watching our house, and how she knew about the party. Anyway, we go inside and instead of opening the boxes with her baby things, Grace goes to the front window and peeks around the curtain.

"What was Gladys saying about a camera taking pictures of our house?" she asks.

I go and peer above Grace's head at the two-story ranch house with its hanging intrusion. "It's a security camera," I say. "But, don't worry. There isn't any crime in this neighborhood. I asked the realtor before buying." But, I can tell the camera makes her uneasy. It makes me uneasy too. This small rotating mechanical ball provides privileged information to my paranoid neighbor, without my consent, which he may and probably will use against me. Not that I'm doing anything wrong, but sometimes people look for things that simply aren't there, especially if you have a lot of piercings and tattoos.

"Can Tracksuit Man see us now?" Grace's face contorts as if she was pushing away the presence of someone watching her.

"He can't see us while we're inside." I pull Grace's hair back away from her face, combing my fingers through it as I stand behind her. Damn that woman for upsetting my Grace. It's unnerving to think of Tracksuit Man at his desk watching live video on his computer, closely monitoring our house. I hide my misgivings well. "Tracksuit Man doesn't see the video. His security company does. And they'll only look at it if there is a robbery." But I'm only guessing at the specifics of the system. It's a white lie, I know. I'm only trying to make my daughter feel comfortable in her new home. That's good. Right?

I point to the security globe and put my head close to Grace.

"See it moving?" I say. We stand there, watching. It's a little hard to see, but I do my best to give a play-by-play of the camera's movements, trying to lighten the situation. It slowly spins from right to left. And, looks like it takes about thirty seconds to complete the scan. We watch it go through several cycles. It takes another fifteen seconds to reset.

Grace asks, "So if I don't want to be on camera, I can run to the car when it's in the other direction?" I'm proud she works through this logic. She's a smart kid. Her reasoning gives me an idea.

"Hey, let's mess with Tracksuit Man. Remember when I showed you how people do weird things when they see the Google Maps street-view car?" I ask.

"Ya! They pretend to kill each other or wear costumes," she says.

"In my closet is a box of our old Halloween costumes," I say. It's all I need to say. She jumps up, disappears, and comes back with the box. She's already opened it and bits of characters burst from the top. She plops it down and the contents are immediately all over the living room.

"Look! My princess mask. And Spider-Man!" She tries each of them on.

I try on the Bill Clinton mask I wore one year while wearing a likeness of the blue dress. Next, I grab my Mardi Gras mask, which has gotten plenty of use. "Look. The masks from Dylan's horror party!" I say, pulling from the bottom of the box. Mine, a latex mixture of blood-oozing stitches, rotten teeth, and crazy eyes on a monster that looks to be several hundred years old. And Grace's, a very good replica of Chucky, which even creeped me out at the time.

She throws the other two masks to the side and dons the horror doll. "Let's play!" She gets the quote wrong, but the attitude is there.

"Here's what we'll do," I say. "We wait till the camera is all the way to the left, then we'll run outside and put on a mask, so it's like we just magically appear. We just stand there, and don't move, facing the camera. Then, while the camera resets, we'll change masks. We'll do it three times, then run inside when it resets, so we just disappear." Grace likes the plan. Her body percolates with the anticipation of screwing with Tracksuit Man. I'm excited too. Something about him watching me be silly sounds gratifying.

So I put the masks in a bag, and we go to the front door. I open it just a crack to peek out through the screen. I tell her, "When I say go, run to the middle of the grass." We barely control our laughter, and I have to pee! Grace's hands are on my back as she waits for the signal. "GO!" I say.

It's a perfect execution. We run back inside, and I wonder if any of the other neighbors see. Gladys probably does, and we'll hear about it later. Tracksuit Man will for sure, if he hasn't already.

We're safe inside laughing. Grace is so much fun! I think this cures her from worrying about the camera. Tracksuit Man put on a show for us when he installed the damn thing, now we've put one on for him. That'll teach him to monitor us. After we catch our breath, we peer out the window to make sure Tracksuit Man isn't outside. We still have to finish unloading the car. Maybe we should have done that first. Grace helps me bring in the boxes and strobe light. She wants to go through the memories the minute they're inside. So do I.

Digging through, she takes out some old dolls and scrapbooks, then gawks at her baby clothes. "They're so cute," she says. And, everything comes flooding back to me. Her wearing the little outfit, how she felt so small when I'd held her against me. How she smelled like cookies, and how, when she looked at me, when we looked into each other's eyes, we saw love.

After we spend several hours reminiscing, I say, "We need to set up for our dance party." Grace immediately changes gears and helps put the boxes in the attic. But before we close the boxes, she grabs a couple things to keep in her new room.

I'm anxious when she removes anything from the boxes. I mean, it's her stuff and I like that she's fond of these things, but I don't want anything to happen to what I've been saving. Inside these boxes are memories, my link to my baby Grace, and I'm not ready to give that up. That's why I was saving them at Mom's in the first place. I didn't want anything to mistakenly be thrown in the dumpster like Grace's old bed. Well, that wasn't a mistake.

We carry the boxes to the back hallway, where there's a door in the ceiling with pull-down stairs to the attic. I have to get a chair to reach the string. I climb the ladder and Grace stands on the chair, handing me boxes from below. When everything's up, she says, "I've never seen inside an attic before."

I tell her, "Okay look, but stay on the ladder and just peek your head in." I like that she's curious, but I don't know if it's safe for her to be up there. Grace climbs and stops when only her shoulders and head are in the attic space above. It's a little spooky up there. She's quiet. I know what she sees. There's a plywood floor, and pink insulation is tucked in between the studs and trusses. A haze of sunlight from the two front dormer windows cast an amber glow on the dust covering everything but the boxes containing our old toys, the ones I just brought up. The ones I can't bring myself to throw away.

"Cool," is Grace's only comment.

⌘

The dance party setup goes smoothly, even though I was only halfway listening to the man giving instructions on how the light works. We use a couple of Grace's bedroom crates to hold the light and phone docking station, and I bring the small speakers Dylan picked out for me from the kitchen. They're surprisingly loud. There's not much to move out of the way, just my work table, which comes apart easily. We put chairs around the edges of the room, creating a dance floor. Grace brings out some of her stuffed animals and sets them around the room to decorate the space. Or maybe they're party guests. After setting up, we go to the store to get drinks and snacks. We also buy streamers. Once we're home, we wait for dark.

Soon we're dancing, and I'm thinking our party is a success. She's no longer in that somber mood. The next morning Grace asks if she can have a friend come over next Saturday. It makes me think she's past the whole soccer fiasco.

Subject #57: Eddie - Session 17
Topic:

Tracksuit Man

It's been a turbulent weekend and it's still Sunday, so it's not over yet. I dropped Grace off at Mom's so I could come here. So yesterday, my obnoxious neighbor pounds at my door just after Grace's playdate leaves. This is the Saturday after the dance party. It hasn't been a good day. Grace is mad at me. I'm questioning my parenting skills again. When I open the door, he screams at me. "What was that horrible woman doing here?" I'm wondering the same thing, but he has no right to ask. This is my house. I can't respond because it's the first time I've been face to face with him since the cattle gate incident, and he's acting as if it's just fine for him to tell me who I can and can't have in my own house. He's nervously twitching on my porch. All I can think is that I do not have the energy to deal with him right now.

And then, get this, he says, "I did not get a security camera to watch you and your daughter do ridiculous things. You're wasting my data." I find this bit humorous. He *did* see our show and it had the intended effect. Then, he looks down at the box of mangled dolls sitting on my porch and shivers as if someone had dropped an ice cube down his back. He turns and walks, but then yells over his shoulder, "The next time any of her toys want to commit suicide, send them out the back window." There he goes again, telling me what to do.

So, it's baffling why he's upset about all this. I'm the one who should be upset. And believe me, I am. He mentioned three things: *that* woman, the security camera, and the dolls. Did one ignite anger for the others? And if so, which is the instigator? Or, is he just nitpicky and anything that happens at my house sparks a huge outrage?

Here's what happened. Grace's friend arrives just after lunch. When I open the door, I'm surprised she's by herself. I assume her mother wants to meet us, but someone drops her off and leaves. Grace is shining as bright as a string of white Christmas lights when she sees Katie, who seems a nice enough girl: she's smiling, a cute blonde with curly hair, polite, although she's wearing bright blue eye makeup that's on alarmingly thick. She looks familiar, but I can't place her. She carries a bag full of stuff. Grace suggests they go outside, but first they put Katie's bag in Grace's room. I didn't think Grace invited her to sleep over, but it's fine if she did.

After they've been out for a short time, I check on them through the front window, making sure they're okay. I try not to let

Grace see me. She took the bag of masks and they're doing the "weird-street-view-moments" for Tracksuit Man's security camera. I laugh. Grace monitors the camera and perfectly times their costume change. That's my girly!

I go to my sewing table, but before I can start working, the girls scream and come running in the front door. They fall on the floor laughing. "Do you think he saw us?" Katie asks.

"His camera didn't, but he did," Grace howls.

I ask what happened.

It takes Grace a minute to respond; she's on the floor giggling in between sentences. "He saw us. He came to the door. He opened the screen and stuck his head out. Then we saw him and ran inside."

Too funny. I wish I'd kept watching out the front window. I would love to have seen that.

They go to Grace's room and play quietly for a long time. It gives me time to catch up on my sewing. I'm at my machine, deep into my work when I notice something outside the front window moving, so I go to the window to check it out.

Raining in succession from above are various-size and scantily clothed dolls. Grace's old dolls. It's as if they are a line of army men jumping out of an airplane. They fall as if in slow motion, twirling about with their arms and legs in unique positions, as if each was a snowflake. Their hair is haphazardly chopped. And although they spin, somehow each doll manages to hold its face toward me, nefariously staring. Each face is enhanced with a thick sharpie. Crazed eyebrows, curly mustaches, condescending spectacles, and cynical smiles cover the once innocent faces of Grace's childhood friends. The shower keeps coming, and ends with each doll crashing to its death on the front lawn, which is now littered with bodies. I'm horrified.

"Grace!" I yell and rush to her room, but as soon as I'm in the hall, I see the stairs to the attic, pulled down. I climb. My hands are shaking, and I yell. "What the hell are you doing?" They freeze. They're standing at the opened dormer window, with their mouths agape. Grace has the same thick makeup on as Katie, and they look at each other. They're smiling.

I notice the opened boxes, precious memories I'd been keeping safe. The contents are maliciously gone through and scattered. A large pair of my sewing scissors sit on the floor, reflecting the sunlight. I didn't notice them missing. Clumps of butchered hair are flung on top of collected dust. It's as if a stranger entered my deepest, darkest space and made a mockery of the things I hold dear. Grace's childhood was hacked up, vandalized, and tossed out the window.

My voice shakes, "Go downstairs immediately and pick up those dolls."

The girls leave quickly with their heads down. They don't say a word. How did I not hear them pull down the stairs? I close the window, pick up my scissors and an empty box, then climb down from the attic. I secure the stairs from below, and set the box outside the front door without saying anything more to the girls. I'm too angry and hurt to watch them or even help clean up. They know what the box is for.

A short time later, Grace comes into the house alone. "Where is Katie?" I ask. My tone isn't friendly.

"Her mom is here to pick her up," says Grace as she heads back to her room and brings out Katie's bag. She goes outside, then when she's back, goes straight to her room.

I holler after her, "Stay out of the attic!"

She yells back, "You didn't have to yell at us!" She never yells at me, and she's right. I feel the good mother scale tip against me. I go to the window to watch Katie's mother collect her, and I'm instantly sick, like I'm on a carnival ride twirling with my body crushed against the wall and the floor drops from under me. Katie climbs in the back seat of an SUV. Psycho Soccer Mom is in the driver's seat. Her window is down, and her head is turned toward my house. I can easily see her face. They slowly roll away. Her face holds no expression.

A cold sweat comes over me. All day, Psycho Soccer Mom's daughter was in my home, playing with Grace. I had no idea this was the girl Grace had befriended. How could I not know? Shouldn't a good mother be aware of who their kid is hanging out with? I mean, my mother knew, even if she didn't necessarily like it. And it's Saturday. Shouldn't she be at soccer?

I take a deep breath. I don't know whether or not this girl is evil, like her mother. And I have to remind myself that she's just a child. It isn't her fault she's the spawn of a lunatic and has Psycho Soccer Mom for a mother. Maybe she feels tortured from having a mother so controlling. I'm not sure whether to feel sorry for her. Maybe she needs to be saved? She's probably too young to know the secret palm, thumb, fist hand signal, but a good mom would make sure her daughter knows. I'll have to remember to explain it to Grace.

Soon after I close the door, I hear some kind of commotion outside, so I look out my front window. Tracksuit Man is knocking on my door. Now what? It's like an urgent, angry pounding. Instead of the cold sweat, my blood is boiling. In a matter of minutes, I've got Psycho Soccer Mom silently calculating my demise with her drive-by and Tracksuit Man on a rampage on my porch. It's like I'm being assaulted on every level. I'm thinking maybe I'll get a security system too, for Grace's sake. And my own.

Subject #57: Eddie - Session 18
Topic:

Abby

I'm back. I called Abby yesterday for more advice about the playdate, after I was here. It isn't long after Katie leaves that I realized the full scope of her destruction. She's like the Tasmanian Devil. It's late, but Abby's home and up. "You can't forbid Grace to see her," she says. "She's at that age where she'll rebel."

"You're right," I say. I know I had to prove any adult figure wrong if they negatively commented on anything I was doing. Maybe that's why Mom never commented.

"Make sure you supervise them closely. Be friendly with the daughter. She's still only a kid. Although you should stay clear of her mother," she says. Hearing this makes me tired. It feels like a lot of work. I've never had to get into Grace's business before, so I'm real uncomfortable about doing it now, and I don't have a clue where to begin. Abby says I should do this even though Katie is clearly a bad influence on Grace: the heavy makeup (on a nine-year-old!), sneaking into the attic and destroying my memories. Grace would never think of doing these things on her own. Abby doesn't change her advice when I try to convince her otherwise, even when I tell her what I found after Katie left.

"She needs time to cool down," I say to Abby. "Then, things will be okay."

But, I'm anxious. Grace is holed up in her room, and in the meantime, I need something to distract myself. I pause, trying not to cry again. I take another deep breath before continuing.

"So, Grace's door is closed when I go to my room. I sit on my bed and reach for my favorite scrapbook on my nightstand. You know the one," I say. "It's been on every nightstand in every place we've lived since we made it." The fabric on the cover is a robin's-egg blue with a gentle silhouette of white primrose lattice accented by a scattering of miniature cherry-red primroses. Abby has seen it many times. The title is written with a gold shiny paint pen: "The Queen and Her Princess." Grace made it up long ago, and I know the story inside by heart. The Queen takes the Princess on a trip to a magical playground made by fairies. In the story, the Princess loves the Queen very much. Maybe that's why I pick it up. Maybe that's why it's my favorite. Anyway, I linger on each page as I flip through. Each time I turn the page, my fingers caress the thoughtfully chosen words, and I stroke the drawings as if they were the side of Grace's soft cheek. How is it possible for one person to feel so much love?

"When I get to page five, I see it." My face, chest, and hands are suddenly cold. It's like I'm dropped into the Arctic Ocean headfirst, and the top half of my body smacks into an iceberg. "On the entire page, and over the original words and carefully drawn picture, written in a thick bright green crayon, are the words I HATE MOMMY." The words press hard into the page, indenting the paper with rage. It's like they're screaming at me, spinning out of control, and it makes me dizzy.

It's like, who did this and when? Was it Grace? Did Katie help her? Did she suggest it? It had to have been written today or recently. I'm sure I looked through the book a couple days ago and it wasn't there. But it's odd she called me Mommy. It's been a long time since she called me that. Is it possible I missed it? I wonder what Katie calls her mom.

Abby says, "She's a tween, not a child, not a teen, and that's hard. Give her some time, then ask her about it."

After I find the bright green words, I hug the book and tears roll down my cheeks. "Was my reaction to the dolls so wrong that it caused her to write this?" I ask Abby. She doesn't respond. But I'm mad at myself for forgetting to choose how to react. How could I get it so wrong?

So, after my crying episode. I place the book back on the nightstand, wipe my eyes, and take a deep breath, bringing all of my hurt to collect at the center of my being. It's joining other collected pain from Psycho Soccer Mom, from Tracksuit Man, from my cousins, Granny's death, even a bit from Dad. It feels like everyone is attacking me. The entire universe is attacking me. My face feels puffy from crying. I get up to get a drink of water from the kitchen, then make a detour on my way back to my bedroom at the half bath to splash water on my face. The mirror doesn't lie. My face is red *and* puffy.

"It gets worse," I say to Abby. "Katie forgot her makeup bag." It's sitting on the bathroom counter.

Subject #57: Eddie - Session 19
Topic:

Mom

So, new day, new drama. Since the playdate fiasco, I try to be that good-mom image I have for myself by inviting my mom over for dinner yesterday for some family time. Grace is mad at me for yelling at her and Katie, and still hasn't quite gotten over me making her quit soccer. I'm hoping time with her granny will soften her. It's only the second time Mom comes to the new house. She has to be curious about how her investment is doing, though she'd never directly ask.

Arjun comes over early to cook for us. He believes a mother should have something nice to eat when you invite her over, which is kind of an insult now that I think about it. But I believe the real reason is that he wants to give me advice on the whole Psycho Soccer Mom thing. He's just as upset as I am. I set the table while

Arjun is busy at the stove. This, I'm good at. My chore growing up. He leaves as soon as Mom arrives, properly asking her how she is before excusing himself. Mom has met him several times and finally stopped asking if we're dating. I just realized Arjun hasn't been a topic for me yet. Next time. Anyway.

When Mom comes in, she says to Grace, "Happy half-birthday!" Grace lights up when she sees the half-cake she brought. Mom's dressed all fancy in her Sunday best, even though it's Monday. She's wearing Granny's broach. I wish I'd put on a newer tank.

Grace's actual half was last week. I completely forgot about it. Some mom, right? But, she didn't say anything either. We used to celebrate it with Mom until a couple of years ago. I'm not sure why we stopped. I guess I was busy, but the whole house thing has put Mom back in our lives. I hope it isn't only about the money. Mom did the half-birthday thing for me until I was ten. When you turn ten, you stop counting the halves. People stop thinking you're cute when you reach double digits, and suddenly you're supposed to know things. It's some sort of unsaid rule.

This will be Grace's last celebration, and I should have done something. In my defense, I've got a lot going on. But bringing the focus back to Mom. She was older when she had me, so her beliefs belong to a grandmother's era. I think she had trouble getting pregnant.

"It smells lovely in here," says Mom, and I can tell she's surprised by the savory aroma. I say nothing about how it got here.

I take the cake from Mom and Grace gives her a long hug. It's a nice way to be greeted, to have someone so excited to see you that they run to the door and give you a heartfelt embrace.

"How do you like your new school?" Mom asks. Grace fills her in and Mom looks pleased. I'm proud of Grace, so I smile too. She gets good grades, even with all the moving around.

Grace likes to read. I think that's why she does well. I started reading for pleasure later in life, but when I was about her age, I carried around my mother's favorite book. It was kind of stupid. I thought it made me look grown up to carry a book no one but a few adults had heard of. I read it over and over again, trying to find a bit of my mother in the text. You know, what about this book did she like so much? She was so much of a "mom" to me and I wanted to see beyond that. I thought this might be another way in. The book is about a family, and it's adult fiction, not middle grade. I didn't understand a lot of it, and didn't like how much the people in the book smoked. Although later I became a smoker myself.

Anyway, I used to quote lines from the book to show off. Something like, "I'm not afraid to be nobody" and "I feel wonderfully unstable." I'm sure I'm not accurately quoting, but it's the gist. At the time, I could barely discern their meaning, but it seems like my current life.

Back then, I underlined certain things and earmarked pages without permission. Kind of dumb, I know. I did it to stand out, make people to think I was smart. Man, I must have been really desperate for attention. I remember someone saying, I don't remember who, that the amount you read directly relates to the level of intelligence *others* perceive you to have. It's all about perception, smoke and mirrors. I tried to fool everyone with this book. My desire to appear to be well read didn't last long. This was when Abby first moved in. Looking back, I can see the other kids probably just thought I was weird. I guess Abby considered me eccentric.

⌘

At my dinner, Grace knows what not to say to Mom. She doesn't tell her she isn't playing soccer anymore. She doesn't tell her about me yelling at her and Katie at the playdate. And I don't tell Mom about Psycho Soccer Mom, the scrapbook, or the necklace Granny gave me. I tell her something pleasant about the neighbors instead. It's what she wants to hear, only good things, like how the lady down the street, Leigh (aka Gladys), helps me with my gardening, and how the man across the street offered to help when our electricity was on the blink. Literally.

Neither is a lie. I don't *like* to lie, especially to Mom. The mention of a man sparks Mom's interest. I tell her he sent over his electrician when he saw our lights blinking, but not to worry, our lights are fine. The lights he saw were the ones we had rented for the dance party. I tell her we were celebrating Grace's half birthday, another lie, a white one. Sorry, Mom.

"Oh, what a nice man to want to help," she says. "Does he have a family? Is he married?" The poor woman is always trying to get me married again. She still doesn't understand I want to be on my own. A man doesn't fit into my image of our perfect little family. I don't blame her. It's how things were done when she was my age.

I tell her yes. He has a family, although I have no idea if that's true. White lie number two. I'm burying myself deep, but these little lies are justified. Then I worry she'll ask me if I'm friends with his wife, and I'll have to lie again. I quickly change the subject. Too many fibs are hard to remember.

"Remember the star you gave me when I was little?" I ask. It works. The man across the street is forgotten. "Is it okay if I give it to Grace for her half?" I already know the answer to this. She perks up when I bring up good times from my childhood. Her experience as a mother was so different from mine. Growing up, she never opened herself up to me like I do to Grace. She'd made motherhood seem effortless. She never wavered. But then, there wasn't anything else she had to focus on. All she ever wanted to be was a wife and a mother, and nothing else.

Oh wow! One of the old quotes makes sense to me. Mom wasn't afraid to be nothing. But was she nothing? She was giving. And trusting. And a caregiver. I'm not sure I'm like her in this way, especially since the ex, but I'm trying.

"Of course," she says. "It's yours to do with whatever you like." I squeeze her arm as a thank you. I'll explain. When I was small, I'm on Mom's lap, looking up at the nighttime sky and that's when she gave me the biggest and brightest star in the heavens. She says it's a wishing star. I couldn't believe Mom owned something so magical. This was well before Granny pointed out my superpower, and technically, Granny didn't give me that.

Anyway, even then, I knew Mom's gift was immense and came with great responsibility. And she trusted me with it. But she warned to use it wisely. I thought it was a silly thing to say. What wish would be unwise?

Grace hears and wants to know right away what I'm giving her. I tell her she has to wait until tonight. But that's all I say. I want to give her the star the same way Mom gave it to me. I hope it isn't cloudy. Maybe someday she'll give to her daughter. Yep, she's got a daughter, not a son.

So, I'm creating the same "fond" memories for Grace I had as a child. I guess you do what you know. The half-birthday cake, the star, and I mentioned the scrapbooks. They all came from Mom. So the scrapbooks didn't start out as an art project with Mom. We first told our stories out loud, taking turns by making up only a bit, then we'd turn it over to the other to continue. Sometimes the same story would go on for days. Mom finally suggests we write them down after I wanted to hear an old one again, and we can't remember exactly what happens. Grace and I skip the whole oral storytelling and put pen to paper from the beginning.

When I reread them, they bring me back to the exact moment Grace and I made them, almost like a photograph, but with sound and emotions, in the text, of course. I'm not schizophrenic. It was my idea to make the covers out of fabric. I've got tons of it lying around. We've made a lot. They clutter all corners of the house.

⌘

So we eat dinner, and of course Arjun creates a masterpiece. But the food is too spicy for Mom. She takes tiny sips of water and blots the corner of her mouth after each bite, real proper like even though my napkins are technically paper towels. "It's fine," she says when I ask if it's too spicy. Grace and I are used to spicy. I've poured two glasses of wine, but Mom barely touches hers, a few sips to be polite. The woman never complains; she always minds her manners, even with her own daughter. I'm in a different category when I move in with the ex, from those you can relax around at home, to someone requiring proper etiquette. People requiring etiquette live elsewhere.

Mom taught me how essential manners are. She'd say, "The purpose of etiquette is to treat others respectfully: hold the door for the person behind you, never blow your nose at the table, always say please and thank you. Eddie, we deserve to be treated exactly the way we treat others. And a person's character is evident in how they treat other people."

I want Grace to respect me, so it's important I set a good example, treat others kindly. But, I need to find at least one person in our new neighborhood I can connect with, like Abby or Arjun. "I wish there was someone I could admire," another quote from Mom's book, or something like that. So, next time Arjun and more about Katie's makeup bag.

Subject #57: Eddie - Session 20
Topic:

Arjun

I promised I'd talk about Arjun when I was here yesterday. It's weird I haven't written his name on the board until now. He's like my security blanket because I'm myself around him. So when he's over making dinner for Mom, I run Abby's advice by him. Grace is in her room, out of earshot.

"Abby's advice is contradicting," I say to him. "She wants me to bring one family member close—Katie—and keep the other at arm's length—Psycho Soccer Mom. It's too hard." Especially when I discovered what's in Katie's makeup bag.

"No. You must keep your enemies close," says Arjun as he chops ginger. I've heard the saying before. Not sure where it comes from, or if it actually works. But, it's been around so long there must be some truth behind it. "Why would she threaten you about your email? You did nothing wrong," he says. I can tell he's freaked out. His face is all tense and his eyes are big.

"I know," I say. "It doesn't make sense, right? Maybe she's bored and likes to create drama?" Although, I have no idea how Psycho Soccer Mom keeps herself busy, if she works or what else she does aside from threatening people. She's kind of like an adult bully. She must have a lot of insecurities to act this way. It must make her feel important.

"If she's close, you'll know what she's up to and can be one step ahead of her. But you need to do it quickly." Arjun waves his knife around as he advises me. It's an appropriate prop. He doesn't usually go against anything Abby suggests, but with this, he's adamant. But he has a point, aside from his knife. If I'm friends with Psycho Soccer Mom, I'd be on the inside. One of them. But only in appearance. I could monitor things better.

"For me to be her friend, she has to be willing, and right now that doesn't seem to be the case," I say, trying to worm my way out of it. The table is set, so I'm standing, watching him.

"Parents need to work together to steer their kids in the right direction," he says. I imagine a caravan of Indian families on the road to some place called Right, the kids taking note of the route. But to be serious, he's pointing out what a good mother does. "The parents need to be in charge," he says. "It takes a community to raise a child." Arjun spouts a lot of cliches. The large knife seems to give him confidence. But, he's referring to his caste system back in India where rules and traditions have to be followed, no questions asked. Except that's not what he did. And Psycho Soccer

Mom helping me to raise my child? I don't see that happening.

So, a bit about Arjun, to get an idea where he's coming from. He's been in this country for almost two years on a work visa. He's an engineer, and his work has something to do with the automotive industry. He makes good money, enough to live in a nicer place than Augustin's apartments or Dylan's frat house, but he says he doesn't need to live lavishly, wants to experience how an average American lives. He comes from a place called Chennai, but his family, his ancestors, are from Andhra Pradesh. I'm probably not saying that right. He says that culturally, they're different. They call Chennai the Detroit of India, so it makes sense he's here. But it's not the *real* reason he's here.

Arjun used to be married. "In India," he once told me, "the man gives his bride the marriage necklace. It unites them forever. She must wear it always." I ask about a wedding ring. He tells me, "We exchange rings at the engagement ceremony." I keep forgetting to ask if there is an engagement ring, one with a huge diamond, and a wedding band. He finally shows me the necklace after trying to explain what it looks like. He's hesitant to take it out of its box. He isn't supposed to have it.

He keeps it in a wooden box; the lid has a lot of white inlay. When he opens the box, I smell something spicy, not spicy like he uses in his food, but more perfumey. The necklace is wrapped in a printed silk, and he handles it gingerly, giving it to me like it's very fragile. As I hold the small bundle, Arjun pulls a long gold chain from the silk. Tied to the ends of the chain is a gathering of gold and jewels, making the necklace a continuous loop. Two drum-like cymbal charms are the dominant feature. They have stones in the middle, which make it look like nipples on a plump round breast. The stones are red. They almost ache. "It's called a mangalsutra, an Indian bridal necklace," he says. "It means she is my mate for life. She is supposed to wear it all of her life, as a commitment to me until I die." Right away, I think his bride is dead because he certainly isn't. And if he can't go home, I wonder if he killed her.

I nudge him to continue as I notice the length of the chain would make the cymbals fall right at a woman's boobs for the rest of her life. God, what would it feel like wearing it all the time. I imaging leaning over my sewing table and the damn thing hanging down and getting in my way, obstructing my sight when I need to be precise. But, I understand the symbolism. At least I think I do. "Why do you have it?" I ask.

"It was a loveless marriage. I was dead the day I put it on her." I'm relieved by his metaphor. He looks so sad. I want to take him into my arms and hold him. And I do.

We've held each other before, not long after we met. There was wine, a lot of wine. And there was a kiss, slow and tender, but there were no sparks. That's when he told me he was gay. We both knew we'd found a very good friend, someone to confide in, someone to accept us as we are. After the kiss, he took my face into his hands and said, "My dear Eddie, my friend. You mean the absolute world to me." We fell asleep hugging each other on the couch, fully clothed. It's nice to have someone to hug. But, back to the story.

"My family chose the design. Just like they chose my bride," says Arjun. "Both are from Andhra Pradesh. It was an arranged marriage. My parents gave my bride's parents a dowry. The black beads are supposed to keep evil away," he explains as he fingers the necklace. I notice there are a lot of black beads. Maybe his parents know more than he thinks.

I ask what his parents had to pay for his bride. "They gave them money, and some land," he says. I don't ask how much. It isn't right to put a figure on a person. He looks as if he wants to tell me more. I give him my full attention, and I wait.

He talks, but he doesn't look directly at me. "Soon after we were married, I took the necklace. She thought it was lost. It wasn't fair for her to be bound to me. She is young and very beautiful. I couldn't love her the way every woman should be loved, even though I tried. She worried about me when she noticed it missing. It is ominous if it's lost or breaks. Bad things will happen. And they did. I left, unable to face my family. I never said goodbye." Arjun doesn't say he couldn't face his family because they would never approve of him being gay. And, he would rather leave his country, his home, than live a lie. I admire that. "I think she knew I took it," says Arjun. "I think she knew why."

After he left his wife and while he waited for his transfer paperwork to go through for the Detroit company, he spent time in a place called Goa, which is like Amsterdam: drugs and orgies. Anything goes. He tried doing several kinds of drugs, which is hard for me to hear, and that led him to shed any inhibitions he had to have his first real gay encounter. When he got to Detroit, he was ready to find a real boyfriend, someone to share his life with.

"I thought I'd met him. I thought he loved me," says Arjun, after he tells me all about this guy he dated: what he looks like, how they met, how he moves. I see a sad sparkle in his eyes. For him, this man is special, his soul mate, and Arjun wants to secure a bond with him. After they make love, Arjun shows him the necklace, tells him its significance, then drapes it over his neck. "He's wearing nothing but my necklace," says Arjun. *This* brings an interesting visualization to mind, and I linger on it as he continues his story. "He looks beautiful," says Arjun. And in my mind, he does.

In the morning, when Arjun wakes, his boyfriend is gone, and the necklace is on the nightstand. No note, no nothing, and he never hears from him again. Arjun searches everywhere, but can't find him. I see Arjun's heart is still broken, and it breaks my heart, too. I'm the only one he has shown the necklace to since.

Arjun and I get along because he's a rebel, too. He left home on questionable terms, and says he won't ever be able to go back. Although when we get together, he talks a lot about his home, so he must miss it. I don't know if he can't or is just afraid to go back because his family won't accept him.

He told me about his necklace a couple months after we met. That's when I told him I had a special necklace too, but I never said why. What I found after Katie left still rattles me, so I grab a bottle of white from the refrigerator.

"Want some?" I ask. Arjun shakes his head. He's leaving soon. I pour myself a glass as I consider his befriend-Psycho-

Soccer-Mom logic.

Armed with a full glass of wine, I share my story while he's making the curry. "Remember I told you I had a special necklace?" He nods. "I keep it hidden in my closet on the top shelf, in a large green, paper-lined gift box that holds my most cherished memories. It's like my vault." He listens closely. I can tell he understands. "Anytime I take the necklace out, I treat it with great ceremony, gently unwrapping it from the dark chocolate velvet. Holding it up to the light to admire it, then I bring it to my heart. The necklace was my grandmother's." I'm giving him details so he understands how important it is. "I can still smell her perfume on the cloth," I say. "It's like she's right there with me. I'll caress it with my thumbs, then look through her old letters."

I remember Gran taking it from the very same cloth when I was a girl. It's a Sarah Coventry necklace, costume jewelry fashionable in its day, with two large teardrop-shaped luminescent pearls, each sprouting from a gold-knitted acorn cap. They hang on a long gold chain that swayed back and forth as my grandmother moved, like a yo-yo that hung almost to her belly. It's vintage. Maybe that's another reason I like it, and this style had recently come back in vogue. It isn't worth much, but Granny has left this world, so to me the necklace is priceless. Her birthday is sad for me, and I wear the pearl-drop necklace on this day every year to feel close to her.

I pause, then tell him about Katie, about the dolls raining from the attic, about how I found out she was Psycho Soccer Mom's daughter, and about my necklace. "Grace knows what the necklace means to me," I say. "She watches me unwrap it every year. She knows someday it will be hers, but for now, it's off limits. And I trusted her." As I pour my heart out to Arjun, I'm checking the back hallway, to make sure Grace isn't there, listening.

"When I see Katie's makeup bag sitting on the bathroom counter, something tells me to look inside. Maybe I want to check out the makeup Grace has caked on her face. I envision unzipping the top and finding cheap kid's makeup and maybe some hand-me-downs from her mother. But, maybe there's something in there she isn't supposed to have, something illegal, something bad I may not recognize. I begin to think the worst, forgetting she's only in fourth grade."

Arjun puts the cover on the pan, turns, then leans against the counter, giving me his full attention.

"When I open the bag, something familiar gleams inside." It's underneath a goulash of varied, colored powders, broken cakes and pencils, all of which had fallen from their containers and were darkened with either dirt or age. I bravely dig in, wanting to uncover the gleam. Then, nestled in the carnage, a glimpse of a vintage gold chain and acorn-capped teardrop pearl catches my eye. I pull it to the surface as if I'm pulling it from the bog. Debris falls loose and drops into the sink and back into the bag, but remnants cling to the crevasses of the necklace and underneath my nails.

"It's my necklace! I can't even imagine what happened for my necklace to get into Katie's bag. And I can't believe Grace is involved. It's like she's turning on me." My heart races, flushed with a mixture of hurt and anger as I relive this moment.

"Then, it's so important you get close to this family," Arjun says. "And, put your necklace in a different place until then. Grace is getting to the age when peer pressure is strong. She will side with her friends." Arjun returns to his pan and stirs. Steam rises.

"I know. That was me at her age. And now, the necklace is well hidden."

"The pressure of parents working together is strong. It worked for me." He's right. It worked for him. He married someone he didn't want to marry. But then it didn't.

I tell Arjun what Abby says. "Parents make all the sacrifices because they love their children more than their kids love them. Children are supposed to leave." It's a thought that leaves me empty, the children leaving bit, but it's how nature works.

Arjun objects. "In India, children don't leave. The family bond is too strong. The children are the ones to make sacrifices." But he left. He's sending me some mixed signals. If his parents knew his secret, they would be against him. I guess the family bond isn't strong enough to withstand a son being gay. He had to leave, but didn't want to. That's a pretty big sacrifice. I don't know what that feels like. I've always wanted to leave. I also never made any sacrifices for my parents.

By the time Mom comes over, I know I can't stop Grace from seeing Katie. They're together at school. I put myself in Grace's situation. I would defy my parents to see the forbidden friend just to spite them. I don't want her to feel like there's nowhere to go but away, like Arjun felt. I have to make friends with Psycho Soc…ugh. I have to stop calling her that. I'll have to start using her actual name. Shelia.

Subject #57: Eddie - Session 21
Topic:

Miss Clark

I didn't come yesterday because I had a beginning-of-the-school-year parent-teacher conference. And of course, Grace and I were late. We're only allowed fifteen minutes, so late is not good.

They didn't have class, so the teachers could meet with every parent in one day. As we run down the hall to her classroom, we pass a single child stationed in a chair outside each door, like they're a security guard or something. I'm breathing so heavy, I get Miss Clark's attention as soon as I'm in her doorway. She's waiting at her desk. And her name is *Miss* Clark, not Ms. And Grace raves about her.

"Please come in," she says, standing. She turns to Grace. "Hello, honey. You can have a seat in the hall while your mom and I chat." She has the tone of someone who wants to take care of you, like a nurse with a terrific bedside manner. Grace sits on the empty chair and picks up a stack of books left beside it as I follow Miss Clark inside.

First thing I notice is her hair. She dons a 1970s Queen Elizabeth 'do. She also wears a buttoned shirt with wide lapels and high-waisted polyester pants. The whole ensemble makes her look like a homemaker from the same era, like she found a look that works for her and hasn't changed it since. It's not like the '70s with go-go boots, flower power, and fringe. That'd be sort of cool. It's more matronly. Maybe a country-western homemaker of the '70s? Although, Miss Clark might not be that old. It's impossible to tell her age. Oh, and then there's the sturdy shoes, nurse shoes or maybe ones a waitress might wear. But she's running after kids all day; I see her reasoning. I can't imagine where she buys any of it. People say Grace is lucky to have her as a teacher because Miss Clark is every student's favorite.

"I'll show you where Grace sits," Miss Clark says as she gives me a quick tour of the room. There's a huge open treasure chest loaded with trinkets any nine-year-old would do almost anything for. Self-portraits and written assignments decorate the walls. They're like family portraits displayed around a home, linking each kid with this space. I find Grace's immediately. I know her hand when it comes to art.

"Have a seat here," she says and points to a small student's desk. I guess I'm meant to get my child's perspective of what it's like to be in her class. When I'm seated, I see it's more than just a meeting. It's a chance for the teacher to guilt parents into volunteering and donating for the rest of the year. Miss Clark sits at the other student desk pushed against mine so we face each other. The desk she sits at has a stack of paper on it. The desks are small, and my legs touch the underside, lifting and making it move with every sway of my body. I slide out from under it and sit with my legs side-saddle like I'm on a horse.

"We need snacks for testing, baked goods for the fair, and parent supervisors for a handful of other school fun-while-we-learn days," says Ms. Clark, I mean Miss. She mentions Shelia. A lot. It seems Psycho Soccer Mom is involved in just about everything at the school, and is held in high regard. So this is what she does with her days. It's going to be hard to find that person to confide in as Abby suggests.

Miss Clark switches gears, and I'm confused. "Grace is having some trouble fitting in." And it's like, my Grace? I stare at her, processing what she said. She must realize my confusion, and elaborates.

"The other kids are more involved," she reveals.

"What do you mean, more involved?"

"Involved with the extras of the school: PTSA and after-school clubs," she clarifies. I'm guessing the extra S in the PTA is students. "The parents, teachers, and students work together to get things done. If Grace wants to be included, you'll have to be involved in what the other parents are doing." As she says this, she's smiling at me, but she's also tearing up, which makes it awkward. Really awkward. It's like she talking from the heart. It's genuine. How can anyone say no to this woman under that kind of pressure?

As I'm wondering why I hadn't been notified about any extra activities until now, she mentions something about Shelia.

"Shelia? Katie's mom?"

"Yes, that's right." She doesn't look up and I realize any plan is going to be hard if Katie's in Grace's room and Psycho Soccer Mom is the room mother.

"Grace quit the soccer team. Correct?" she asks. "I hear some encounters you've had with the other parents were a little...rude." She says the last word like she knows it will be painful for me to hear, scrunching her face and lifting one eyebrow. I'm feeling a little defensive. I'm not sure if she's referring to the Psycho Soccer Mom incident or the comment I made to one of the bag-of-orange-slices ladies, but I maintain a calm outward appearance. Although, the rebel kid inside me is rising.

I've been accused of being rude before, but never of not being involved in my daughter's schooling, or her life for that matter. That's my mom. And soccer's not a school function so why does she care? Unless Shelia has something to do with it. A proverbial light bulb illuminates. Both Abby and Arjun are right. I'll have to watch out for Psycho Soccer Mom *and* get along with her. She's everywhere at Grace's school.

"I've always been involved in Grace's school functions," I say, then reassess the initial "nice" label I gave her. Things seem to be a little backward, a mom telling the teacher what to do with someone else's kid. It's clear. Abby's plan won't work for Miss Clark. Arjun's is my only option.

Miss Clark mentions Shelia again, and I ask, "What do I need to do to help?" My new plan is in motion. But, I'm not comfortable about it. I hate to pretend I like someone. I'd rather tell them to their face that I don't.

"You can be Shelia's assistant," she says. Perfect. I try to grasp what being Shelia's assistant entails. All the while, Miss Clark is looking directly at me, waiting for me to accept. The moisture in her eyes never fully forms or goes away. The longer I ponder, the more fidgety I become. I can't think of an excuse.

Miss Clark puts several sign-up sheets in front of me before I answer. "What does the room mother need help with?" I ask. Yes, I cave, but it's the plan to protect Grace.

"That's up to Shelia. She's in charge." Wow. Even Miss Clark acts as if she's under her control. Miss Clark shuffles through papers and puts the room-parent sign-up sheet on the top of the pile. For some reason, the woman needs five assistants. Four of the slots are already taken. When I hesitate, thinking about Psycho Soccer Mom's threat, Miss Clark reminds me our time is nearly up. I pick up the pen, and as I'm signing, wonder if Psycho Soccer Mom was saving this spot. Strategically. Just for me.

Miss Clark immediately takes the pen from me after I sign, as if she's afraid I'll change my mind and cross it out. She also whisks the papers away. "With you involved, Grace will be able to do so much more. It's good to be on Shelia's good side, if you know what I mean." Did I see her just wink? I know what she means, but do I really? "There'll be perks for Grace," explains Miss Clark, like she's hinting at something.

Arjun will be happy I've got my in with Psycho Soccer Mom. Miss Clark hands me a syllabus for the upcoming year. "Here's what Grace will be learning. Do you have any questions?" I have many, but I'm not sure if she's the person I should ask. I shake my head.

Miss Clark puts the treasure chest sign-up sheet in front of me. With less than a minute left, she's pressuring me to commit to something else. Boy, is she good. The list is already long, like everyone is donating something. I wonder how many cheap toys any kid needs.

She stands to greet the next mom and kid when they appear at the door, leaving me to finish. I sign, and as I stand to leave, reach over and grab a handful of trinkets from the treasure trove and stuff them in my bag. My way of dealing with what's coming. I think Miss Clark sees me, and so does the other mom, but they don't mention a thing.

Subject #57: Eddie - Session 22
Topic:

Me

Back. I don't know if it's the traffic coming here, the unavailable parking, or the series of events since yesterday that's making me worked up. Maybe it's everything piling up. Arjun's watching Grace while I'm here. Okay, I get a message from Psycho Soccer Mom the moment I'm back from yesterday's session, like she knows when I get home. It's one of those calls that goes straight to voice mail, where my phone doesn't ring. She's having her first Room Mother meeting, and gives me an hour to be there. All assistants must attend. For some reason it's at her house, not the school. Her voice message sounds cordial, so I'm thinking maybe she wants to put the whole threaten-me thing behind us. She must think I want it too by agreeing to be an assistant.

Driving to her house, I feel as if I'm going to throw up, and my stomach spasms as I try to decide what I'll say to her. Then, this is crazy, I begin to feel sorry for her. Maybe she's desperate, and having these assistants coming to her house is her weird attempt at friendship. I mean, she sounded nice on the message, like she's happy I'm involved. But, I have to tiptoe around this one. I take a deep breath as I pull up to the house.

My stomach quivers as I walk to her front door. I'm imagining it's a gauntlet, and there's a crowd throwing things at me. They're pointing and laughing. I knock.

Psycho Soccer Mom opens the door. "Hello! Come in." She's smiling and I'm back in the twilight zone.

"Hi," is all I can muster. It's like an alternate reality. Instead of exuding her usual confidence, she looks soft, like a different woman than the one I saw at the rental store. Or the soccer field. She wears no makeup and has on an oversize ragged sweater. Her hands tightly grip the large folds. It makes her look vulnerable. I feel a bit of empathy.

"Sit down. Would you like some coffee?" she says.

I'm blown away. This isn't the same woman who strutted up to me, flicking an email in my face. Why is she suddenly so nice? Then it dawns on me—I'm the only assistant here. There should be four others.

"No, thank you," I say. "Where is everyone else?" I'm nervous. It's feeling like an ambush. The smile she greeted me with remains stuck on her face.

"Attendance is mandatory, but I've scheduled *our* meeting separately. I'd rather it be more one-on-one. That way, we can get to know each other better." I'm smiling and nodding, but now I'm freaked. Does she mean only *our* meeting or do all the assistants get the special one-on-one treatment? The room feels warm, but I think it's me. She has a sweater. She isn't dewy. I've surely walked into a trap.

"I'll be right back. Make yourself at home," she says, and goes to the kitchen, leaving me engulfed in her life. I hear dishes rattling. The opulently carved furniture is oversize for such a small space. Deep earth tones and heavy textures press upon me. They're exaggerated by multiple framed photos of various family members, all of them watching me. Her team, so to speak. It's like they're waiting for me to make a move, and are ready to tattle. The house is homey and cluttered, yet organized. Clear containers holding parent donations are stacked along the floorboards. I can't place the smell. It isn't repulsive, but foreign, like someone else's house, someone else's life.

I sink into the sofa and I'm quiet, trying to hear what's going on in the kitchen, to see if anyone else is in there. Psycho Soccer Mom enters the room with a mug of bitter coffee. I'm glad I didn't accept. It smells stale, as if it's been sitting on the coffee burner since yesterday. She sits in a chair kitty-corner to the couch, facing me. She sips her mug and waits. The pause is long and awkward, so I start talking.

"I want to tell you how sorry I am for the whole thing about your husband not being at practice. I totally misspoke." After I say this, I'm like, what the fuck? Why the hell am I sorry? But, for some reason, I continue. "I know it couldn't be helped, and the girls were just fine. Besides, there was a dad there watching them," I say, not believing *this* is my response to her silence. I've just sold my soul. I know I have a plan, but I'm way overdoing it.

But, I sound sincere, saying what she wants to hear, and it's the only way I can get in good with her. Her smile leaves and her face becomes hard like a carved marble bust looking at me. Then her smile creeps back, but only on one side of her mouth. It's devious, and I'm not sure what to make of it, but she seems satisfied.

I move to the edge of the couch and take a deep breath, then let it out. Heat emanates up from the scoop-neck of my top. She sets down her mug. "Well then," she says, then slaps the top of her thighs with open hands. "That's that."

It's like any history we had is forgotten. She tells me what's expected of me as a room mother's assistant in a tone like we've been friends forever. She leans in and uses hand gestures and her face is animated. "Grace and Katie will help us run the classroom. Katie really likes Grace." And all the while, I'm afraid to change the smile plastered on my face. If I change, it might prompt her to do the same.

Although, Grace will love being an important part of her class. This might be good for her, as long as I can monitor the situation, as Arjun suggests. I relax. If Psycho Soccer Mom continues to be nice, maybe I can tolerate this assistant thing. Perhaps it isn't such a bad idea.

I drive home baffled. I expected Psycho Soccer Mom to berate me. Or threaten me again if I got out of line. The last thing I expect her to be is nice. I have to wonder if I misjudged her? Abby's warning flashes through my brain. There may be some nefarious agenda she's yet to unfold.

So then, I picture Psycho Soccer Mom as a cartoon character, a dark figure wearing a trench coat, collar up, with a broad-brimmed fedora. Dark glasses masked the identity of the silhouette peering at me from the bushes. Or maybe she wears a cape, and drapes it over her arm like Dracula, hiding the bottom half of her face and shielding the rest of her body. I can hear a heinous laugh emanating from behind her shroud. Regrettably, the cartoon image of her is the one that feels more real, but I can't say why. I wish it were the other way around, and the nice version of her felt like the real one. That's the image I have for me and Grace fitting into this new community. We're involved, in a good way.

⌘

I tell Grace the news as soon as she's home from school. Me and Katie's mom are now buds. She wants to know all the details—what extra fun things will she and Katie be in charge of? She's beaming as she calls Katie. She's happy, so I'm happy. Okay, maybe I can do this.

I tell Arjun everything is going to plan when he calls to see how my meeting went. He's proud I actually went through with it. I'm not sure why. He knows me well enough to know that I don't take shit from anyone. But, it would *appear* I am taking shit from Psycho Soccer Mom. However, it's not real. All smoke and mirrors. I'm doing this for Grace.

I don't tell Abby.

Subject #57: Eddie - Session 23
Topic:

Psycho Soccer Mom

All right. I have like a week and a half to catch you up on. I've been busy making friends with Psycho Soccer Mom, and it's an odd, high-maintenance friendship. But, something happened that changes everything, so I rushed right over. So. I don't hear from her for a couple of days after the room mother's meeting, which is curious because it seemed she would be calling me daily. When she finally does call, she asks me to do her a favor.

"Eddie," she says. "I won't be home and I'm expecting an envelope that needs to be signed for. Can I have it sent to you, and I'll pick it up later?" It's a simple request, but it's weird she doesn't ask a neighbor. Maybe her neighbors aren't home or they're like Tracksuit Man and she doesn't get along with him. I don't know.

"Sure," I say. "I should be home most of the day." She probably knows this. The delivery guy with her envelope arrives a little past noon. I sign. Favor done. I examine the package. It's from the county clerk's office. It has the name of a company, and underneath, my name and address. I set it by the door.

She stops by before dinner to pick it up. Katie's at her side. "You're a lifesaver, Eddie," says Psycho Soccer Mom. "I would've been in line for hours." She holds up the favor, shaking it. "I owe you lunch," she says as she's leaving.

Lunch? What she owes is an apology for threatening me. But lunch with another mother is one step closer to fitting in, even though Psycho Soccer Mom isn't my ideal companion.

⌘

We do lunch the next day. It's actually quite nice. At lunch, she gives me a bag of goodies filled with promotional items with the school's name printed on them: drink cups, back sacs, phone cases, thumb drives, and two T-shirts, one for Grace and one for me. "You'll want to show your school pride," she says. I notice the trademark on the items is from the same company name as the envelope I signed for. Grace will be happy.

We've repeated lunch several times since, and she's opening up to me like I'm a real friend. We actually have a few things in common. She's lived here forever, even went to school, K through twelve. And she stayed. Much like me still living at my mom's when everyone else had left. That's why she's so involved. I kind of get that. It's all she's known. She even married her high school sweetheart, Coach.

The last time we had lunch, she confides in me. "Eddie," she says. "I ran into my friend Jennifer. She went to college, has her dream job, and makes a lot of money. At first I envied her but what I do is more important. I make sure our kids get a good education, and have fun." Her eyes are watery, like she doesn't believe what she says, and is ashamed of how she turned out, or she's super emotional about it. It was pretty freaky.

So she grabs my hand, hard to where I can't pull away, and says, "I just wish my husband would recognize all I do for our kids, for him." She looks down and pauses. This is after three margaritas. It's pretty awkward. I get the feeling she was popular in high school, and all of her friends went on to bigger and better things. It makes me think of Abby and me. "I'll get the check," she slurs while rubbing my hand.

We're done and she heads to the bathroom as I leave. On the way home, I begin to see a soft spot in her and think maybe there was something else going on in her life when she threatened me, and she misdirected her anger. People do that. A lot. We seem to be friends now, but not friends like me and Abby or Arjun. But Grace is involved in school, and she's happy. Maybe I don't need to protect Grace from this woman? Maybe I let the threaten-me thing go?

I get a call from her the next day, and she's laughing. "Eddie, we can't go back there for margaritas ever again." She must have embarrassed herself after I left. I, however, left in full control. "I told them you were going to pay the bill, then I pretended to go to the ladies' room and bolted. You were the last to leave." She's still laughing and my stomach sinks. I had a weird feeling when she said she'd pay, other than the hand rubbing thing.

I'm rolling my eyes, and ask, "Why did you do that?"

"I told you about my husband not paying me much attention. I have to get excitement somewhere," she says.

"I'll go pay our bill today," I say. Running out on the bill is something I'd done in high school. We're not in high school. "I'll leave a large tip to make up for it."

"No, no," she interrupts. "I already took care of it. They called this morning. They know me, but said they might press charges against you, something about Grace's dad. Eddie, do you have a police record? Does he?"

"No!" I can't believe she thinks this and how do they know about Grace's dad?

"Don't worry. I calmed them down. I don't know what they're talking about, but they made it clear you're not welcomed there," she says. And I'm like in shock. What the fuck just happened?

"I don't know what they're talking about either," I blurt. But the truth is, I do.

Then, Psycho Soccer Mom says she wants to meet for coffee. I'm glad it isn't for drinks. And, she's not asking me. It's more of a demand. "Meet me at the Palace in fifteen minutes," she says without explanation, giving me no time to object.

The Palace is a diner in town serving all-American everything where waitresses wear those pink one-piece dresses that zip up the front. Psycho Soccer Mom is sitting in a booth when I arrive. She's facing the door and doesn't take her eyes off me as I make my way to her. I can't read her expression, but it ain't friendly. There's only a few other people in the restaurant. It isn't quite lunchtime, so maybe she chose this time of day so no one would overhear us. When I sit, air escapes the plastic cushion of my seat, an exasperating sound that makes the situation even more awkward.

"Is something wrong?" I ask, but she waits to answer. A young girl, maybe just out of high school, brings two coffees and two pieces of pie then leaves. Psycho Soccer Mom has ordered for us both.

"Of course there is," she snaps a little louder than a whisper, then looks around. It must be something to do with her running out on the check. She lowers her voice. "I need you to do something." I'm curious, but I don't want to hear it. This isn't the same woman I'd been having lunch with, more like the day-after-margaritas-woman, the woman who flicked the email at me.

"You may not know this, but I'm very prominent at all the schools in the district, not just the elementary school," she says. I don't answer. She tells me about her son, who is in high school. "I have a tip that I need you to check out. You are perfect for this mission because of your..." She gestures in circles at my body.

She's referring to my tats, my unsuburban style. I know because the Cs still sarcastically comment on it—"Oh, that look is going to get you far in life." My first thought is that Psycho Soccer Mom wants me to pretend I'm in high school, which is ridiculous, but I'm wrong.

"My son is in his first year of high school, and we just got around to getting his required physical. He's very busy. He plays in a rock band," she says, looking proud. "We were late handing in his paperwork, and they were letting him slide until now. We see Dr. Hawk. You should make him your doctor; he's very good. Tell him I sent you." It's odd how she switches her tone from matter-of-fact, to sheepish, to supportive, like mixed personalities that confirm my nickname of her.

She continues, "At the appointment, the doctor confided in me. He wants me to take care of something important. And I want to hand it to you. But you mustn't tell a soul." It's like she's flipping back and forth from the friend at lunch to the psycho mom on the soccer field. It's making me dizzy.

So I'm sitting in the booth watching her eat pie as she's telling me the town's good doctor relies on her, a volunteer parent and a crazy one at that, to do something important, and that it's hush-hush. But what does this have to do with me being a fourth-grade room mother's assistant?

She looks around again, then leans forward. "Eddie, high school is the time when the kids start drinking and doing drugs." Why doesn't she think I know this? Has she seen my so-called style? And besides, it begins in middle school, elementary for some.

"My son is being tempted." She switches to a whisper. "The doctor and I have an inside tip. The drug dog comes to the high school every day to sniff around, but kids are clever." She pauses, tightening her lips when the waitress comes to refill the coffee. Her head gestures toward the young girl as a warning that she's probably one of them, one of them kids on drugs. She puts her fork down and waits. When the girl is gone, she continues at a normal level. "Eddie, they're hiding drugs in the ceiling, so the dog can't find them."

She's right. If the kids are hiding their stash well above the dog's reach, they're pretty clever, but I'm still wondering what this has to do with me. I don't have to wonder long.

"I know where they are, and I need you to get them," she says. "And bring them to Dr. Hawk." She is insane. What exactly did the margarita restaurant tell her about me? I'm not going to transport drugs across town. My first thought is that this is some sort of setup, and the doctor isn't involved at all. She wants me to be caught in possession, or make it appear I'm dealing to the high school kids. But why? Is she still afraid I'll tell everyone she and Coach left the girls unattended? It's so ridiculous. Then something even weirder happens.

Shelia looks beyond me when I hear someone enter the almost empty restaurant. I turn to see a man. He walks to the waitress and kisses her on the cheek, then comes to our table.

"Hello, Shelia," he says.

Psycho Soccer Mom introduces us. "This is Dr. Hawk. I was just telling Eddie about the ceiling at the high school." He acts like he knows what she's talking about. I'm speechless. Dr. Hawk grabs the to-go order waiting for him on the counter. After he leaves, she tells me the waitress is his daughter.

"Why don't you tell the school and have them search?" I finally muster. I'd think she'd want the school involved. The guy with the dog should check the ceiling, not me. There has to be something she's not telling me.

"What I'm asking you to do isn't wrong. You'll be turning drugs in. That's good. Eddie, if you don't want to help, I can find someone else to be my room assistant, but Grace would lose her position as well. The student's position is attached to the mother's." And there it is. She wants me to do her bidding or she'll take away Grace's happiness. Isn't that blackmail? She sits back all satisfied-like, waiting for my response.

Grace loves that I'm helping at school, that we're both helping, and I *need* to be involved so I'm around to protect her. But what Psycho Soccer Mom is asking me to do is wrong. Even if getting drugs out of the school is a good thing, it's an unusual way to get there. And to take it out on Grace? That's pure evil.

She pats my hand. "And we can't let the school know it's there." There's that hand touching again. There *is* something she's not telling me. Her son must be involved. I wonder if he's dealing, and again I feel sorry for her. Images of my ex come flooding in. I know firsthand a person would do almost anything to help a loved one.

"What about the guy with the canine? Can't he do it?" I ask.

"If he finds it, he'll have to file a report. We don't want that either." I secretly wish she'd blackmail the canine guy to do it instead of me. But he's probably an outsider, so she has nothing on him. I hate myself for wishing this woman upon the poor man and his dog, but I don't want to be the one to find anything. Red flags are going up all over the place.

"Sorry, I can't," I say.

"Eddie, you owe me this. I saved you from the restaurant. Without me, you'd be in jail. I haven't told anyone about it, but I can and I will." She's sitting with a smugness that makes me want to punch her.

"I didn't do anything wrong," I say.

"People will believe my story, not yours. The other mothers won't let their kids play with Grace if they know her mother is a common criminal. We're good people." It's another threat. I regret helping myself to the treasure chest. She probably knows about that, too. I sit, not responding either way. How can I possibly respond?

"So you'll do it this weekend," she says, nodding once. "Grace can play with Katie at my house. There won't be many people at the school." She has it all planned. There is no way I'm doing this. I feel as if I'm sinking down a dark hole. The air is thin, with an invisible force strangling me. Abby was right. I shouldn't have listened to Arjun. I shake my head.

"I can't. What if I find something? What am I supposed to do with it? And what if someone finds me with drugs?" I imagine the police coming. There are loud sirens and a stand-off. I'm in handcuffs, sitting in the back of a squad car, and Grace sees me through the window. The look on her face says it all. I've betrayed her. I'm a hypocrite. Especially when I've been so vocal against drugs. I'm abandoning her and I'm going to jail. And if I don't do what Psycho Soccer Mom wants? I'll be the local thief, a thug. But it's better than being a drug dealer. Maybe I can still go to the restaurant and clear this all up. The trinkets are another story, an embarrassing one.

Psycho Soccer Mom gives me a piercing look. "You will." There's a long pause. "Eddie, I know about Brian."

Everything stops. Even the blood in my veins. How does she know? We've been living here less than two months. I'm in shock and she's the only thing I focus on. Everything around us has vanished as her voice booms. "I even went to see him." She smiles. I don't move. She takes something out of her purse and slowly unfolds it. I recognize the colors and thick lettering at the top. I more than recognize the face, now creased and faded. "I showed him pictures of Grace. He might want to see her. I told him I know some people, that I could make it happen if I wanted. And the other parents would be interested in your story."

I can't breathe. This is full-on blackmail. First she threatens me, now she's blackmailing me. My plan has gone terribly wrong. I was supposed to get close to her, so I could monitor her every move, to protect Grace. I had an ulterior motive with our friendship, but she was doing the same thing, only she's better at it than I am.

This sort of thing shouldn't happen in real life, only in the movies. It's as if that invisible force has a hold on my ankle, and is dragging me under the table, farther into its hole. The waitress pours more coffee. I haven't touched mine. Neither of us looks at the young girl. I only see a blob of pink in my peripheral vision, and an arm holding the pot. And steam. The steam surrounds Psycho Soccer Mom's face. It looks as if it's floating in some sort of cloud, a toxic one.

I weigh the possibility of her bluffing. You'd think leaving the girls unattended on the field might result in a reprimand, or at most, a dismissal from coaching. I mean, it's inappropriate but not illegal. Why is she going to such extremes? I'm lightheaded, and have to tell myself to breathe.

"I see you understand," she says. "I'll call you later with exact details." She gets up and leaves. I don't move and look at the now empty spot where she sat. The plastic-covered booth retains the indent of her back. I'm surprised she doesn't finish her pie before leaving, or even take it with her. It's cherry. Grace will be happy about spending the day at Katie's, and she won't know the reason she's there. I'm not doing a very good job of protecting her from this woman. How can I be a good mother? I can't even protect myself. The waitress comes over and gives me the check. I make sure it's paid.

Subject #57: Eddie - Session 24
Topic:

The Ex

Tomorrow's Saturday. I still don't know if I made the right decision. I wrote "The Ex" on the board today. It's time. It's because of him that I'm the only person in the world in charge of protecting Grace. Sure, other people help here and there, but ultimately, it's all up to me. Once you hear, you'll understand why I'm agreeing to do Psycho Soccer Mom's favor, if you can call it that. And what I'm about to say isn't a secret. Way too many people know about it already. I'll say his name once, and only once, in order to make things perfectly clear. So pay attention.

Brian.

This is all his fault.

He's Grace's dad; my ex. You'd think once someone is out of your life, you'd be done with them. Nope. Grace has never known her father, except when she was a tiny baby. He's been in jail the last several years. Before that, he was into drugs and started dealing, which is what landed him in jail, partly, and is why I kept Grace away from him. I don't talk about him. And she doesn't ask. Who wants to hear their dad is a big loser?

We met right before I graduated high school. He's a couple years older, and he was wise to what the world offered, and he was hot. Back then, he worked at the Natural Foods store and had a holistic approach to life. You know, the mind and the body are one; only natural things went in his body and in his mind. No processed anything. He was cool, at first. He taught me how to meditate and had this incredible passion for everything he did, including me. That's why I fell for him. He took me under his wing and showed me a life very different from my parents'.

The problem is, he considers some drugs a natural substance. "It's grown from nature," he'd say, as he'd get high in our apartment. But then he stops caring about this. I knew he smoked pot when I met him, and that didn't bother me. It wasn't until later, after I moved in with him, that I discovered he was using crack, then heroin. He was spending too much time in the bathroom and it was suspicious. I'd be banging on the door, and he wouldn't answer. It had to be drugs or porn. He'd have the shower going with the door locked, but when he finally came out, he wasn't clean, and there weren't any wet towels thrown all over the place like when he actually took a shower.

"What were you doing in there?" I'd ask him *later* because, at the time, asking was useless.

"What the fuck do you think?" he'd say, and laugh me off. I never knew how to respond to that. I guess a part of me didn't want to know the truth.

After I found out I was pregnant and we planned to get married, I found drugs behind the toilet, taped to the bottom tank. I went looking because of my suspicions. "I'll quit," he said, and I believed him, or at least I wanted to. He lied. Didn't even try, and he found some new hiding places. I found those too. Soon after the wedding, he left his paraphernalia out lying around, on the table or in the kitchen, like he didn't care anymore who saw it.

I never got the wedding I wanted. We did a quick city hall thing. I had to drag him to the courthouse when I was in my last trimester. Abby flew in just for the weekend. Looking back, I think he was high. He put his habit before everything else, even Grace. When Grace becomes more mobile, I quickly realize she shouldn't be around that kind of environment. Soon she'd be able to easily grab his carelessness.

Maybe I wasn't so quick to realize. It took many no-wet-towel shower arguments before my epiphany. At some point I'm afraid to come home for fear I'll find him dead, lying on the floor in the locked bathroom. So I left. Mom helped me leave. Grace was just beginning to talk.

Abby wasn't in town when I left, which was good. I didn't want her to see the loser he'd become. Maybe he always was one. She found out why I left, months after I moved back in with Mom, after the divorce. Mom says a divorce is better than never being married at all, for Grace's sake. Grace was born within wedlock.

This is important to her. I never told her the extent of the drug use.

So, I leave, and want to break off all contact, but he comes around every so often to visit Grace. We never fought for custody. He didn't want it and I want Grace to have a dad in her life, just not this one. That won't change, and it's not up to me to take him away from her. This means I have to be extra vigilant whenever he's around. She's almost two at this point.

Then, word gets back to me he's dealing to support his habit. I contemplate wanting to help him, for Grace's sake. We get on good terms, and I'm thinking that maybe he's doing okay. He's nice to me and brings presents for Grace. He even lets me use his car when mine is broken.

So one day, my car won't start and he picks me up from Mom's to drive Grace to daycare and me to work. I put her car seat in the back, after pushing a bunch of dirty clothes and garbage on the floor to make room, and the smell is overpowering. I have my window open the entire way so Grace and I can breathe. But he drives way out of the way to some house in the city instead of going to Grace's school, which is closer. It's incredibly annoying because I'm already late for work, and now, I'm aggravated.

"I have to take care of some things," he says. "Take the car and come and pick me up after work."

"What the fuck? It was closer to just take me," I say, but whatever. As I drive to Grace's preschool, I'm thinking that with the condition of his car, and the way he's slacking on his hygiene, he's using again. When we're at Grace's school, I leave the car seat with her, thinking there's a strong chance I might not have the car or even a ride by the end of the day. When he's like this, he isn't reliable.

So I'm at work, and a couple hours in, I notice people gathering around my car. Then, a police car pulls up. I'm afraid to go out there. I'm thinking he robbed a bank or something using this car, which he now wants me to drive. People do dumb things like rob banks when they need their next high. I shouldn't have let him get back into our lives. Suzanne's watching out the window and she's quiet. I'm staying back, but watching too. More police cars come and so does an ambulance. They hang yellow police tape around my car. Several officers make their way to each shop in the plaza. It's only a matter of time before they come here.

By the time the officer comes to the fabric store, the ambulance and police cars block my car, so I can't see what's happening. My hands are shaking. My knees buckle. Suzanne sits me down in the back so I can't see out the window. The policeman asks me questions. The first one being, "Is that your car?"

⌘

Fast forward, because I don't want to relive that moment. But here's the gist of what landed my ex in jail.

He sells heroin to a kid. It's laced with fentanyl, and the kid dies. But he doesn't just die right away, although my ex doesn't know this. They knew from the autopsy. He's with the kid when the kid shoots up, so my ex panics and throws him in the trunk because the idiot doesn't know what else to do. He doesn't want to get into trouble, but maybe he could have saved him.

The kid's in high school, so he's underage, and lived near the Natural Foods store with his family. He'd been missing for three days when they found him in the trunk of the car I'd been driving with Grace in the back seat, just foam and plastic between him and my baby. His family had filed a missing person, so it was easy to figure out who it was, and with the car, they knew what happened.

He gets twenty years. I think maybe this is the best thing for him. He'll sober up. Maybe he can lead a halfway decent life once he gets out, but the images of the kid's grieving parents still haunt me. I put myself in their situation all the time, imagining what if it had been Grace? Parents will go to the extreme for their kids. And his did.

Before the trial starts, a group of parents hang flyers all over the neighborhood, near the Natural Foods store. The flyers had a large picture of Grace's dad, a good likeness, with the word "Monster" in thick red letters at the top. I see the flyers everywhere and people start to associate Grace and me with him. I get whispers and comments wherever I go. They even put one up on the glass of the fabric store, but Suzanne took it down, not before I saw it though. Grace and I become outcasts through no fault of our own. I know the power society can have on you if you're not on its side.

Rock bottom is when I pick her up from daycare, and as we're leaving, she sees one of the monster flyers stapled to a pole. "Dada," she says as she points. It's horrifying. I rip it down and quickly push it deep into my purse. For some reason, I don't throw it away. I still have it. Not long after this is when I start working from home, and cut off all contact with her dad.

⌘

When Psycho Soccer Mom unfolds the paper from her purse at the diner, I know exactly what it is. If she has a monster flyer, she knows the story behind it. Kids can be mean, but evidently, parents can be meaner. She's trying to protect her son just like I'm trying to protect Grace. I can't let us become outcasts again. This time, Grace is old enough to understand.

I get the feeling Psycho Soccer Mom isn't bluffing and will ruin everything for me, so it isn't ruined for herself, when all I'm trying to do is to be a good mother.

I never liked drugs. I want to feel in control, and drugs do the opposite. I know what they do to people and how addicts hurt the people around them. So, Psycho Soccer Mom's request to look for drugs in a ceiling of the high school, where my kid doesn't even go, naturally freaks me out. But, she wants to save her son from becoming like my ex. That part I get. Maybe that's why she's asking me. This is why I agree to do this, with my own limitations of course. Ones I don't tell her about. If there's anything there, I'll leave it and anonymously phone in a tip. No one will know her son is involved.

If I can help prevent one kid from becoming a drug addict, I'd like to do it. But she'll need to do more than this. It would crush me if Grace turned out like her dad. She must think if anyone found out her son is involved, it would affect her position as room mother. It's the only thing she has, aside from her family, that makes her feel good about herself.

Subject #57: Eddie - Session 25
Topic:

Beth

Okay. I'm supposed to do that drug search later today and I thought I'd come in to gather up some courage, or maybe talk myself out of it. I mean, I want to help steer her son away from that sort of life, but still. I'm just glad the lab is open today because I'm feeling pretty unnerved. I spoke about my ex last time, so it's befitting I fill you in about Beth. My old neighbor? Plus, it relates to what I might be doing later today. She's the only neighbor at Augustin's apartments I avoid. I think she runs in the same circles as my ex. She wasn't the other woman or anything like that. She's not his type; his mistress was the horse, the Big H. You know: smack, junk, tar, the dragon? Anyway, Beth's a junkie too.

The first time I see Beth, she comes across as this quiet, mousy woman. Very thin and pale. She wears wire nondescript glasses. No makeup. Light brown hair. She's the kind who blends in to the background instead of standing out. Total opposite of me. If Miss Clark has the hairstyle of the Queen, then Beth wears a Princess Di cut but doesn't quite pull it off. It's combed dry into place. No product, so it falls down, but not over her face. It's too short. It's like she's lazy about her appearance. Or she doesn't care. Or has given up on it long ago.

Also, she doesn't look you in the eye, like at the mailbox or in the parking lot. It makes it impossible to say anything to her. Once, I finally get fed up and yell, "Hello?" It comes out louder than expected, and echoes underneath the railed walkway above us. Kind of rude, but hell, she deserves it.

She glances back, but keeps going, and huddles her mail closer. It's like she doesn't want you to see something. That's what first reminds me of my ex. The avoidance. Especially when he came out of the bathroom. This is why it takes me off guard when she finally says something to me, because I'm trying to be nice to her and she brushes me off.

Here's how I know. She wasn't new to the complex, but kept to herself, so none of us really know her. It's Halloween, and we were having a cookout. We're in the Yard. Grace is dressed as a '70s hippy. I'm a pirate. I thought, hell, why not invite Beth? It's a party. Right? And maybe I've had a couple of drinks. So, I go to her apartment, which is at the end of the row, holding cupcakes, thinking they'll lure anyone. I knock.

When Beth answers the door, the look on her face tells me I'm bothering her, or interrupting something. After I invite her, she glares at me holding my cupcakes and mumbles, "No, thank you." Her words are stern, like she feels like she's above us or something. She basically tells me to fuck off! That's all she says: "No, thank you." I don't like being told no.

I reply, "Okay!" in a tone that says fuck you back. I turn and walk. I'm just trying to be nice to the bitch and she treats me like I'm some low-class animal. No smile. No reason of why she can't come. I don't need that.

Then, as I'm walking to the Yard, I realize what she's holding when she answered the door, and everything starts to make sense. Thin, pale, unhealthy looking, off in her own world, doesn't look at you when she walks by. This is my ex leading up to me discovering his stash. When Beth came to the door, she was holding a needle and syringe. Beth is a heroin addict. Now I'm imagining what goes on in her apartment. She lives alone and doesn't need the running shower.

I think back to the times I've seen her at the mailbox, always wearing long sleeves, but then a couple of times she didn't, and there were little scabs all over her arms. She kind of hid them when she saw me coming. Her clothes are cheap. I know where her money goes. I don't know why I hadn't noticed these clues before. I wonder if she knows who I am, or knows of my past. Maybe she avoids me because of my ex.

When I bring my cupcakes back to the Yard, Arjun is the only person I tell. I don't like to say bad things about people unless they're standing in front of me. And, I don't want to get close to someone I might find dead because of their habit. I tell Grace to stay clear of Beth, and we make it a point to turn and go the other way if we see her. I don't care if she notices. In fact, I hope she does.

⌘

It's very unusual for a heroin addict to hold a job as long as Beth has. From what I gather, she's worked at the school for a while. She must have her habit under control, if that's possible. Every day, I expect to get a letter from the school saying that one of their staff unexpectedly died of an overdose. Because that's what happens with heroin. You either quit, or you die. Or, you land in jail like my ex, and in jail it's the same—you quit or you die.

But Beth's position at the school is chill. She's what they call a rover, working in the office part-time and running the computer cart on computer days. Grace says the computer person is absent a lot. There isn't anyone to fill in for her, so they skip an entire week. I have to wonder why they keep Beth around. Grace doesn't seem to recognize Beth, and I'm trying to keep it that way.

When I come by the school and Beth is in the office, we both pretend we don't know each other, keeping it short and sweet. She seems like she's always uncomfortable, like she's unsure of how to do her job. But I've seen her jump into action when Psycho Soccer Mom is around. Everyone does.

Hearing myself say this, and having watched everyone do exactly what Psycho Soccer Mom says, there has to be more to this than saving her son. Of course I want to help save a kid from getting into this lifestyle, but threatening to tell everyone at the school about my ex, including Grace, to get me to save him is totally uncool. I don't want Grace to have to go through that, so later today, I'll be at the high school secretly look for drugs, which is not, I imagine, how any good mom spends her Saturday.

Subject #57: Eddie - Session 26
Topic:

Me

I hope it's okay that I'm here twice in one day. I have to tell someone what happened. I'm not supposed to discuss this with anyone, so the confidentially of these sessions is perfect. Okay. I drop Grace off at Psycho Soccer Mom's, as instructed. And just to say, I had no choice in doing this because of that damn "monster flyer" Psycho Soccer Mom pulls from her purse. In my mind, I see her unfolding it again and again.

Here's what happened.

I drive to the school, noting any details that might help me not get caught. There's a lot of cars. I thought the school was supposed to be practically empty, but fall sports teams are practicing and a steady stream of students and adults go in and out of the building. I drive around the school to see how many entrances there are. As I drive, what bothers me most is how many windows the one-story building has. There are square pods extending from the main structure, and they're connected by energy-inefficient walkways made entirely of glass. If I'm in that hallway, it's like I'm a fish in an aquarium. Doing this "favor" without being seen is impossible.

There's a circular drive at the front with awnings shadowing a bank of doors. I see students with dyed hair, piercings, and tattoos here. The look seems common for the high school kids, different from when I was in school. Psycho Soccer Mom was right. I look like I belong. I think of my cousins' remark. This is exactly how far my look has gotten me, a minion for Psycho Soccer Mom.

I drive to the back of the building. The rear parking lot is abuzz with activity of a different sort. In the middle, students carry instruments, while to the far right they have sports equipment. I'm confused. Psycho Soccer Mom's details are too vague, and I'm not sure where to start. I should have asked to see a picture of her son. If he's involved, I'd know the type he hangs out with, and where to go. I consider calling her for more instruction, but then think that if I attempt and fail to find anything, at least I'll have done what she asks, and have kept myself out of jail. The only problem with this theory is that she'll probably send me again. But, maybe it would buy some time.

I decide to start is where the colored hair/pierced kids hang. I park, then put on a baseball cap and my large dark sunglasses. My disguise. The sun is out, so the dark glasses don't look suspicious. I grab my large Mary Poppins umbrella from the back seat and head toward the circular drive.

When I'm near the front bank of doors, a pierced girl comes out. I keep my head down and go in. I stand, waiting for my eyes to adjust. There's no way I'm not taking off my sunglasses. There's an office on the left, and through a window, a lady works behind the counter, helping several students and parents. And it's like, why are they here on a Saturday?

The woman is too busy to notice me. There's a long empty hall that continues past the office. Opposite the office is a large trophy case holding an array of gold-plated cups. To the right are two smaller hallways stemming from the main corridor. The school is dreary, old, and run-down. I'm angry. Kevin, my realtor, said the schools in this district are stellar. I refocus. Two sets of gray metal doors cut the corner where the two smaller halls meet, creating a gathering space in front. A woman exits these doors, and I can just glimpse cushioned stadium seating in the dark room where students rehearse some sort of play.

"Hi, may I help you?" asks the woman. She's middle-aged, an employee with a badge on a long braided string. And she's not matronly like Miss Clark, but acts bored and annoyed.

I'm quick. "No, thank you. I'm looking for my daughter. She should be in there." I point at the doors to the right of the theater with my umbrella.

"Is it raining outside?" she asks.

I think I'm caught and say, "No, but I thought it might."

The woman shrugs and continues walking down the empty hall, away from me. I head to where I pointed my umbrella, to the right, down the hall, trying to make it look as if I know where I'm going. Thick brown plastic wedges hold the doors open. The kind where dirt and hair collect at the bottom. It's the entrance to another corridor, empty except for a stack of boxes at the end. I feel like this is where Psycho Soccer Mom wants me to look, even with her sketchy details.

I pull the wedges and let the fire doors close. This shuts off any noise coming from the rest of the school. My combat boots click on the linoleum and the sound echoes softly against the painted cinderblock walls. The inset institutional-ceiling lighting casts an eerie glow. A fixture at the end slightly flickers. Looking up, I'm pretty confident this is where the "tip" said to go. The drop-down ceiling is the giveaway, white compressed ceiling boards, stained and resting on hanging metal supports. This type of ceiling is absent in the foyer and the long hall near the front, where pipes and ductwork are exposed. And, no one would hide something in the fishbowl hallways where everyone can see them. This hall is private.

I psych myself up and begin. When I raise my umbrella, I can reach the ceiling with my arm extended, with a few inches to spare. I'm clever for bringing it. I gently poke at a single hanging board, trying to determine if there may be something lying, hidden on top, something adding extra weight. A rush of adrenaline flows through me, anxiety flared with excitement, as I poke several more. I soon recognize what an empty tile feels like.

I methodically make my way down the hall, checking each tile. It's monotonous. But then, I feel something different. I stop. Shit. I'm dreading what I have to do next. The hallway is suddenly hot and stuffy. I don't have a ladder, so how am I supposed to see what's up there? Clearly, I hadn't thought this through. Maybe I should leave. The unfolding flyer flashes through my mind.

Then, I notice the boxes at the end of the hall are stacked on and around a desk, a student's desk, the kind with a chair connected. Perfect. So, I'm clearing boxes off the desk when I hear the door handle click behind me. I stand straight to face whatever is behind that door. Face my demise. A high-school kid comes out holding a paper-filled folder. He pauses, looking from me to the boxes. I say hello, and he nods and walks away, letting the door where I removed the wedges slam behind him. My breath shakes, like I'm traveling over a bumpy road, and my hands tremble, but I pull myself together and continue. I clear the desk, then carry it to the suspicious ceiling tile. It's not heavy, just awkward.

As I carry the desk down the hall, I feel mechanical, like a robot in a dream, without control over my own body, as if *I* were on drugs. I want, no, *need* to make all this Psycho Soccer Mom blackmail shit stop, but I can't stop my body from moving forward and down the hall. Then, I think of Psycho Soccer Mom's son, how maybe I can make a difference in his life. Maybe this is the one thing that changes his path in life, that will save him from ending up like the poor kid in my ex's trunk. I have to believe that if I find drugs and don't bring them to the proper authorities, but call it in instead, I'm actually doing something good.

So, when I'm on the desk, I have to stand on my tippy toes to reach the ceiling. I'm just able to raise and maneuver the tile from its foundation. It's tricky, but it works. I'm not used to holding things above my head, so my shoulder muscles tighten and begin to ache. I put the board back down on the tracks, leaving it misaligned, to give my shoulders a rest. I squat to sit on the desk with my feet on the chair. Here's when I realize I can't just peek to see what's there. If I tilt it, whatever it is will slide down and hit me in the face. I don't want a mouthful of drugs. I have to take the whole tile down.

I'm up on the desk again, raising the board like Atlas holding the weight of the world, when I hear a click at the far end of the hall, and I drop it. The board falls misaligned on the slats. Two kids open the door. They've got their phones out and they're laughing. They look right at me, then turn and leave. The door slams shut. They don't seem concerned that a stranger is standing on a desk in the hallway.

I raise the tile, tilting it just enough to set it free from the slats. I'm real careful, so whatever's there doesn't move. I don't want the bag tumbling onto the floor either, breaking open, drugs scattering everywhere. If that happens, with my luck, that's when a teacher comes in.

But that doesn't happen. I lower the tile to just above my head, barely resting it on my baseball cap. I have to concentrate to keep my balance. As I do this, I'm trying to figure how best to get off the desk without disturbing what I'm holding. I squat, bringing one foot to the desk chair, carefully balancing while I bring the other down to the floor. It's hard with my chunky boots, but I make it. So, I'm standing upright on solid ground, still holding the ceiling tile above my head.

I think once this favor is done, Psycho Soccer Mom will leave me alone. It's like I'm having to prove myself to her, showing her I'm loyal, like she's some mob boss or something. Now, I have to get this large tile around the bill of my baseball cap, and it's awkward. If the drugs are anything but pot, I'll be clueless to what they are. But, as soon as I bring the board around the brim of my cap, at eye level, I immediately recognize what the extra weight is.

It almost looks like a pair of rolled-up, gray-woolen socks, except for four stiff evaporated legs promising never to scurry again. I jerk my arms forward, away from my face, sending the board and what weighted it, crashing to the floor. As it pummels to the linoleum, the stench of decay ejects upward, a smell I recognize. It forces my gut to heave. I grab my sunglasses and umbrella and head down the hall toward the exit, leaving the hall in disarray. I take several steps before I let go a full body shiver and let out a terse scream. It echoes louder than the tap of my boots. The only thing I can think is that Psycho Soccer Mom just punked me.

Subject #57: Eddie - Session 27
Topic:

Tracksuit Man

I'll jump right into it, continuing with what happened after I left here last. I'm so creeped out by the flying dead rodent that after I left here, I go home and shower. This lab has the same kind of ceiling tiles as the high school, by the way.

I have a while to figure out what to say to Psycho Soccer Mom because it isn't time to pick up Grace. So, I'm taking a long hot shower, scrubbing myself to get rid of the heebie-jeebies. After, I put my clothes in the washer and walk around the house in my robe, knowing that secretly searching for drugs isn't the good-mother image I want for myself. I'm trying to figure out why. Why is it so important that Psycho Soccer Mom has *me* do all these crazy things for her? Is it because I called her and her husband out at the soccer practice? Am I somehow a threat to her? Is it because

I'm an outsider? Maybe she fears I want some of the school positions she holds? I don't. Is it my looks?

This is running through my mind when I notice Tracksuit Man in my backyard, and I'm like, what the fuck?

I don't immediately go outside. I'm in my robe, and don't want to come across as vulnerable, plus it's old and a bit tattered. So, I throw on yesterday's clothes and storm outside, but he's gone, which sucks because now I can't yell at him. I should've come straight out, robe and all. Why should I care what he thinks?

My gate is closed, and nothing's out of the ordinary. Back inside, I look out my front window. He's just getting to his when he turns and sees me looking. He smiles, and does an up-nod, then goes inside. I can't figure out if the gesture is friendly or nefarious. And what was he doing in my backyard? Him, in his tracksuit. Although, he's wearing only the bottoms with a fitted tee, which is a good look for him. This is when I realize it must have been him who sent the police.

I don't think I mentioned. Back during Grace's dance party, just about a month ago, the doorbell rings at 10:06, at night. Grace didn't hear it, and continues dancing and singing while I open the door. Two policemen are on my porch, and right then, the streetlights go out, rolling outages to conserve energy. It accentuates the flashing lights on the squad car parked in front of my house, making their appearance even more dramatic. The lights mimic our strobe light inside. When police show up on your doorstep, it can only be bad news.

"Hello," I say. "Is there anything wrong, officer?" I've taught

Grace to always be respectful to the police: yes sir, no sir, thank you, officer. I hide my alarm. I think they're here to tell me someone is dead.

"Sorry, Miss," the older portly one says. "We got a call about a loud music disturbance." Then he adds, "At 10:01." Then he rolls his eyes. I relax, silently congratulating the men for such a quick response time. Grace comes to the door. The music and lights are still going.

"I'm sorry, we're having a little dance party." I open the door wider and let the officers see it's only us. "Is this too loud?" I ask. I want to be transparent and show Grace that I'm complying. This is what you do if you have an encounter with the police. You don't run. You do what they ask. I'll be damned if I'm anything like my ex.

"Not really," he says while the younger one turns to look around the neighborhood. "Maybe just turn it down a little. Keep everyone happy." It's clear he's annoyed with the caller, that dispatch sent him here.

I apologize again, and as they walk to the car, the portly one says something into the device on his lapel. As I watch them go, someone is peering from the front curtain of Tracksuit Man's house. He doesn't even leave when I notice him, like he wants me to know that he called the police. I should have asked the police who sent them, but I don't know if they're allowed to say.

I close the door and tell Grace (so she isn't frightened by the police at our door), "I can't believe the police busted our party." Grace looks pleased. I turn down the music a couple of notches, and we dance slower, an interpretive dance rather than a mosh pit.

The following Monday, when Grace is at school, I'm in the kitchen when the front doorbell rings. I'm thinking it's Tracksuit Man coming over to complain about the music, although I'm wondering why he took an extra day to do it. I peek out the front window, and there's a man holding some sort of toolbox standing on my porch. I open the door.

"Hello," he says. "I'm an electrician. I was doing some work for the man across the street. He said I should come to see if you need my services. Says your lights keep flickering." It's like what? He calls the police on me, then pretends my party was due to faulty wiring. I'm thinking he's messing with me like Psycho Soccer Mom.

I look across the street to see if Tracksuit Man is watching, but the sun is glaring on his windows, and it's hard to tell. "No, we're fine. But thank you," I say, close the door, and watch him leave out the front window. Tracksuit Man emerges from his garage, saying something. They both turn and look. They see me. Tracksuit Man waves. It was very odd.

This isn't the only time I see him staring at me from his house. He doesn't try to hide it. It's like he's challenging me. A couple of times when he knocked at my door, I pretended not to be home. He probably knows I'm inside because it takes a long time for him to go away. It's like a game we play. He boldly stands at his window so I can see him watching me, and I boldly ignore him when he knocks.

⌘

I consider getting a security system not too long after I saw Tracksuit Man installing his. I had a company out, and it turns out I already have a system wired in the house, but it's old. The guy says it'll work, but I'd have to pay a monthly service fee. I just can't afford that right now. I'm barely keeping up with the bills as it is. It would seem that only those who can afford to pay are safe.

So yesterday, I'm off my guard, and open my door before checking who it is first, because I'm heavily involved with my work—a double pinch pleat curtain in a heavy brocade fabric, which is a little late in getting to my client with all this Psycho Soccer Mom shit happening. It's Tracksuit Man. I'm about to slam the door in his face before he complains about something stupid, but he says, "Wait! I want you to make me some curtains."

A million things flash through my mind, first of which is, why? Then I realize he asked nicely and is standing there with a pleading puppy-dog face. Was I quick to judge him? The way people judge me? Which I hate. A stream of weird things he's done play through my mind: the cattle gate, the light bulbs, the water. Nope. I think I know his type. He's wearing that T-shirt again, with a pair of jogger sweatpants. His arms are a little more muscular that I imagined under the initial full tracksuit. Is this another setup like the drugs in the ceiling? Is he working with Psycho Soccer Mom and she's asking me questions about his wife to throw me off? But, I haven't mentioned that yet. Anyway, I'm going back and forth on whether this is a trap or if there's more to him than I think.

Subject #57: Eddie - Session 28
Topic:

Psycho Soccer Mom

Okay. Yesterday, I mentioned that Psycho Soccer Mom asked me about Tracksuit Man's wife. Boy, it's really hard not to say what happened all at once, but I'm trying to stick to the rules for the study. I guess it's making me think about things from different angles. But still.

So, after the high school mission, when I go pick up Grace, I tell Psycho Soccer Mom I'm late because when I get home, I find my neighbor in my backyard. "I had to chase him away," I say, which isn't exactly true, but I think she'd like to hear this about me. It makes me sound daring, unafraid, and strong. It's also a distraction, a procrastination in telling her I didn't complete what she'd hoped.

She may think I'm lying about going to the school at all. And

I'm still not entirely sure there were drugs in the ceiling. Maybe it was a test? Grace and Katie are busy creating some posters for an upcoming school event, so I start to tell her what happened.

"Shush!" she says before I can get anything out, then head-gestures to the girls. It's rude, her shushing me. I imagine this is how she and Coach interact with each other, maybe Katie, too? Certain things can't be said out in the open. It's like we had the same father growing up. Then, she mouths, "I'll call you later." She summons Grace, but before we leave, she hands me a bag of goodies filled with the same promotional items she gave me earlier. It's like my reward for following directions. Although she doesn't know yet that I've come empty-handed.

"Is it okay that you're giving me this? Should I pay you?" I ask, thinking of the unpaid margarita bill.

"Of course, I'm the President of the PTSA. Gifts are at my discretion." Then she asks, "Which neighbor?" I'm wondering why it matters.

"The guy across the street," I say. She suddenly puts her hand on Grace's shoulder, preventing her from walking toward the door.

"Do you ever see his wife?" she asks.

"I didn't know he's married, but I haven't seen a woman there. Although, we never talk, so," I say. Grace is listening, so I don't fill Psycho Soccer Mom in on his bizarre details. Why should I tell her? "You know him?" I ask. I thought those without kids would be safe from her control. They live in a world where things are rational. Then I remember I'm talking about Tracksuit Man. He's far from rational.

"Not really," she says, releasing Grace, and we leave with no further mention of the school or my neighbor. I had so many questions when I came here, but now I'm leaving with a million more.

⌘

She calls later. "What do you know about your neighbor across the street?" she asks. Again with the neighbor? She's more interested in him than the high school. In fact, she doesn't ask me what I found there at all, after everything I went through. I don't know whether to be upset or relieved. I tell her only general things because I don't know her motive. But, why doesn't she ask about the school? I should let it go, but I don't.

"Don't you want to know about the drugs?" I ask.

"I already know, Eddie," she says, all snarky. I go quiet. She must sense my confusion, and says, "It's my job to know." If she knows, then someone was spying on me. Maybe the two kids who came in the hall and left? Maybe the boy with the folder?

"Then you should already know about my neighbor," I say. It just sort of comes out, and she's quiet. I'm worried I've overstepped.

"Eddie, you've done well; I'm going to let Grace into our gifted and talented program. The high school job was important, but something more urgent has come up and I'm counting on you. It will require you to do a little monitoring of your neighbor. I'll need to do some planning. Let me work out some details. We'll meet later at your house, and I'll go over what's needed." She hangs up without saying goodbye, leaving me baffled. What could be more urgent than getting drugs out of the school, especially if her son is involved?

I'm curious. Why does she want to spy on Tracksuit Man? I almost want in. It'd be fun to spy on him, you know: do unto others, give him a dose of his own medicine. He's been monitoring me from his window and with his security camera since we've moved in. And going in my backyard without permission is totally unacceptable.

But a good mom wouldn't do something she knows is wrong. Although, Grace has been wanting to get into the GT program. And if I knew what Tracksuit Man was up to, it might ease the tension I have about him. And, if I help with the monitoring, Grace might get more perks. I'm flipping back and forth, talking myself out of it, then back in. But the real question is, why does Psycho Soccer Mom care about Tracksuit Man, and what does he have on her?

Subject #57: Eddie - Session 29
Topic:

Miss Clark

Man, I'm at this lab so often, I should have moved here. Anyway, I can't believe how much has happened in just one day. So, while Psycho Soccer Mom's planning her thing against Tracksuit Man, she calls to say she's got another mission for me, a side mission. I don't feel good about this one, either.

"I'll email instructions along with a letter," she says. "Sign the letter, bring it to school, and, Eddie, hand-deliver it to the office. Do this quickly." She hangs up and never tells me what it's about. This whole thing about her giving me missions is stupid. I need to figure a way out, one that doesn't impact Grace.

So when I get the email, and I'm literally heartbroken when I read the attached letter, so much that I can't finish my breakfast. The email itself doesn't expand on what Psycho Soccer Mom told me over the phone. I have to read the attachment to see what I've committed to.

The letter she sent is supposedly from me and to the principal of the school, Mr. Barneyak. I'm claiming Miss Clark should be dismissed immediately, that unless he fires her, which I assume with the way this letter is worded, that hiring and firing takes place at his discretion, that I will bring the matter to the PTSA, who will then take it up with the school board.

Miss Clark is Grace's favorite teacher, so I'm thinking there's no way I'm doing this.

I'm staring at the letter on my screen as I consider. Psycho Soccer Mom is the president of the PTSA, so Shelia is giving me a letter to give to the principal, and if he doesn't do what I want, what she wants, the letter will end up with her and she'll get it done.

I have to stop Psycho Soccer Mom from forcing me to do things that are the opposite of what a good mom should be, but something else is going on here. Either she's got something in for Miss Clark or Mr. Barneyak. Or maybe she's taking care of them both with one swoop. Then I think, if Mr. Barneyak doesn't do what she wants, and the letter reaches the school board, it will be public knowledge. It's as if Psycho Soccer Mom would prefer to let Miss Clark go discretely. Why?

In the letter, I'm claiming that during class, Miss Clark habitually goes through her social media on her school-provided iPad, and she does this in front of the kids. She's shown them several photos of herself in seductive poses wearing practically nothing. If you know Miss Clark, or you've even seen Miss Clark, you'd have a hard time believing this. I have to see it for myself, and immediately look her up.

It's astonishing. Miss Clark's matronly stout body is all over her page. She's showing bits of her I'll never be able to unsee. But, there are also several photos with her at school with some kids. In these, she's fully clothed. She's smiling. Innocent. A proper teacher. This version of Miss Clark, the teacher version, is taken from a distance, no selfies with kids, and most of them aren't very clear.

There are a dozen photos, and no other information about her, except where she works. The photos are such a contrast that it's curious, unbelievable. The almost-nudie photos are cropped tight to where you only see a bit of the hair on her head. It's the same body type, so it looks like Miss Clark, but there is a possibility that these aren't her at all. Maybe it's a friend? A girlfriend? A lover? Maybe this is how she wants others to view her and they're photos she found on the internet? Or *maybe* someone has hacked her account?

Poor Miss Clark. This has to be a fake. I wonder what she did to make Psycho Soccer Mom want to get rid of the school's favorite teacher? I know I did nothing to put me in this situation, but I can't get the image of Psycho Soccer Mom unfolding that flyer out of my mind. I rationalize. Good teachers come and go, but her threat to me is about family. I print the letter, but before I give it to the school, I want to ask Grace if it's true, verify Psycho Soccer Mom's information. If it is true, I have no problem in handing it over. If it isn't, I won't ruin the life of a woman who is nothing but nice.

Then, I get a call from Psycho Soccer Mom. "Eddie, where are you with the letter?"

I didn't realize she'd be waiting for me.

"I wanted to check it out with Grace first. This doesn't seem like Miss Clark. Do you think someone set up a fake account?" I say, immediately regretting I told her the truth. I should have lied about my delay.

"No, Eddie, it's her. I've had it verified. Bring the letter right away." She's firm.

"I don't know. Grace will be so upset if Miss Clark leaves. This account can't be real," I say, like I can persuade her to change her mind.

"Eddie, what did you find at the high school?" she interrupts, and the topic switch is jarring.

"What? I thought you knew. Nothing. I didn't find anything." I'm like, why is she mentioning this?

"Ah, but, Eddie, you did," she says. She knows about the rat, or mouse, or whatever it was, and I'm trying to figure out why a mouse is important. I don't have to wonder long. My phone dings. A text from Psycho Soccer Mom. It's a photo of me on the desk, with my hands on the ceiling tile from the angle of the two kids that came in the hall. I'm thinking, so what?

Shortly after, she sends another photo. I don't recognize this one. It's the ceiling tile, on the same desk I left in the hallway. On it is an array of pills, and a bag of weed, and a bag of a white powder. I feel sick. I know her plan.

I think of what would happen to Grace if this got out. So, I try to rationalize. I'm giving them one letter. And, it's coming from a parent that's new to the school who doesn't have any clout. Why would they believe me over a long-standing stellar employee? Maybe they'll check into it first before actually firing her. It's only one letter.

⌘

Maybe I can warn Miss Clark before handing the letter over, so I rush to the school. I need to get there before Grace gets on the bus. But, when I enter the office, Psycho Soccer Mom and Beth are both there, and now I'm alone with them. It's clear where Psycho Soccer Mom got the drugs for the photo.

When she sees me come in, Psycho Soccer Mom thanks Beth and steps back to give me access. The office is stuffy. Opposite of the chill in the hallway, and there're papers stacked everywhere. Psycho Soccer Mom doesn't leave, but just stands there watching. She nods once, slowly, prodding me to deliver.

I tell Beth to let Grace know I'm here, then look at Psycho Soccer Mom, who gives me this death stare. It's boring into me like a beetle or a worm, making me flustered. So much so that I take out the letter and tell Beth I have something to give to Mr. Barneyak, even before I ask Grace if it's true! I'm watching myself hand it over, unable to do anything as if I'm watching a horror movie and I want to scream to the heroine the monster is behind her. Psycho Soccer Mom grabs the letter from Beth and opens it.

"Eddie, you forgot to sign this." She thrusts the letter and a pen in my face.

I sign.

She sees her mission is complete and she leaves.

With Psycho Soccer Mom gone, Beth reads the letter, sighs, and gets a sad look on her face, but isn't surprised. She's friends with Miss Clark. I've seen them together. Beth wears long sleeves and scratches her arms like every ten seconds. Her hands are blotchy and red. Miss Clark evidently took Beth on as a charity case. Maybe she's a sponsor and Beth is trying to quit. Do you have to be a recovering addict to be a sponsor? Maybe Miss Clark does have a secret life?

With what I've seen Psycho Soccer Mom do so far, it's wise to have someone in the office on her side. Poor Miss Clark. Poor Grace. I hope they don't say why they fired her. Deep down, I know it can't be true.

Then something weird happens. Beth reveals some interesting news. It's kind of under her breath, but it's definitely there. "It's the sixth one today." I know there's no hope for Miss Clark now. There's no need to ask Grace about the social media incident. Poor Miss Clark. I helped dig her grave, and for what?

I'm so upset about this, I came right here from the school. The student outside said it was okay that Grace waits for me in the lobby. I feel like I'm doing the complete opposite of what a good mother would do, all because of Psycho Soccer Mom. I need to stop this before Grace finds out I'm involved.

Subject #57: Eddie - Session 30
Topic:

Abby

I feel like things are getting worse. Abby has to go to LA for work and her flight gets delayed while she's changing planes in Detroit. By the way, changing planes in Detroit isn't a route from London to LA. She has an ulterior motive, other than seeing my new house. I haven't been keeping her up to date since the whole Psycho Soccer Mom threat thing. Anyway, she has hours to kill and shows up on my doorstep unannounced.

When I open the door, I know I'm caught because Psycho Soccer Mom is here. "Abby?" I say. She's on my porch looking beautiful, even though her hair sticks up all over the place. She tilts her head up as she smiles, showing perfect teeth.

"Surprise!" she says. "I tried calling, but it goes straight to voicemail."

My fault. I forgot to charge my phone. Fortunately, Grace and I are home. Unfortunately, Psycho Soccer Mom and Katie invited themselves over because she's ready to plan details on the Tracksuit Man mission, Psycho Soccer Mom brings more school cups, mugs, pens, and water bottles to soften me after the Miss Clark incident.

Abby has to be aware I'm acting a little strange toward her, taking way too long to let her know I'm happy to see her. We hug, but it feels forced.

"Grace, look who's here," I yell. Grace comes running, squeals, then hugs Abby. She drags Abby by the hand to the kitchen. I bring in her suitcase, then follow. "This is Shelia," I say, looking at Abby. "Grace's room mother. We're working on a project. And this is her daughter, Katie. Everyone, this is my best friend Abby." Abby smiles as she's hugs on Grace and greets them. She knows who this woman is. Something behind her eyes changes. I'll hear about it soon enough, and with the look she gives me, I know I'm in trouble.

"Grace, I've got a present for you," says Abby, pulling a bag of taffy from her purse. The only time Grace ever eats taffy is when Abby brings it from one of her faraway places, so it's a special treat.

"Yay!" Grace jumps up and down. "Come and see my new room." She grabs Abby's hand again, leading her to her room. Katie and I follow. Psycho Soccer Mom stays in the kitchen, checking her notes. She has no interest in the tour, or in Abby. She barely looked up when I introduced them. We linger in Grace's room. Grace wants to show Abby every new thing she's gotten since seeing her last.

Back in the kitchen, Abby asks, "So what are you two working on?" She isn't afraid to pry.

I'm not sure how to respond or how much to reveal, so I let Psycho Soccer Mom take the lead. "Something for school," she says, eyes still on her paperwork. Psycho Soccer Mom is cordial, but maintains full control of what she will and will not share. "A fundraising event," she adds. This raises more suspicion with Abby, because I'm not one to do charity events since middle school.

Somehow Abby knows Psycho Soccer Mom is lying. "And you're having it here?" she asks. Maybe she sees the hand-drawn map of my neighborhood marked with x's and arrows, from my house to the house across the street. She knows where Tracksuit Man lives, and she's clever. I can't see myself hosting such an event. It sounds so… suburban, so hoity-toity. Surely, Abby's thinking the same thing.

Psycho Soccer Mom notices Abby's gaze and tucks the map under a stack of notes, then puts them in a folder. "We haven't decided yet." She crosses her arms like she's waiting for Abby's next pitch, finally looking her directly in the eye. It's a physical barrier, an arm-chain she puts in front of herself to lock her secrets inside. No one's getting in unless she says so. The room is thick with tension, but I don't think Grace notices. She's sitting on the kitchen floor with Katie eating taffy.

It takes longer to get to our house from the airport than

expected, so Abby doesn't stay long. I'm relieved when she leaves, which is something I've never felt before, but I don't want Psycho Soccer Mom to let something slip about our plan. More likely, it'd be me. Psycho Soccer Mom has more experience in these kinds of things. If Abby finds out what we're doing, she'll wonder why I'm involved, then I'll have to tell her about Miss Clark and my letter, the ceiling photos, the margaritas, and the resurfaced flyer of my ex, although she may understand that. I'll tell her at some point. I just need more time to decide exactly how.

Abby's visit enables me to sprout some inkling of a backbone and I finally ask Psycho Soccer Mom why we're planning this, and to my surprise, she tells me.

⌘

Anyway, Abby calls after she's settled at her hotel in LA. Our guests have long gone, and Grace is in her room, asleep. I knew this was coming. "Dee, what are you doing? You're friends with her after what she did to you?" Her voice sounds tight. I explain how Arjun convinced me, but instantly regret it because it feels like I'm blaming him for what I'm doing.

"But, don't blame Arjun. This was my choice," I say. Then, I tell her about the extras Grace has been getting.

"You mean the school merch in your kitchen? I can't believe you'd follow a psycho lady around because she gives you a free cup," she says, which really hurts. So I'm going to have to tell her more to save face.

I mention Tracksuit Man spying on me and how I caught him sneaking around in my backyard. Then explain what Psycho Soccer Mom said after Abby left. "His ex-wife openly tried to seduce Psycho Soccer Mom's husband, and was so ashamed when everyone found out, she fled the neighborhood. The Coach wanted nothing to do with her, of course," I say, repeating it exactly the way Psycho Soccer Mom said it, but now that I hear myself repeating it, it doesn't sound plausible, if you consider the attractiveness of everyone involved. Although I've never seen Tracksuit Man's wife, she must be at his level. Isn't that the way it works?

"What does this have to do with what you're planning?" Abby asks.

"Psycho Soccer Mom heard that Tracksuit Man's wife is moving back into the house. She just wants to know if it's true," I say. "I'd like to know, too. That's why I'm helping. If she moves back, maybe he'll leave me alone." I try to make our plans sound reasonable, while keeping the details vague, like we haven't quite decided how to handle it.

"Why doesn't someone just ask him?" Abby says, which would be the most reasonable thing to do. "If she doesn't want the wife back, there's no telling what she'll do to keep her away, especially after threatening you. Dee, people can do unthinkable things when it comes to love. Stay away from her."

I try to convince her it's no big deal, but it worries me, too. Psycho Soccer Mom has already done some horrible things to me.

"I'm protecting Grace," I say, trying to make her understand.

But who knows what Psycho Soccer Mom will want next? I know I need to put an end to this soon. Abby always said I was a procrastinator. It's just that things have gotten better for Grace ever since I've started "helping."

But is it worth it? Poor Miss Clark. They let her go the day after they got the letters. Mr. Barneyak didn't waste any time. Grace has a substitute until they find someone permanent. They sent a letter saying Miss Clark suddenly resigned. Didn't say what prompted it. She didn't take her treasure chest. It's considered school property since the donations came from the parents.

"She's was very nice when we had our initial room-mothers' meeting. And the women at the school include me now, even the ziplock orange-bag lady."

"Dee," says Abby. "You're becoming just like her." Her comment crushes me.

"That's harsh," I say, thinking she's turning on me. "You always say I exaggerate. Maybe what I've told you about her isn't so bad?" I want to put a barrier between me and Abby, a folded-arm chain, but I don't want to lose her. I think of the time we became blood sisters near the tetherball pole. We have so much history, and our friendship is crumbling. Why can't she understand? Even a little? She doesn't know what it's like to have a child in school, all the parent politics I have to deal with. It's not the same as in the business world, where people make rational decisions. I don't want to return any hurtful words, so I'm quiet.

"Well, I've met her, and it feels like you were accurate. She seems like she's over the top," Abby says.

"I'm doing it for Grace," I finally say, and we hang up soon after. I'm bitter. It's not an angry or a mean hang-up, more like a parting. I think she feels it too. My stomach is tight and I feel like hitting something. I'm glad Grace is asleep. I don't want her to see me so upset. Abby's never been unsupportive, so this feels strange, like it isn't real. Why is she judging me now? I'm trying to do the right thing, make good choices for Grace. But I have doubts, especially when I think of Miss Clark. This is such a horrible thing to say, but I wish Abby hadn't come by.

Abby can make me tell her anything if she knows what to ask. Lucky for me, we end the call before she asks *why* I'm involved.

Subject #57: Eddie - Session 31
Topic:

Gladys

It's bothering the hell out of me that Abby's upset. And I don't want Grace to know. I can't stop thinking about our phone conversation or how disappointed she looked when she left my house. I'm hoping Grace didn't notice. She didn't say anything. A child shouldn't have to worry about her mother. After leaving yesterday's session, the image of Abby getting in the Uber and the look she gives me doesn't go away.

When I get home and get out of my car, Gladys is waiting for me at my house. I don't know why I shouldn't expect her to appear any time I'm outside. But she's there, arms and legs stiff, and she's smiling, lips tight, making her mouth look too small for her head. It's like she's almost bursting, like she can't wait to share something with me. I'm not in the mood for her, or her gossip, but that quickly changes when I learn her gossip includes me.

"You've become friends with Shelia," she says. This is how she starts. Straight to the point. It doesn't surprise me she knows. She still monitors my house. "It's...interesting to see her in the neighborhood again," Gladys says with this crazy smirk. She moves her feet slightly, giving the impression she's anxious. She's trying to lure me into her gossip. I bite.

"Oh, yeah? What do you mean again?" I prepare for a long-winded explanation, and get it. She first fills me in what everyone else on the street has done since the last time we spoke, so I flip through my phone, regretting my decision to engage. She doesn't get my hint.

As she gets to gossip about me, although I'm not sure if she knows I'm involved, she stops and looks at my head. "Your hair is fading. It's not quite purple anymore, is it? More of a bland gray," she says, right out of nowhere. So rude. Right?

Anyway, she says there were eight letters from parents complaining about Miss Clark. I'm fuming. Seven would have been enough to get her fired. With so many of us, you'd think the guilt would be diluted. It isn't. Especially when Gladys tells me what happened when they escorted Miss Clark out.

"They let her take one box of personal items," says Gladys. "That's it. She had to leave everything else behind. Supplies she's been collecting for years. Learning games she purchased with her own money!" Jesus. I'm picturing how sad she must have looked, carrying her one box. But how does Gladys know what goes on in Miss Clark's classroom? She doesn't have kids in the school.

"After she left, everything else was thrown away. They didn't keep it for the next teacher. Shelia said the new teacher should buy all new stuff." So, that's how Gladys knows. She must be friends with Shelia.

Such a waste. Does that mean parents have to donate new supplies? "Miss Clark was crying the entire way out." Ugh. My initial image has more detail. "Teachers lined the halls to watch her go. They booted her out after the end of the school day, so the students didn't see, but staff was required to stay late."

Finally, Gladys gets around to answering my question, the one about Shelia being back in the neighborhood again. Although I can't let go of the image of Miss Clark and her box. There's mascara running down her cheeks. But, wait. Miss Clark doesn't wear makeup. I adjust.

Gladys switches to Shelia, and I'm expecting her to say something like she was friends with the lady who used to live in my house. Because if what Shelia said about Tracksuit Man's wife's pursuit of the coach is true, Shelia wouldn't be in this neighborhood unless she was trying to track down her husband and use my house to spy. Maybe she's reusing plans she made then. But, I'm wrong. Gladys points across the street.

"Philippe." That's all she says, then scratches at my arm as if her fingers are nibbling it. She stares at me and waits. She's making me work for this? So annoying.

"What's up with Philippe?" The question comes out exasperated as I move slightly away from her reach. I don't think she can tell me anything I don't already know. But, I didn't know the details on Miss Clark, and wish I was still unaware, but just because I don't know about something doesn't mean it didn't happen.

"His wife and Shelia's husband had an affair," she says, and I'm a little shocked Psycho Soccer Mom's story is true. Then, Gladys says, "They used to be friends. Shelia and Gretta, that's his wife. She's a cute little Asian girl with a German name! She and Shelia practically ran the school. I'd see Shelia's car in front of their house all the time. When Shelia found out about the affair, she tried to get them back and went after Philippe."

This bit I find amusing! I cannot see Psycho Soccer Mom trying to be seductive, and I'm happy to get the image of Miss Clark out of my mind.

She goes on, "But he wanted nothing to do with her, and Shelia threw a fit. She bad-mouthed Gretta, got her thrown off some of her posts at the school." Wow. Psycho Soccer Mom must have been humiliated. Maybe this is when she turned evil. She was reacting. But given the situation, I don't blame her. I start to feel sorry for her.

"You do not want to cross her," says Gladys. She's pointing her finger, scolding me as she talks. "One day, Shelia was on their front lawn screaming and throwing things at the house. The entire neighborhood heard and came to watch. I wasn't sure if she was yelling at Gretta or Philippe, but she wouldn't stop. I had to call the police. In the end, Philippe and Gretta got an ugly divorce, and Shelia and her husband eventually got back together. Gretta moved away with their son. And I hear Philippe never gets to see him. It was such the scandal."

Gladys is all puffed and proud telling her story. But, the image of people coming out to watch sticks with me. It's like what they did with Miss Clark. No one intervenes or helps. They just let it happen. It sickens my stomach. I regret the show Grace and I did for Tracksuit Man's camera, making a similar spectacle for everyone to see. And I notice Gladys called the police. It seems the po-po spend a lot of time in this neighborhood.

Gladys's features flare with amusement, a strange juxtaposition to the story she's telling of Psycho Soccer Mom throwing things at the house to save her marriage. It seems Philippe is the innocent one in this mess. But then I feel for Psycho Soccer Mom, too. Some of her ways, although unconventional, begin to make sense. It's what people do when they're in love, and get their heart broken.

I grab my bag from my car and close the door, lingering on the fact that Tracksuit Man has a son. And an ex-wife. And rejected the seduction of Psycho Soccer Mom. He's getting more interesting, and innocent, each time I see Gladys. The sad thing is that a boy is involved. What that poor kid must have gone through, seeing all these adults behave so poorly. The police coming because of some domestic-disturbance love-triangle has to be rough on a kid. Parents should never put a child through this. My mom would never do that. I know I'm a better mom than that.

"How old is the son?" I ask, on my way to my front door.

She says, "Oh, about Grace's age." It makes me feel worse.

Subject #57: Eddie - Session 32
Topic:

Psycho Soccer Mom

Yesterday, I get the call. Psycho Soccer Mom says the mission is a go. Tonight. On a Sunday! It happens when I'm laying a silky fabric out on my worktable, one that's difficult to keep flat, and any movement or slightest push makes it ruffle. Stopping means I'll have to measure everything again, so this whole Psycho Soccer Mom dictator mess is getting in the way of me earning a living.

"Eddie, Philippe is meeting with a woman who wants to move into the neighborhood and take over my role as president of the PTSA," she says. "I need you to tell me everything that's going on, what they do and what they say." She doesn't say the woman is Gretta, or that she's worried about her marriage, which is weird because that's what we talked about after Abby left.

Instead, she's afraid of the competition for her role as

president. I wonder if she's embarrassed her husband had the affair and she's pretending she wants the info for business reasons, like she doesn't want me to know she's hurting. It makes me think her school leadership roles are the only place she gets respect. The "I hate mommy" written in green crayon comes to mind. I haven't asked Grace who wrote it, but Grace doesn't talk to me this way. Katie probably says it to her mom all the time.

I take notes of what Psycho Soccer Mom says on the back of a curtain order, an order that's way past my promise date. I don't have time for Psycho Soccer Mom's love life. Although, I'm curious to see how Tracksuit Man lives. I'm thinking I'll be like a scientist with binoculars monitoring wildlife. I wonder what kind of books he has, or what his favorite TV shows are. Is he a neat freak? With the matching sweatsuit, I'm guessing he's anal. "How do you know the woman is coming tonight?" I ask.

"It doesn't matter. I just know," she says.

She must have a huge outreach program. Gretta doesn't live nearby, so I'm told. And if Gretta wants to move back, even if they don't get back together, no one can stop her from moving into the school district. So, I don't know how Psycho Soccer Mom plans to prevent this, which kind of worries me. While all this flies through my mind, I'm writing instructions, then remember, I don't have binoculars.

With no binoculars, this suddenly becomes real. I'm no longer in some romantic movie playing a female 007. Instead, I'm a mother about to do something she'd be ashamed of if her daughter found out. This isn't what I signed up for when I moved into this neighborhood.

"Eddie," she continues. "Take photos, record what they're saying, write it down in case you forget, or in case the recordings aren't clear. And don't let them see you."

This is disturbing.

"No," I say. I had imagined myself only looking out of my front window, noting who comes and goes, and when. That bit earlier about seeing him in his own habitat, actually inside his house, was just fantasy. I have no intention of going to his house or even getting that close. A busybody watching from behind curtains is one thing, but getting so close that I can record what they say without them knowing? Red flags are up all over the place. It's too intrusive. I fail to see how this information will help Psycho Soccer Mom's "Maintain the Presidency" cause. What will Grace think if I'm caught?

My pen bears down on the paper, making thick lines. "How am I supposed to record them and take photos without them noticing? If I go to his house, they aren't going to talk in front of me. And we don't have that type of relationship where I can just pop by for a visit," I say, logistically try to wiggle my way out of this mission. I think I'm making a strong case, but she pushes back.

"I don't care how you do it, Eddie. Just get it done." There's anger in her voice. My scribbled lines become dark patches on my notes. Then, "Hide in the bushes for all I care."

At this point, I drop my pen and give her the finger, even though she can't see the gesture. I want nothing to do with her.

Isn't this illegal? It's not the kind of person I am. I don't follow the instruction of some lame soccer mom. I'm the rebel with the tattoos and purple hair who shuns insane authority figures. I'm the woman who if you don't like what I'm doing, then Fuck You. I thought she knew this about me. But then, as Gladys pointed out, my purple is fading.

Then she drops the mother of all bombs. "Eddie, you wouldn't want Grace to see the flyer, would you?" I revisit her pulling it from her purse, then slowly unfolding the photo of my ex, the red word MONSTER shouting at me. "Or, to see the photos of you at the high school with drugs? Or the letter you wrote to get Miss Clark fired? I've got a large envelope ready to give her. It's got photos, phone numbers, everything she needs."

That last "or" is especially painful. It's something I did that negatively effects Grace's life. She still tells me how much she misses Miss Clark, how sad she is that she's gone. What kind of mother takes away the best teacher ever?

I take a deep breath and curl into myself. But wait, there's more. "I can remove Grace from the school play, the gifted program, recess kickball captain, the advanced art program, the list goes on. And, Eddie, you can't come back empty-handed like you did with the high school. You must bring me something or Grace gets the envelope."

That bitch! My brain feels like it's flipping in twenty different directions, not knowing which way to land. I flick the arrow and it's spinning. Unfortunately, it lands on Psycho Soccer Mom, when all the other options are Grace.

"Okay," I shout. It's like I'm stuck. Shamefully, sometimes it's easier just to go along with things. Once I agree, her voice becomes pleasant, like we're having a fun conversation between friends. Meanwhile, I'm sick to my stomach. She gives me the details: what the woman looks like, what kind of car she drives, but she doesn't know the exact time she's coming over so she wants Grace to sleep over at her house tonight, even though it's a school night, so I can focus on my mission. I instantly object.

"No, she can sleep at my mother's," I say, wanting Grace to be far away from what I'll be doing.

"No, she will sleep here," says Psycho Soccer Mom. "We have to make things seem as normal as possible, and I'll have an urgent project for them to work on for school. No negotiation." I'm pretty numb by this point, and agree to let it happen.

I can't tell Grace why she's going. I hate lying to her. For the rest of the day, I just go through the motions. I'm out of my body and watch me move around my house as I work on the curtains. I watch myself bring Grace to Katie's. I watch myself waiting for night to fall, watch me make macaroni and cheese that doesn't get eaten. I'm a puppet, and a psychotic lady holds the strings. "Oh, and, Eddie," she says before hanging up. "Before you do this, make sure there's nothing in your trunk."

Subject #57: Eddie - Session 33
Topic:

Me

I've got more to get off my chest so I'm back. Twice in one day. Grace is at school and I'm too agitated to work. Whatever image I had of myself as a good mom when I moved in, *this* is not it. So, back to the mission.

It's dusk. I'm looking out my front window, and I don't know if just me or there's a green haze over everything. Grace is at Katie's, and driving home I realize what a poor choice that was. The first thing I do when I'm back home from dropping her off is look in the back of my car, but there's nothing. The lights in my house are off so nobody can see in. I wait by the front window for what feels like a very long time. But when I check, it's still early in the evening. Time moves ridiculously slow.

Finally, a car pulls into Tracksuit Man's driveway, and it's the car Psycho Soccer Mom warned me about. She's even got the license plate right. A woman gets out. But so does a boy about Grace's age. My stomach drops.

The son. It hadn't occurred to me he might come with his mom. I hesitate. This changes everything. I can't spy on them if a kid is involved. But right then, Psycho Soccer Mom texts me for an update and any morals I may have had go completely out the window. I revert to puppet status. I don't have a choice and say, "The subject just arrived and I'm letting them settle before I make my move." It needs to be completely dark, so I won't be seen.

I'm dressed in black, head to toe, and I'm still trying to figure a way out of this. But if I wait any longer, I'll miss something important, or my subject may abruptly leave and I'll miss her all together. Grace will get the envelope; she'll know about her father; she'll know what I've done. I might as well get this over with. I feel like throwing up.

I text Psycho Soccer Mom to let her know I'm in motion, and go out the back door. Someone may be watching the front. (Gladys.) It's cool outside now that the sun has set. My footsteps disrupt the dew beginning to form on the grass. I slink along the side of the house and go through my gate. Right when I get to the front, I stop, remembering Tracksuit Man's security camera.

It's almost impossible to see it moving at night. He's probably got the night-vision feature. So in my head I map out a path of things I can crouch behind in case I'm in the camera's direct line of sight. I keep low and crawl to my driveway, peering around my car, then dash to the curb and hide behind a street lamp.

For some reason, I think I'm thin enough. Now that I'm at the street, I can just make out a red illuminated light moving in the camera, but it's difficult. My trash can is still on the curb from yesterday. It gives me wider cover. From here, I watch the camera go through several rounds, so I get the timing right.

When I see the camera pass me, I run across the street and duck behind Gretta's car. My breathing is heavy. I'm at the back and take a photo of the license plate. Psycho Soccer Mom will want to see this. I'm proud I'm clever enough to take this photo. But the flash goes off, so I huddle near the driver's rear tire and wait to see if anyone in the house noticed. I turn off my flash. Everything's still quiet. After a while, I look through the car's windows to look into the house. Lights are on in the living room and in the back of the house in what looks to be the kitchen.

I make my way between the wooden fence and Gretta's car, monitoring the camera the entire time. When it's safe, I get on the ground and crawl up to the house like I'm in one of those army commercials trying to get people to enlist. Crawling on your elbows is harder than it looks. The night is cool, and the air feels almost exhilarating. I have a high like I am in full control, but then a light goes on upstairs. It casts a spotlight onto the grass just beyond me. I stop. I see a shadow of a smallish person in the rectangle. They're at the window, so I tuck my arms and roll into the line of bushes under the living room window. I catch my breath, then slowly rise. As I do this, my hair gets caught in the branches.

The branches attack me, scratching my face. I can't see very well over the bushes, so I push my way through, using my arms as a machete, like I'm making my way through a jungle. The ground is wet and my shoes are heavy with mud. When I reach the brick, I squat in the space between the house and the hedge, positioning myself just high enough to where I can peer inside. In this spot, I actually have a good view of the entire room. No one's there.

I'm more relaxed now that I've made it into position without being detected. But when someone comes into the lit room, I'm on high alert again. It's the boy. He moves around a lot. I've never noticed Grace moving so much. Maybe it's a boy thing. He's carrying a backpack. He yells something toward the kitchen, but I can't hear him. Moments later, Tracksuit Man and Gretta come into the room. They're each holding a cold beverage. They're smiling and laughing as the boy empties his backpack onto the table.

Clearly, Tracksuit Man and his ex get along. I could never see me doing the same thing with mine. The backpack spills pieces of boy toys, which are now scattered all over the table, and the boy assembles them. My subjects look as if they're having a pleasant conversation, like a Hallmark movie moment, but I can't hear. Tracksuit Man must have some beefy windows. I don't see bitterness or anger. It looks like a happy family. I think Psycho Soccer Mom is right. They're getting back together, and Gretta and her son will move back into the house. For some reason, this disappoints me. Why should I care? Psycho Soccer Mom will have competition, so maybe that's a good thing. And me? I'll be left alone. By Tracksuit Man anyway.

I take out my phone so I can send a video to Psycho Soccer Mom, and double-check to make sure my flash is off, then hold my phone up and record while I watch them. I'm holding as still as possible. It feels like I'm in this position for a long time, recording, so I straighten my legs a bit, but I'm still bent over. I'm pretty confident no one can see me.

After a while, Gretta gets up and goes to the kitchen. A couple minutes later, she sticks her head in the room, says something, and Tracksuit Man and his son rise. The boy knocks some of his toys off the coffee table as he runs to the kitchen, and Tracksuit Man stays behind to pick them up. I watch him. He's careful, gentle. He's somehow different at home.

When he leaves the room, Tracksuit Man turns off the lights. The room inside is dark. At this same time, the white light from the rolling street lamps pokes its way through the large tree branches in his front yard. The beam hits and saturates the window, and...it's startling. The glass suddenly reveals a hideous woman on the surface, and she's staring right at me.

I gasp. The woman looks odd: aged and worn. The bulbous cheeks I'd known for so long, erupting when I grin, are gone, and so is the voluminous smile that puts others at ease. This is not the 007 image I'd imagined or the good mom image. What I see is an old biddy of a woman with a nasty expression, tight lips, and furrowed brow. My hair sticks up like a crazy person. The image hits me hard, and I jerk back, trying to get away from it. Well, as much as I can with a row of hedges behind me.

I can't believe what I'm looking at is me. What the fuck am I doing? My mind goes blank. Then I realize, I'm a Peeping Tom. I'm a friggin' Peeping Tom. Oh my God! What the fuck is wrong with me? My thoughts go immediately to Grace. What would she think if she saw me here? Abby is right. I am exactly like Psycho Soccer Mom.

The wind blows and the branches scrape against the glass. It gives me chills like fingernails on a chalkboard. Gretta peeks into the living room and tilts her head as if she hears something out of the ordinary. The sound of scratching, of course, *that* makes it through the sealed glass. She crouches as she creeps toward the window, my window, the one I'm plastered against. I duck. When did I become a psycho? What kind of mother have I become in such a short time? I'm sitting in the mud, wedged between Tracksuit Man's house and his bushes, trying to figure out a way to get home without getting caught. I'm doomed.

⌘

I want to make sure Gretta still isn't at the window when I leave, so I wait her out. All the while, I'm thinking about Grace. Is this another thing Psycho Soccer Mom will use to get me to do more of her bidding? Does she have someone else hiding in the bushes, taking pictures of me, ready to show Grace if I don't do what she asks, like at the high school? When will it stop?

I have to escape before Gretta leaves. As the night progresses, it's getting colder and I'm shivering. I didn't think I'd be here so long. I should have dressed in layers. Maybe it's nerves. Then suddenly, everything goes black—the rolling streetlights. This attempt to save energy usually pisses me off because whenever I'm walking to the house or the car, the lights go off. This time, it's a godsend. But…

When I crawl from the bushes and look left, I see bright lights flooding the darkness and a fierce spotlight slowly moving back and forth, searching over the ground ahead of it, so I duck back behind Gretta's car. There's a low rumble in the distance, and a car stops at the curb on the wrong side of the street, several houses down from where I'm crouching. A door opens, and a dark-suited leg plants itself on the ground, then grows to full form as a man stands and comes out from behind the door. The driver stays inside. The first man closes the door and shines his flashlight. I scatter to the side of Gretta's car.

Someone called the police. He'll see me if I try to run across the street. I'm thinking I'll be arrested. I'd be the creepy neighborhood lady arrested for being a Peeping Tom. Grace's mom, arrested for being a Peeping Tom. I'm unhinged and totally mortified.

I have this vision I'm in the back of a squad car. Why do I keep having this same fantasy? I've never had it before moving here. Grace is crying. How can I do this to her? I plead to God that if I get out of this, I'll never listen to that Psycho Witch again.

The only thing I can think to do is to call Arjun. Both the car and the man creep closer. I duck lower. The car's lights shine down the street, obstructing my path home. The policeman walking shines his light at Tracksuit Man's bushes, then walks to the place where I was hiding. He looks on the ground and notices footprints. He follows them to the driveway. Fuck.

But then, like a miracle, Tracksuit Man and Gretta open the front door and he turns and goes to the porch. It's like the Lord God and heaven above are shining down on me. I have a window of opportunity. I dash around the fence and dial.

Subject #57: Eddie - Session 34
Topic:

Arjun

So I'm still on what happened last Sunday, while I'm on Psycho Soccer Mom's mission. Today's about Arjun. When I call him, he answers right away. Thank God, he's in his car and not far. Through the slats of the privacy fence I see the patrol car stop in front of Tracksuit Man's house, and suddenly I have to pee. The driver gets out and meets up with the other officer, who is already at Tracksuit Man's door. While they talk, Arjun pulls up several houses down. I'm on the phone with him the entire time, so he's getting the play-by-play. He knows which way to come down my street, and to turn around before he gets to the fence I'm hiding behind. He has his headlights off, and like a true getaway car, keeps the motor running.

I make my way to his car, hiding behind whatever I can find, and making sure my path isn't too close to the street or any house where someone else might see me and call the police again. I jump in, and he takes off. "Slow," I say. "We don't want to attract attention."

He inches forward, and when he gets to the stop sign, turns on his headlights. This is when I start crying. I never cry.

"I'm sorry. I'm sorry," says Arjun. "You shouldn't have taken my advice." His regret comes pouring out. But, it isn't his fault. This is all on me. I chose this. I shake my head.

He was so proud when I told him I was taking his advice over Abby's, but now his hands are trembling and his eyes bulge, like he's a scared little kid or an animal cornered. It was unfair for me to get him involved. Now he's nearly the basket case I am when he's usually the calm one. I cry harder, but try to keep it in so my shoulders jerk up and down.

He's careful to drive the speed limit, use his turn signals, and fully stop at every stop sign. When I calm down, I tell him what he doesn't already know about my spying mission. His hands still shake. I realize that by having him pick me up, I make him an accomplice. From the look in his eyes, I think he knows it, too.

"Eddie. Where is Grace?"

"She's at Katie's," I say. My voice trembles. Knowing she's at Psycho Soccer Mom's makes me more upset. My stomach clenches and shoulders tighten, rising to my ears, and it's hard to breathe, partly from crying, partly from panic. We drive around, afraid to go to my house. Then, he heads toward the highway, carefully changing lanes. I am a terrible mom.

"Get on here," I say when I see an entrance ramp to the highway. I want to get as far away from the situation as I can. We're quiet. It's like Arjun and I are both trying to process what the fuck just happened. I'm trying to control my breathing. My face is wet. He has no tissues in his car. I use my sleeve.

"Should we go get Grace?" asks Arjun as he merges on. And I'm realizing I'm leaving Grace behind. I sit up in my seat to figure out what a good mom would do. What's wrong with me?

"Yes! I need to get Grace. Get off at the next exit," I say. My voice sounds like it isn't coming from me. I hear it fill the car's cabin. Arjun moves to the right lane, turn signal on, then gets in the exit lane. "No! Stay on!" I'm screaming and pounding on the dashboard. Arjun brakes and drives over solid white lines to stay on the highway. Someone beeps at him, a long angry honk. His expression lets me know he's bewildered. "I can't let her see me like this. I need to calm down first." She'd freak if she sees me crying. Besides, what do I say to Psycho Soccer Mom?

"What are you going to tell Psycho Soccer Mom?" Arjun asks. It's like he's reading my mind.

"I'm not sure," I say. My voice is still trembling. I'm watching red tail lights rush by. The traffic gets heavier as the gathering of illuminated red increases in front of us. There's orange barriers with yellow flashing lights forcing cars into two lines. Arjun chooses the far lane, which moves slightly faster. I'm quiet again, and the show of moving red is oddly soothing. But, I can't forget. Grace is still in the trenches. "We need to go get her," I say, breaking the long silence.

The car rolls to a stop in the standstill traffic, even though we're supposed to be in the fast lane. Arjun looks ahead, assessing the situation.

"I'll tell her I never went," I say. "Deny I was ever involved, but someone saw me. Someone called the police." My voice is calmer, but my stomach isn't. Even if Psycho Soccer Mom didn't send one of her minions to take pictures of me, someone knows. And with her web of intel, she'll know soon enough. "I think it was Gretta."

"Maybe Gretta, or whoever, saw a person, but they don't know who it was?" he says. This is a ray of hope, but only a single thread. I pray it's true, but with Gladys in the neighborhood, something will get back to Grace.

"Get off at the next exit," I say, monitoring the construction, which is difficult with the blinding flashes of yellow. It makes no sense. They're trying to caution you, but they make it harder to see.

We're sitting in traffic when Arjun says, "You remind me of me." He's smiling, not a happy smile, something more toward understanding. He glances at me, but only for a second, returning his eyes on the stopped car in front of us. I don't understand the connection. We roll forward a few feet.

"How?" I ask.

"Doing what others tell you instead of doing what you know is right." I don't see myself this way, and process his remark instead of getting defensive, which is what I'd normally do. Maybe Arjun is thinking of his family. The traffic moves slowly. I'm still looking for that exit.

"How can I make things right with Grace after everything I've done? How did you make things right? And what should I say to Psycho Soccer Mom?" I ask, turning in my seat to face him. The seatbelt makes it difficult to move. I tuck my legs to my chest in a fetal position.

"I didn't make things right. I was a coward and ran away. But it is important you make things right. You have Grace to think of. You can't run away from her," he tells me, and I realize that's exactly what I'm doing. I really am terrible. He's looks straight ahead as we creep.

It sounds like something a mother would say—*make things right*. I can tell he misses his. Maybe this is what she said to him before he left—make things right with his family. Maybe it was after. I see a sign for an exit up ahead.

"So you think I should come clean?" I ask. "With Grace?"

"You should tell the truth and do what you believe in your heart to be true." His words are like an ancient Indian guru. I try to listen to what my heart tells me. But I only hear his engine. And then I hear a text coming in. I look at my phone. It's Psycho Soccer Mom.

ARE YOU STILL IN POSITION? WHATS HAPPENING?!!

"Fuck!" I say. "Psycho Soccer Mom wants to know what's going on. There's an exit coming. Let's go get Grace, now!" I'm instantly anxious, and don't reply to the text. What can I say?

Arjun moves slowly with traffic, nudging his car into the right lane, and since Psycho Soccer Mom is waiting for a response, the slow pace feels even slower, like I'm running but not getting anywhere, a fight-or-flight urgency, but I can't do either. We finally come to the exit, and my voice gets all pitchy and high. "The exit's closed!" A new text comes in.

EDDIE! ANSWER ME!!

EDDIE! WHAT'S GOING ON???

The urge to get Grace is too strong. I don't want her in that house one second longer. She'll be angry, and I'll get the silent treatment for the rest of tonight, at least, maybe in the morning too. I deserve it. I'm angry with me too, for letting this get as far as it did. I'm stuck in a world where Psycho Soccer Mom rules, and I have no option but to follow her blindly. I'm also stuck in traffic.

EDDIE! She screams in her text.

And then it happens. She texts me a photo of Grace. She's in Katie's bedroom. They're both sitting on her bed, smiling. Then she texts me photos of the contents of her secret envelope: the flyer, newspaper articles of what happened (she actually did her homework), pic of me standing on the desk in the high school, the drugs, and maybe worst of all, the letter I sent complaining of Miss Clark. All I can do is scream. It's a loud, long, high-pitched wail like I'm in some horror movie; maybe I am. Arjun looks at me, terrified.

"What?" says Arjun. I'm stomping my feet on the floorboard and pounding my thighs as my wail continues. This goes on for several minutes, and it's crazy that Arjun can maintain control of the car, while I'm having a freak-out right beside him.

"She's going to tell Grace, like right now," I say. It comes out desperate.

Arjun thinks quickly. "Text her you want to show her what you saw in person, and that you're on your way." It'll buy me some time. I quickly text her. She replies with another photo, a selfie with her and the girls. Her hair is wet. It makes her less attractive. The pic is followed by a command.

HURRY. I'M KEEPING TRACK OF THE TIME. IF YOU'RE NOT HERE SOON, I'LL...

She leaves me dangling, letting me finish the sentence. I know how it ends. My attention's on the traffic, then I see it. A sign saying the next exit is in one mile, and the three exits after that are closed. We have one chance to turn around. The lane beside us begins to move and Arjun joins it. We're finally moving again, although slowly.

"There!" I yell when I see the off ramp just ahead. "Get over!"

He pushes his way in, coming only inches from the car beside him. Everyone around has no problem letting us know they're angry. "Is your blinker on?" I ask. He clicks his turn signal. I feel like getting out to direct traffic, because we are *not* missing this exit. I sit up in my seat and put my hand on the door handle, but there's no room for me to open the door.

Finally, the guy in the next lane behind us stops and lets us in, but not without laying on his horn for several minutes first. It's not like we're taking cuts; we're only passing over. I roll down my window and give him the finger as we leave on the exit ramp. It's a huge relief to get out of traffic. This feeling doesn't last long. I get another text.

FIVE

I show Arjun. "What does that mean?" I ask. My urgency to get Grace is in full force, so I start briefing Arjun about what's in the envelope, and the photos she texted me, so he'll understand why I did what I did. Maybe he won't.

FOUR

Another text. "Oh my God, she's counting down. Go faster." My mother used to count down to get me to do something when I was in trouble. Psycho Soccer Mom is treating me like a child. My explanation of the envelope quickens, thinking if I talk faster, we'll get there sooner. With everything out in the open, we discuss what to do next.

THREE

This text comes sooner than the last, less time in between. "She's not giving me time to get there," I say, on the verge of another freak-out.

"Tell her you're almost there," says Arjun. "It will help if you communicate with her, so she knows." I text Psycho Soccer Mom, adding TRAFFIC.

Arjun and I continue devising my game plan. He's afraid to give too much advice, not wanting it to backfire, but what he said earlier about truth stays with me. While many parts of the world are beautiful and kind, there are people in it who are evil. I pray I'm not one of them. It's best Grace hear the truth from me. I'll tell her as gently as possible, while letting her know I love her. Because really, that's all I've got.

TWO

This two doesn't faze me. Well, it does a little, but I've got a good plan. And although I'm nervous about implementing it, I'm moving forward. I text back. JUST AROUND THE CORNER.

⌘

We park in front of Psycho Soccer Mom's house, and I text Grace from the car. I tell her to gather her things and come outside immediately. I wait until now to text her so I don't cause suspicion. I don't tell her why. She calls back, demanding an answer. I say she has two minutes to meet me on Katie's porch and I hang up. I hate talking to her this way. I sound like my parents. But, sometimes when you're the mother, you have to take charge. When I go to the door to collect her, Arjun comes with me. Their garage door is open. It's filled with packaged individual bottles of water and other boxes stacked to the ceiling. It's too dark to read the labels to know what's inside the boxes.

We have to wait a long time after I knock. I can't imagine what they're doing inside, and my stomach is tight. What if she's showing Grace the envelope while I'm standing on her porch? I'm thinking maybe I'll text Psycho Soccer Mom to distract her, when finally, Coach answers. I tell him I'm here for Grace.

He looks clueless, like he doesn't know she's here. And then it hits me. Psycho Soccer Mom probably has no communication with her husband. Maybe that's what led to the girls being left on the field without supervision. Their relationship must have never gotten over the affair scandal. Her role at the school really *is* the only thing she has.

Grace comes up behind him with her arms full. Her face is red and tense, like she's holding back tears. I can tell she's furious. I just hope she's mad about leaving and not that Psycho Soccer Mom told her something she shouldn't have. Grace has to go around the coach to get outside because he doesn't move. Katie stands beside her dad, also looking confused, which is a good sign. I'm amazed at how smoothly this is going, without incident or a scene. We're halfway to the car when I hear it.

"Eddie! What are you doing? What did you find?" I look back as Psycho Soccer Mom pushes her husband out of the way and runs out the door. She's in pajamas, and there are curlers in her hair. The pink foam ones. Who still uses curlers? She carries a large manila envelope. "STOP!" she yells, and it echoes. We obey, almost afraid to move any closer to the car and our escape. "I demand that you tell me what happened!" She puffs herself up, trying to control me and my daughter.

Something in me sees her like a balloon, big, inflated, floating above everyone to draw attention to herself. Her own virtual party. But I see she's also thin-skinned and fragile, and if I took a pin and poked her, she would easily pop and be hurled chaotically away from the force, most likely screeching as she deflates. She's wearing pink fuzzy slippers. They match her curlers. She must have stepped in mud when crossing her lawn because the fur gathers in clumps of wet earth.

The sight of her dirty slippers somehow makes me think more

clearly and I suddenly remember that I have a superpower. I carry a pin, and if I choose, I don't have to listen to her. I also remember my plea with God. I know I'll have to come clean with Grace. It's time anyway. She's old enough to hear the truth, and she needs to know exactly what Psycho Soccer Mom does to control everyone. It isn't right. Grace should know there are unkind people in the world and what she should do when she meets them. Maybe I've sheltered her too much. But I want to shelter her for just a bit longer, at least until I have the chance to tell her the truth. I stand my ground.

"I will call you in the morning. Right now, I'm taking Grace home," I say. My voice is confident. My powers make me invincible. I feel the wind blowing my hair away from my face as if I'm standing in front of a huge fan. It feels like I'm floating, not like a balloon, but propelled by my own power like I'm the Starship Enterprise.

"No! You need to tell me now!" Psycho Soccer Mom tries to get up in my face, but Arjun steps between us even though he needn't.

"She said she will call you in the morning," says Arjun, with a voice as confident as mine. He pronounces every syllable, suddenly losing all traces of his accent. OMG! I love Arjun. He's this skinny Indian guy and Psycho Soccer Mom could probably whip his butt, but that just shows what a bit of confidence can do. And quite frankly, I'm ready to take her on all by myself.

I look back at the house and see Coach isn't there. He's gone back inside, seemingly wanting nothing to do with what's happening on his front lawn. Maybe he's seen it too many times before. Maybe he witnessed Psycho Soccer Mom yelling on Tracksuit Man's lawn.

The garage door closes, most likely by Coach. It's as if he separates himself from her. She stands alone in her front yard, without anyone to help intervene, like Arjun did for me. Katie stands at the front door, looking scared. Poor Katie. It's a very dysfunctional family. I almost want to take her with me. Almost.

Arjun motions us to the car and we leave Psycho Soccer Mom standing in her lawn, fuming. The only thing that would make this any better is if it started to rain.

Subject #57: Eddie - Session 35
Topic:

Grace

Same night, but now the topic is Grace. We're quiet as Arjun drives us home. I know if I don't tell Grace everything tonight, I'll chicken out. I made my deal with God so I can't renege. Either I do this or the whole Psycho Soccer Mom controlling thing will continue, maybe even get worse, and I am so completely done with it.

I guess when there's no love left in your marriage, you try to get it elsewhere, and sometimes settle for admiration. My marriage was dead, but I had more than enough love with Grace. Psycho Soccer Mom's problem is that she forces admiration from others, and what they give is pseudo love.

Anyway, any signs of the police are gone by the time we're home, so is Gretta's car. Arjun pulls into my driveway and asks,

"Should I come in?" He thinks I need some backup when I tell Grace. Or maybe he wants to be sure I tell her.

I shake my head and say, "I got this." It's hard to leave the security of his car, so I wait before making a move. Getting out means having to do something hard. Grace looks out the window, away from us, and I can't tell what's going through her mind. She's sitting behind Arjun and huddles up against the door. It's like she's trying to distance herself from me. She waits until I get out before reaching for the handle. Arjun helps bring in her sleepover stuff, setting it just inside the foyer. He gives me a hug before leaving. The house is strangely quiet.

"Let's go sit in the kitchen," I say, and Grace heads there without responding. As I sit with her, she focuses on the medallion tattoo on my right upper arm. It was always her favorite. She used to trace the design with her finger when I held her, when she was small enough to hold. Arjun told me the pattern's called a mandala.

Grace's stare tells me she knows what I'm about to say is important. This has got to be the hardest thing I've ever done. I long for the days when I didn't have to explain anything. Where to begin?

I go to my room and dig out an old photo from the memories box in my closet. I wonder if she'd seen it when she found my necklace. She waits patiently in the kitchen, staring straight toward the cupboards. I kiss her on the top of her head when I return, then give her a picture of me and her dad when we first started dating. She redirects her stare to the picture, doesn't give me any hint to how she feels about it. There's only one way to do this. I start from the beginning.

I tell her how we met, how he was different back then, how the drugs came between us, and how I had to protect her from his new way of life. I tell her several times that what he did had nothing to do with her. He was broken before she was born, but he loved her in his own way. She listens intently, without asking questions or commenting. She stares at it as if it's an illustration to my story.

I tell her he's in jail, and why he's there, that he was responsible for a teenager's death because of drugs. I don't tell her the details of the trunk. That's too much for a child to hear. Maybe when she's eighteen. I say it's up to her if she tells anyone where her dad is. I ask her if she wants to know more. She nods.

I let her know he gave her good genes before he turned bad, after she was conceived, and that's why she's a good person. I'm not sure she understands that part, but I go on to say that it was the drugs that turned him. He started taking them after I was pregnant, so the drugs aren't a part of who she is. I tell her this is why I am so strongly against any kind of drug use. She nods. All she can do is nod and stare. I wish I knew what she's feeling.

Then, I explain everything about Psycho Soccer Mom, how she threatened me, how she tried to blackmail me, and what she had me do at the high school. I try to explain why I did the things I did, that I was trying to protect her, but now I see it was wrong. I tell her it's okay to be wrong, as long as I try to make it better. I tell her what Psycho Soccer Mom has done to other women in the community: how Jack's mom was forced to make him quit baseball tryouts so Katie's brother would make the team instead of him (I don't know if she knows who Jack is, but the details reinforce the story), how she made everyone leave girl scout camp after one night when they were supposed to be there three because the lady at the cafeteria said something she didn't like, and how she wanted me to spy on Tracksuit Man's ex-wife because she didn't want competition in the PTSA.

Then, I tell her about Miss Clark, and as I do, tears come. My tears, not hers. This one's the hardest, and I think of what I just said to her, as long as I try to make it better. This is when she finally stops looking at the photo and looks at me. She's disappointed. I see it in her eyes. My daughter sees me as I truly am, and I need to make it right. I promise I will. But, I don't say it out loud. Instead, I'm quiet. The promise is for me.

After a while, I tell Grace it's up to her if she wants to be Katie's friend because Katie is innocent. She can't help that Psycho Soccer Mom's her mother. "Katie is welcome in our home, but for now, I don't want you going to her house, at least for a little while until we get things sorted," I say.

I think Grace understands. It's hard not to bawl because she's so brave about the whole thing. Maybe because I'm totally honest with her, and am giving her room to make her own choices? After this conversation, I'm numb. In my head, I hear both Abby and Arjun cheering.

"You can keep the photo," I say. It's more hers than mine, anyway. She takes it with her and quietly goes to her room. It's already late and way past an appropriate bedtime, and she needs to process everything I've said. There will be questions tomorrow. As she leaves, my heart aches for her. There's so much love I feel like I'll burst. But then calm sets in because everything is out in the open, nothing is hidden. I've popped the balloon and feel lighter than air.

⌘

I'm in bed when I start to worry I've dumped too much information on poor Grace all at once. She was quiet, and listened, so I don't know what she was thinking. How can I not ask her how she's feeling? It wasn't a conversation. I was monologuing, again. I'm terrified she hates me for lying to her for so many years. I don't sleep. My social anxiety hits me, playing through my mind like an Instagram loop. Hours pass, and I can't scroll past this worry. I continually revisit our conversation, making sure everything I said can't be misinterpreted. But, I'm sure it has. I don't want to be cranky in the morning from lack of sleep, so I try to calm myself by absorbing the stillness of the room.

The room is mostly dark, except for the thin blade of light coming from the single streetlamp outside, which is back on, always when you don't need it. It finds its way through a slit in the curtains and draws a straight line on the floor, beginning at the window and ends its point at the framed photo of me and Grace, stabbing each one of us in the heart. I study the intrusive beam and have to change my assessment. The line of light has narrowed with specific intent of sectioning Grace from me, coming between us, or maybe it's me that has. The light only briefly distracts me, and my thoughts return to Grace. I worry she'll never forgive me. I worry I'll always be a terrible mother, and the good image I had for myself disappears in a puff of smoke.

⌘

I look at the clock. It's just after three, and I'm willing my limbs not to move, but then I'm convinced that if I reposition myself— first by bending an arm and a leg, then lying on my side, finally I lie flat—sleep will come. It doesn't, so I reposition the bed linen by folding it neatly under my arms and smooth it across my body. The next thing I know, it's morning. And the first thing I think is that Grace isn't in her bed. She ran away. That's what I would do.

Subject #57: Eddie - Session 36
Topic:

Me

The sessions where I talk about me seem to be the most therapeutic. It's exactly what I need right now. Is it possible to feel relief and angst at the same time? This is what I constantly feel when trying to protect Grace from the world, especially one with Psycho Soccer Mom in it. There's a war going on inside my body, and I'm not sure who is winning.

So, it's the morning after the Tracksuit Man mission. This is three days ago. I wake up freaked out feeling Grace isn't in her bed, that she ran away because of everything I laid on her. It's barely light out, so I tiptoe and quietly open the door to her room. I see her face, and this is all I need for the tension to gush from my body. It leaves me wobbly. Maybe it's from not enough sleep?

I try to sleep for another hour. But, my eyes won't stay closed no matter how much I force them. When I notice something moving near the ceiling, I sit up to focus, but my eyes are sore from all that forcing. When I rub them, it feels like an eye-massage, if that's a thing. I look again, and my room is full of ladybugs. I have no idea how they got there, but something tells me it's a miracle. Ladybugs are supposed to be lucky. Right?

I get my kitchen stepladder, quietly so I don't wake Grace, and gather the bugs into a plastic cup. I'm like almost giddy, which is weird because if I were collecting any other kind of bug from my ceiling, cockroaches or spiders, I wouldn't be so happy. I'd be Febrezing them.

As I put them in the cup, I count each one. There are fifty-seven. I'm holding an envelope over the cup as I take them to my garden, padding along the grass in flip-flops and now my shoes and feet are wet with dew. It feels fresh, like a new beginning, like hope. I cradle the bugs so I don't upset them. When I'm at the garden, I want to make a wish on each bug as I ceremoniously set them free near the overgrown blackberry bush. But, I want two wishes, so I'm torn.

I alternate between them. First, I wish for Grace to be okay with everything I piled on her last night. Then, I wish for some guidance on what to do next. So in the end, I make each wish twenty-eight times. (I'm doing a lot of math this morning.) But, there's one bug left, so I wish for Arjun to reunite with his family. I think it's something he wishes for, too. I saw it in his eyes last night. As I let Arjun's bug go, I consider getting a ladybug tattoo.

I leave my garden thinking I'm selfish for only allotting one bug for Arjun. Sorry. As I walk back to the house, I notice a ladybug clinging to my shirt. She must have jumped on me after I set her free. I already made a wish upon her and don't want to overstep, so I say the rhyme, "Ladybug, Ladybug, fly away home." When I try to nudge her, she crawls onto my finger and roams around in my hand. I speak to the bug as if it were Grace. The lack of sleep has me not thinking too clearly.

"I'm sorry," I say, thinking how I let Psycho Soccer Mom control me. "I'm not a good mother." The bug stops moving, almost as if it's listening. "I'm sorry I kept things from you your entire life. I'm sorry if you're hurting. I hope we can get through this. I love you more than anything."

I fear the events of the past couple months will change our relationship forever. What would I do without Grace? Not that she'll physically leave me, but emotionally withdraw like I did with my mother, which might even be worse. This bug must sense I'm upset because she appears to be staring at me. It's weird when a bug looks at you like that. I came outside with so much hope, and now I'm a mess. There's so much I can't put into words, but I try. "But please know you are my heart, my life, my weakness, and you are my choice."

I can't believe I'm so stupid. I only want to do what's best for my daughter, but have made a mess of things. Am I evil if I consistently choose poorly? Maybe I've been trying too hard to be the cool mom so Grace would like me. Maybe I should relax and lie low, like my mom did. Maybe that's what a good mom does? Let go and let God. Right?

I already made my wish, but I'm having a hard time getting this bug to fly away, so in my mind that justifies me making another. I don't know the exact rules for ladybug wishes. I whisper, which I should have been doing all along in case Gladys is listening, "Let go and let God." I'm letting go of Psycho Soccer Mom, and her pressuring me to do the wrong thing. That's over.

With delicate breath, I poof the ladybug away and watch it take flight. I don't see which direction it flies because a small pool has formed in my right eye, blurring my vision. Collecting together, the moisture becomes a single drop. That one drop holds a bouquet of emotions, each carefully arranged and each taking up a proportionate amount of space. My one tear encompasses everything I have endured since being evicted, and everything else I buried inside me my entire life: love, betrayal, loneliness, fear, and even hope. As I stand in the yard, my tear moves to the lower ledge of my lid, then gently makes its way over the ridge, flowing softly down the curve of my cheek. That one tear enables me to feel alive again. And even though technically I have a superpower, aka I'm a superhero, that one tear makes me human.

⌘

Psycho Soccer Mom might always be a problem in our lives. But half the battle is simply acknowledging what the problem is, right? So, I'm halfway there. To move forward, maybe I let her do whatever she does and I won't be a part of it, even if Grace doesn't get to do the fun things. They were things she was handed because of me. It's better for her to earn it.

So, with the tear gone, I see the ladybug is back on my shirt. It's like, what's with this bug? I hear Grace calling me from the house, and I'm eager to see how she is, if she's mad or hurt. "Go," I say to the bug. But it stays. "Go. Move!" I'm almost yelling at it. It finally flies to the garden. People say I'm intimidating when I yell.

Grace smiles when she sees me.

"I'm worried how you're feeling after what I told you last night," I say.

"I'm fine," she says as we go inside and she sits down to breakfast. "I kind of already knew about my dad being in jail."

It surprises me, but then it doesn't. She's pretty smart and has been listening to me and her grandmother, and me and Abby talk all of her life. She's put the pieces together herself. It's something she's grown up with, and she understands I was trying to protect her. I'm not sure how this is even possible, but I love her even more.

"Katie tells me a lot of what her mom does," says Grace. "She knows she's crazy. We couldn't believe you became friends with her." She's smiling. Life through the eyes of a child is pretty incredible. Grace is quiet, then says, "I'm sad about Miss Clark." And here comes my angst.

"I know," I say. "I am too. And I'm going to make things right." I failed her. She had a good, caring teacher, and I got rid of her, only to be replaced with someone more compliant to Psycho Soccer Mom, no matter their qualifications. When Grace gets up from the table, I give her a long hug.

While she finishes getting ready for school, I bring my coffee to the living room and look toward Tracksuit Man's house. Hiding in those bushes seems like a lifetime ago. I'm a completely different person since then. I want nothing to do with Shelia. I want to concentrate on my business. Grace can make good choices; she doesn't need me to help.

I notice my old books nestled on the table. I took great care to arrange them, like an art installation. Sandwiched between two books on the history of textiles is my fabric printing journal and the book from Mom. The one I'd weirdly carried around and quoted. I hadn't wandered through its pages for years.

I grab the book and return to the window, setting my coffee on the sill. Opening it, I stand sideways, so the sun lights up the entire page. Outside, crows nestle on the ground near the street, searching for their breakfast. I'm searching too. I don't know what for. We had some in my yard growing up. I'd watch the same ones year after year. First there were two, then three, then four. It was evident which were the parents, from their size and their behavior. Crows stay together as a family. The crows near the street must live here. I switch my book with my mug. As I grip it, steam rises from the heavy ceramic cup, weighted with a strong French roast.

I hear Grace in her bedroom. A dog barks outside as if an alarm on some neighbor's porch went off. The sun moves. Outside, smaller birds come to feast; they are polite and work around the crows. My coffee becomes bitter as it cools and recedes into the cup. Maybe I'll add sugar. I remember reading that three grains of salt will take away the bitterness too. There's more than one way to achieve something. The heat of the sun dulls the room. The dog still rings. I wish someone would kindly turn him off.

I randomly open the book again and read. I'm sucked in through its wormhole where I see the mother as she watches her son shave; he stands by her as she sits and smokes. I smell her stale cigarette, and hear her words; she worries about her darling daughter. I try to send her a message telepathically. It's normal to worry, but don't do anything crazy. The bathroom is hot with steam.

The sun nudges me as it finds its way up from my book and shines in my face, pulling me back to the dull heat of my living room. I hear movement. It's getting closer, and makes its way to where I stand. "Ready?" I say. It's a very happy morning.

⌘

Wow, it felt great to go through all this. Some needed me time. I'll get back to the crazy when I'm here next. This session is like the calm before the storm.

Subject #57: Eddie - Session 37
Topic:

Psycho Soccer Mom

Here we go. Shortly after Grace gets on the bus—I'm still on last Monday—Shelia shows up, and she's frantic. I'm using her name. She isn't worth the energy of so many syllables. Anyway, it's like she was waiting for Grace to leave. "Let me see all the photos you took and I want to hear any recordings," she demands as soon as I open the door.

It's typical for her to treat me this way. But, this morning is different. I'm calm and she doesn't affect me. I feel like I'm still standing in the sun at my front window, like I'm watching her from behind a plate of glass.

She makes a move to enter my house, but I don't budge from my doorway. I'm holding the door with one hand and the jamb with the other, like I'm a human barrier. "I got some great photos,"

I say. "And video." She's nodding, with her eyes wide.

"Gretta threatened Philippe with a knife. She was screaming and crying, and her makeup was running like Tammy Faye." Then I backtrack. "She grabbed the knife only after Philippe fist-punched her in the face, then as he swung her around, her shirt rips off. She's holding the knife shirtless. One boob has come free from her bra." I'm having fun with this, and keep going. "They struggle as Philippe tries to take the knife away, and she falls against the coffee table and knocks out her front tooth. Then chokes on it."

None of this happened. I already said what I saw. But, it's fun messing with her. When I feel she's taken up enough of my time, I say, "The truth is, Shelia, that none of that is true. I made it up just to fuck with you. I've already deleted any photos I took and I won't be spreading any rumors about my neighbor." It's like, oh my God! Go me! The look on her face is something between confusion and alarm, with a bout of nausea. I don't tell her what actually happened. It isn't her business.

"Eddie, remember what I can do," she warns me, and takes the dreaded envelope from the massive purse she's got slung over her shoulder. She's expecting me to instantly become the sniffling amoeba I'd been in the past.

"Do whatever you want," I say nonchalantly. "Grace knows everything. I told her last night. I showed her the flyer; I kept one. But we'd love to see what you have in your envelope. Please hand it over. Or you can give it to Grace yourself." I'm smiling.

"Did Gretta get to you?" Her face is angry, like with puffs of steam coming from her ears. She's red and her eyes dart back and forth. She's still wearing her pink curlers. And the muddy slippers.

"No, Shelia. Common sense did. I'll be listening to that instead of you from now on." I close my door in her face. She's still holding the envelope. I don't lock it. She wouldn't dare come in. My hands are steady, and I'm light, like I could fly simply by hopping off the ground and jutting my arms out in front of me. I don't need a starship.

I'm peeking through the front window as she gets in her car. Before she drives away, she texts me.

BE CAREFUL EDDIE. YOUR BUSINESS IS ABOUT TO BE AUDITED. NOT THE SEWING, THE ONE YOU SIGNED FOR.

Subject #57: Eddie - Session 38
Topic:

Tracksuit Man

I'm here six days in a row now. That must be a record, and one of those days I came twice. Anyway, last time, I left you with another what-the-fuck moment. Like, what business is Psycho Soccer Mom talking about in her text?

Soon after she leaves, there's knocking at my door. I think she's back, ready to clarify. I'm ready to face her, so I rip open my front door, but it's Tracksuit Man standing on my porch. He's holding a bag. And all I can think is, he knows.

"Wait. Don't close the door. I need to talk to you," he says. I'm flushed, because I'm sure he wants to talk about last night. I can't respond, can't even move. He continues. "Please, Eddie, I need to apologize, and I bring a truce offering." He holds up his bag. "Can I come in? Please."

I'm still shocked, but in a different way. Apologize? For what? I open the door and he steps inside. He's wearing jeans.

He hands me the bag and gestures for me to look inside. It's more than weird. I halfway think it's a trap, like something will bite me or there's a pile of shit inside. Maybe from that barking dog. But I'm wrong. I bring out an old book with a gold-embossed spine, *The Art of Dyeing Fabric*. I open the cover. It was published in 1869. He stands there, smiling at me. It's a nice smile. A flock of questions burst through my mind, but the predominant ones are: Why? And how did he know?

"Leigh told me you're into fabric, and I've seen you in your garage reupholstering furniture," he says. "She also told me about the aphids. Said it looked like you didn't have any experience with gardening. You weren't home, so I put ladybugs in your garden. I hope you don't mind. Did they help?"

He clears up several mysteries in one swoop. This is a different man than the one etched in my brain. I thought the worst when I saw him in my yard when he was being kind. Why is he suddenly being nice to me?

"I wondered where they came from," I say. I'm not sure what to do next, so I just stand there, looking at him. It's not awkward for me, because questions are still swirling, so I'm preoccupied. But he looks nervous. He fidgets with his hands, finally tucking them into the front pockets of his jeans, then diverts the nervous energy to his feet by kicking at something that isn't there. It's sort of charming, like he's suddenly shy.

"Well, I have several apologies to make, and a lot of

explaining," he finally says. "I think we got off on the wrong foot. Do you have some time? Can I sit?"

This keeps getting weirder, but I'm open to whatever the universe wants to bring.

"Sure. Sit here," I say, gesturing to the couch, which is buried in fabric. I move it out of the way, and we sit on opposite ends, facing each other. I'm still holding my gift. He takes a deep, cleansing breath.

"Hmm, do I start from the beginning? Or do I work backward?" He's talking to himself. I don't respond. "I'll start with last night."

I freeze. Oh shit!

"I'm sorry," he says. "But Gretta, my ex-wife, called the police. She didn't know who was outside." He doesn't say anything about me hiding in the bushes and looking in his window. I appreciate that. It's humiliating he knows it was me. "She did it before I could stop her. She's the one who suggested I come over and explain. We know why you were there. And we don't blame you. Shelia can be pretty forceful."

This takes me off guard. He understands, but I don't admit nor deny anything.

"We've gone through it. Shelia's got this weird hang-up with Gretta. She's always trying to compete with her. Maybe since Gretta never took her seriously, never listened to her the way the other women do, no matter how hard Shelia tried to force her hand."

Wow, I think I like Gretta, but I also like my image of her

toothless with a boob hanging out, which isn't real. Tracksuit Man continues.

"When she heard me and Gretta were separating, Shelia tried to make the moves on me just to get at Gretta. We laughed about it. When this didn't work, Shelia started spreading rumors that Gretta and her husband were having an affair." I think about how Shelia's story fits this. This one's more believable, given the people involved.

"She said some nasty things about Gretta, and our son heard about them. It was all made up, totally ridiculous, but the other kids started teasing him. We explained everything to him the best we could, but the PTSA or even the school board wouldn't do anything about Shelia. And it isn't just in the elementary school. The district is small, so there's only one PTSA for the entire district. That's when we agreed Gretta should move away with Josh, our son. This was years ago, at the end of kindergarten. They rarely come back here for that reason."

That poor child. Kids can be so mean, but it makes me even more angry that the entire thing was started by an irresponsible child-like adult. I still don't respond.

He continues, "I usually spend time with them at their house or we have a cabin by the lake we all go to. We're still great friends and still very much in each other's lives. Gretta was here yesterday to pick up some papers. She planned to be quick, but somehow Shelia found out about it. Shelia tells everyone she caused our divorce, but it isn't true. We've been talking about separating for years. We're the best of friends, just never meant to be married."

I'm kind of envious of this last remark, and imagine how different Grace's life would be if her father was like him. I don't think we'd have it so hard. I focus on Tracksuit Man. It's odd how open he is, like we've been friends for a long time. He sounds sincere. I might actually like him. But what if this is another trap? Maybe Shelia sent him over.

"That's why I was so upset when I saw her over here a while ago." The entire scene comes back to me, the one with the dolls when Katie visited. I'm still not sure about him. He was pretty unhinged.

"Sorry about that, by the way. I hate to see her corrupt another parent. She digs her claws into people, and it upsets me. It happens too often. So if there is any way I can help, please let me know." He seems genuine, but there are still some issues that need answering. Now might be the best time to ask.

"What's with the cattle gate when I first looked at the house?" I ask. He purses his lips in a thoughtful way. I'm thinking he'll either deny it or conveniently forget it. But instead, he shrinks.

"Yeah, that was weird, I know," he says, and I'm puzzled. "Sorry about that, too. Shelia came by earlier that day to tell me one of her minions was interested in the house and was going to come by to look at it. She warned me to treat her well. I don't know why she involved me, but I certainly didn't want one of them living across the street, so I did the opposite."

That sounds like something I would do. I want to ask about the light bulbs and the rant with the bottled water, but I start to have empathy. Besides, I don't think he knows I know about those things. He's transparent, and he wants me to come clean about yesterday, but I still don't know who I can trust.

"What do you mean by helping me?" I ask.

He exhales and leans forward with his elbows on his knees. His hands rub his face like he's manually trying to organize his thoughts. Then he sits straight.

"You're obviously a strong woman and probably don't need my help on anything, and please don't be offended, but I'm offering to help you get her back. Or rather, make things right," he blurts.

And it's like I can't believe what I'm hearing. I'm quiet for a while because I'm excited, and I don't want him to know.

"How do you mean?" I ask.

"Well," he says, then pauses. "What she wants most is power, control over people, right? That's why she never got along with Gretta. We take her down; get her kicked off every committee she's on."

I like this idea. It would just about kill her. And it almost sounds evil, but if we did this, she wouldn't be in a position to treat people so poorly, or to blackmail them. And she wouldn't be in a position to make Grace miserable. Besides, if she wasn't on all these committees, she could focus on fixing her relationships in her family.

I'm back in the twilight zone. Tracksuit Man is in my living room and we're having a friendly conversation. Well, he's doing most of the talking. Did I really get him so wrong? I'm wishing

Abby could see me now. Tracksuit Man and I want the same thing, for Shelia to leave people alone. I'm considering his offer. We'd be saving the next person, who is probably already in the crosshairs of her scope. I like the idea of paying it forward.

I want to know more, and offer him tea to keep him here a while longer. When I bring the tea to the living room, I ask, "What do you have in mind?"

"Well, to beat her at her own game, we need to think like she does. Her big thing is blackmail. Do you have anything on her we could use?"

I think of her crazy incidences: the time she threatened me at soccer practice, asking me to search for drugs in the high school, and last night's spying episode. And Miss Clark.

He must know Shelia blackmailed me. But does he know what she has on me? I appreciate him not asking. That's a sign of a true gentleman. He's sharing more with me than I am with him. This makes me trust him. I'm not ready to mention last night's episodes, so I start with soccer practice.

"She threatened me," I say.

He wants the details. When I mention that this happened when I was on the phone with my ex's lawyer, he gets excited.

"Eddie, they record those calls to use in court if needed. They probably have the whole thing recorded."

I don't know what he does as a living or why he knows this, but this knowledge is a godsend.

We brainstorm and come up with several good options to get back at Shelia. It doesn't take long before we're laughing, and I'm actually having a good time. This is when Arjun calls to see how I am after my talk with Grace. I take the phone into the kitchen and I fill him in about Tracksuit Man.

Arjun says he'll leave work and come right over. He's not convinced Tracksuit Man's intentions are good. When I'm back in the living room, Tracksuit Man says, "You have a lot of school merchandise. Are you involved in the sales?"

"No," I say. "Gifts from Shelia."

When Arjun gets here, he has groceries. It's odd, right? He tells me he's rushing over to save me and then stops to pick up food. But that's Arjun. I introduce him to Tracksuit Man. "This is my friend Arjun." But when I go to introduce Tracksuit Man, I hesitate, and Tracksuit Man notices. I've used the nickname so much that when he's standing in front of me, that's the only name that comes, but I catch myself. "This is my neighbor ... Philippe," I finally say. They shake hands.

"Please call me Phil," he says to both of us.

I contemplate how this new name registers with this man I'm meeting for the first time. Phil. I let it roll through my brain. Phil.

⌘

We move to the kitchen table, and I refill our tea. Arjun is making a curried spinach dip, while Tracksuit Man and I, I mean Phil, continue planning. As Arjun stirs the dip, he's listening and watching Tracksuit Man. To him, Phil is still Tracksuit Man. Arjun is ready to step in if things start to turn. He's like my chaperone.

When Grace gets home from school, she's stunned to see me getting along with our neighbor—yes, he's been here a while—and that Arjun is okay with the whole thing. She's hesitant, but joins us because Arjun puts a new dip on the table, a red pepper hummus made from scratch. She sits by Arjun and takes on the same devil's advocate role he does. She's quiet at first, but then sees how Phil is very different than we assumed. My Grace is perceptive that way.

Soon, Grace softens like I did. Phil is funny when interacting with her. He's clever, and he knows how to talk to a kid. He must have a good relationship with his son. That's what it seemed when I peered in his window. So now Grace is in on everything we're doing and even helps us plan because she knows what goes on in Shelia's house. She reinforces my image of the lack of mutual respect in Shelia's house, and promises not to say a word. I don't have to worry about her breaking her promise. She knows what I've been through.

I open a bottle of wine and empty it into two large glasses. Arjun still listens while he gets up to find something more substantial to go with our wine. He finds chicken. He can do a lot with a chicken. By the time dinner is ready we have a plan, and it's a pretty damn good one. I open more wine. Now that I've had wine, I'm more relaxed. While we eat, I tell everyone the story of me hiding in Phil's bushes, and he fills in the bits of what was happening on the inside with Gretta calling the police. Everyone laughs. I ask how he knew it was me, then suggest he saw me on his security camera.

"No, Gretta heard someone outside. She's got incredible

hearing. Then she saw you looking in the window. She didn't know you were my neighbor." He pauses. "She said someone from Team Shelia was outside when she was dialing. Later, when I saw the officer outside with the flashlight, I saw you running away. That's why we went outside, to distract him and tell him it was a false alarm. I knew Shelia must have been behind it. I didn't want to get you into trouble." Wow. Tracksuit Man saved me. This just about puts him in the same category as Arjun. Almost.

"I rarely check that camera," says Phil. "My company made me get it when I started working from home. They're paranoid."

I guess I am too. I wasn't the reason for the camera. But, then I was on Team Shelia when Gretta saw me, so I technically was the reason. Thank God I quit. "God, what do you do?" I ask.

"I'm in cyber security. We were recently awarded a contract with the government. They insist on extra monitoring," he says, which actually makes me feel comfortably secure for about a second until I realize the government has probably seen me prance around in masks.

After dinner, I make Arjun a large bowl of ice cream, and I put a gulab jamun on top with syrup. It's an Indian fried dumpling. He leaves a can at my house for such occasions. It's his reward. While he eats, he watches me and Phil clean up. I also give him a bowl of chips. That's my culinary contribution. I taught him to let the ice cream melt and dip the chip in it. The salty sweet is heaven, with a dumpling on top. See. I teach him some things about food too.

As Arjun brings his bowl to the sink, he whispers in my ear,

"He's flirting with you." He's got this smirk on his face, and I feel my face flush. Then he says, "I'm going to check on Grace in her room."

I could punch him because it's so obvious why he's leaving. I'm not sure if he's right that Phil is flirting. If he is, I'm not sure I'm comfortable with it.

So, I'm alone with Phil, drying a pan, and he takes the pan out of my hands and just stands in front of me, staring. I'm getting hot and bothered, which is stupid. I'm supposed to be this badass lady, and here I am, getting nervous like a schoolgirl. He sets the pan on the counter, then takes my towel. I'm just standing there. He takes my hand, and when I don't move away, he comes closer, bringing his face inches from mine, and then stops.

I'm thinking our chaperone is gone, so why is he stopping? I don't want him to stop, but he hangs out there. It seems like forever. He finally starts moving in, in ultra-slow motion, only after I slightly lean forward, like he's waiting for my permission. His eyes wander all over my face, taking in every detail. He touches my hair with his free hand, then tenderly moves his touch down to my jaw, bringing us closer. Then we kiss. It's a slow, thoughtful kiss. It's a good kiss.

All during this kiss, I'm thinking how I'd been noticing him from afar, little details, without really realizing it, *and* how I'd been thinking a lot about him lately. But a boyfriend doesn't fit in with my image of being a good mom. I guess the woman in that image is celibate, never thinks of sex, like my mom.

"I didn't think you liked me," says Phil.

"I don't," I say.

We both know I'm lying.

⌘

Arjun clears his throat as he enters the room, making extra noise by stomping his feet. He even bangs the bowl I have on the counter holding my keys. Phil and I separate, and I pick up the pan, put it in the cupboard. Arjun pauses and just looks at us, then demands I tell Phil how Shelia came between me and Abby. My best friend. He still thinks it's his fault, but he's wrong.

Abby doesn't think Arjun did anything wrong by giving advice. He was trying to help. He must have had the idea to mend my relationship with Abby while talking to Grace, who most likely had some input. She doesn't want Abby out of her life. Neither do I. But Abby and I will be okay. We have to be. Although I owe her an apology.

Phil sides with Arjun. "You should call her now and set things right. Friends are important."

Grace comes in the kitchen and sides with the both of them. All three are ganging up on me, but I like they feel this way.

"Abby's in London and it's in the middle of the night," I say.

"Then promise me you'll call her tomorrow," says Phil.

"I promise. I promise to pour my heart out to her, explain why I did what I did, and why I didn't treat her like I should have when she was here. I'll beg her to forgive me." I hope she supports our plan. She has a good head for these types of things, so I should have listened to her in the first place. Sometimes I'm an idiot. My tone, as I make all these promises, suggests I'm kidding. I'm not.

When Phil says it will take a couple of weeks to get everything in place, Arjun suggests we see if Abby can be in town to help. I like his suggestion.

⌘

It's late and Grace is asleep. We got a lot done, and we're exhausted. I walk Arjun and Phil to the door. Arjun is the first to step out. Phil turns and touches my face. "And, Eddie," he says. "I'm happy to help you with anything. You know, like moving some of the enormous sofas you're reupholstering, or whatever. Just let me know."

"Manly, are you?" I say, and he laughs. Even though it's dark, I can see him blush. Manly, yet blushing. Interesting. He kisses my hand and leaves. I can see Arjun standing behind Phil, giving me two thumbs-up. "Go home," I tell them as I laugh, then watch them walk into the night.

Subject #57: Eddie - Session 39
Topic:

Beth

I had to break my streak yesterday and take a day off from this. It's been a week since the kiss. The first time I see Phil after the kiss, I make sure to wear my glasses. They're bifocals, thick black cat-eyed frames with rhinestones decorating the corners. I don't need them to see, and there isn't a prescription on the top part, only the bottom which enlarges everything when I look down, so it's helpful when I'm sewing. I make sure to wear them because boys don't make passes at girls who wear glasses. It has to be true because my mom used to say this to me when I was little. I guess back in her day, it was devastating for a girl to wear glasses. I'm counting on it to be true because now isn't a good time to start a relationship, especially with a neighbor, especially with this whole Shelia plan going on. I need to concentrate.

At this point, Phil, Gretta, Arjun, and I have been busy gathering what we need for our plan for almost a week, and we've done a lot in this short amount of time. We're quietly enlisting others, and Team Eddie is growing. But, it's important we make sure everyone keeps it on the down-low, so Shelia doesn't become suspicious. She has many tentacles out there; it's hard to know who to trust. People are happy to help. They've had enough. And the most unreal thing is that our most unlikely ally is Beth.

She approaches me first when I'm at the school. This was last Friday. I'm thinking Shelia's behind Beth's approach, but then maybe she's heard about our army and wants in. She was friends with Miss Clark, remember?

"Augustin says hi," is how she approaches me while I'm sneaking around the school doing reconnaissance. This throws me for two reasons. One, I didn't know she's friends with Augustin. More importantly, it proves she knows I'm her old neighbor.

"You've seen Augustin?" I say, admitting to knowing all along who she is.

"Ya," she says. "I drove up for the day to see his farm last weekend."

Oh my God. She's close enough to him to visit? I thought I was the only one to receive his special invitation because of Grace. I'm focused on her face, trying to figure it out. She partly looks at me as she talks, but mostly looks away. And she doesn't open her mouth very wide, so it comes out quiet. She almost looks terrified. Do I do that to people? Then I think she's frightened I'll blab about her drug use, and she'll lose her job, like Miss Clark.

"You got to see his farm!" I say, and she smiles. "I didn't know you were close." It sounds like a weird or odd thing to say, but I'm trying to figure out why she's suddenly opening up to me. I mean, she hasn't said anything personal to me the whole time I'm here. Or even since never.

"Ya, we've been friends ever since I passed out at work. He was my emergency contact when I first moved here and started working. I didn't know anyone else."

Wow. What a drag. To have your landlord, who you barely know, be your first person of contact. But it's just like Augustin to take someone in need under his wing. I still think it's drug related. It makes sense.

"You fainted?" I ask. I try to keep my voice down.

"I had a seizure. I'm a diabetic. Type one. I'd forgotten I put him as my emergency contact, and never changed it." She's looking at me more directly now, and I feel like an asshole. I assumed the worst of this poor woman with her thin pale frame. Her long sleeves that I thought were to hide the needle marks is probably because she's cold. Poor circulation and all that shit. I hear diabetes is a horrible disease. All of her health problems are totally not her fault. I'm such a loser!

"Oh, no. I'm sorry. About the diabetes. That's got to be tough. How is Augustin? What's his farm like?" I feel my face redden, and I'm trying to be extra nice.

"Ya, I manage. His land is beautiful. He's got fifteen acres, and he bought one goat that he says he's practicing with before he gets more."

I laugh, easily seeing this, but in my mind, the goat is a bit of a handful for him.

"It sounds nice to have so much land." I sound upbeat. I wonder if she's aware of what I thought about her or that now I see her differently.

"Ya, but I'm not sure he should get any more. The goat follows him around everywhere, and he treats it like a dog. He even has a bed for it just inside the back door, and there's a food and water bowl there. Inside his house." Beth tucks some hair behind her ear. She's letting it grow. She has clips holding back her bangs. "It was nice to get away. Especially after what happened to Miss Clark. The whole thing doesn't make sense."

Oh God. She's right. It doesn't make sense. What I did will forever haunt me. But I think she knows something. Does she know my letter and all the others were made up? I wonder if Shelia bothered to change the wording on each one she sent. Beth would know. If she read mine, she must have read the others. But, I have to ask carefully. I'm not sure if she'd join our team or trust me since I'm one of the parents who got Miss Clark fired. I poke.

"What do you mean? I don't think it makes sense either." I look around to see who might be listening, and lower my voice. "Can we meet for coffee later? After work?" I want Beth to feel comfortable confiding in me. I think I need to get her out of this toxic surrounding where someone may be listening. Working in the office, she'd be an asset if she joined us. We'd have access to a lot that could help our cause.

"How about the Palace?" she suggests, and I shake my head.

She must not know the diner is Shelia's office.

"We should meet at the coffee house in the next town over. The coffee is better there," I say. I think she understands why I choose a place not in this town. Arjun comes over to watch Grace. I arrive at the coffee shop early. Beth is exactly on time.

⌘

I'm sitting at a table in the back, away from prying eyes. Various art objects cover the walls, paintings, three-dimensional installations, car hubcaps, even an elaborate shrine dedicated to Elvis. There's also strings upon strings of lights. "I'm sorry we didn't hang out more at our last apartments. I thought you didn't like me," I say, as gently as I can. It's all true. "And I'm sorry if I said anything rude to you back then. Sometimes my tongue gets away from me. It's one of my many flaws." I don't tell her what I had thought. I can still picture her holding her syringe. But now, her image is frail, and I want to hug her.

After the waiter takes our order, she tells me where she's now living. "It's not as nice as Augustin's place. I don't make much working at the school, so I can't afford anything better. I spend most of my money on diabetes medication."

"Doesn't the school provide insurance to cover it?" I ask, sort of horrified. She's in a situation she'll never be able to get out of.

"The school's insurance isn't that good, especially since I'm not a full-time anything. Shelia's in charge of getting insurance for the district. She chose something cost effective." This explains

Beth's clothes. The school specifically hired her for two part-time positions to get out of giving her full-time benefits. Can they even do that? My anger mounts, giving me more reason to move forward with our plan.

Even though Beth is the first to mention it, we dance around the subject of Shelia's wrongdoings. Neither of us wants to be the first to say why we're there, just in case. But I'm the one who called this meeting, so it's up to me. The waiter bring our drinks, and after he leaves, I take a deep breath and dive.

"How is Miss Clark? I feel bad about being involved. But...I had to." I word it this way because depending on her response, I could say I had to protect Grace from what Miss Clark was doing, or I had to because Shelia made me. She answers in a way that doesn't address either of these.

"She isn't good. Those kids were her life. It doesn't make sense. I wish there was something I could do for her."

There's that logic again. I'd almost forgotten she said this earlier.

"What doesn't make sense?" I ask.

Beth adds cream to her black coffee, no sugar.

"Miss Clark doesn't use social media. She doesn't know how. We've talked about it when I asked if she wanted me to set up a Facebook page for her class," she says as she watches the spoon she's swirling in her cup.

Right away, I know the Miss Clark account is fake, but I need to figure out how Shelia is involved and why.

"Someone must have set her up," I say. Even though I know

who it was, I try to get her to tell me more. "Do you know anyone that would want to do this to her?"

Beth continues to stir her coffee even though it's well blended. She's not drinking it. It's like stirring helps focus on something else besides me and our conversation. Maybe it's her way of dealing with anxiety. I don't even know if coffee is something a diabetic can have. I wonder if she ordered it because it's what I ordered.

She puts her spoon on the table after clanking it on the rim. "No. She's always been the same. She's nice to everyone. She isn't one to ruffle any feathers."

No, she isn't. She's fair. She's kind. And look what I've done to her. "Is there any way of finding out who set up the Facebook account?" I ask. "Aren't you the computer lady at the school?"

"There is a way, but I'm not that savvy. I only know the basics." She looks down at her untouched mug.

"Beth," I say. "Do you want to help Miss Clark? Really help her? With me? Find out who did this?" There's a spark in her eyes. First time ever. A fire. Although it's barely perceptible, it's there. "But I don't want you to do anything you'd feel uncomfortable doing." She gets this faraway weird look, like she's been there before, like Shelia has gotten to her too. She contemplates.

"What would I have to do?" she asks. She sounds hesitant. Nervous.

"Look at the letters that got Miss Clark fired, the ones like mine. What were there, eight?" Beth nods. "See if they all say the same thing. The exact same thing, word for word." By the movement of her eyes, she's already scanning them. She looks floored, then confused. I'm sure they're a match. "The office keeps them filed. Right?"

"They do. It's required," she says. Her expression asks, *Why?*

I don't want to lose Beth, and we don't want the letters to go missing. So right away, I come clean. "Shelia was behind the letter I wrote, and she must be behind the others as well. She blackmailed me into doing it." Beth doesn't ask what she's got on me. This tells me she's a decent person. But then, Beth shrinks like an abused animal, and I can tell something's wrong. "Did Shelia get to you, too?"

It's almost as if Beth is afraid to move. She looks small in the wooden chair. She looks at her hands clutching the cup in front of her. And then I see it. The slightest ever nod. I gently put my hand on her arm. For some reason, I'm suddenly all touchy-feely, but I don't want to scare her away. I use a tone that matches hers. "Don't worry. You don't have to tell me what it is."

We sit for a while, and when I think she's ready, I continue with the plan, still using my Beth-inside voice. "If the letters match, we have some proof that Shelia was the one who wanted Miss Clark fired, not the parents, and that she forced them into signing the letter."

Beth agrees to do some digging, and to give me a list of parents involved. I'll see if I can recruit the people on this list to join our team. But we still need to find out why. Why did Shelia want everyone's favorite teacher fired?

Subject #57: Eddie - Session 40
Topic:

Me

For the last several days, I don't come to any sessions because we've been building an army. Arjun, Phil, and Gretta meet at my house the day after I talk with Beth. We're all excited to have someone on the inside, and I'm a hero for at least a couple of minutes. I tell them about the fake Facebook page, and Phil says he's knows a guy who can figure it out.

Then, get this, Gretta suggests I make up with Shelia, to get back in her favor, so she won't suspect our revolt. It isn't something I look forward to, but I agree it has to be done. I'm going to have to do a bit of groveling, and I'll make sure Grace knows what I'm doing, so she doesn't think I'm heading down the "inappropriate mother" road again. Gretta makes a list of what Beth should look for in the office.

After the meeting, everyone leaves but Phil. "Did you speak with Abby?" he says, running his fingers down my arm, then gently takes my hand. Darn! The glasses aren't working. I pull my hand away and readjust the glasses, thinking maybe they're broken, and I have to jiggle them to get them to work properly.

"I did," I say, turning away from him.

"Everything okay?" he asks. "I thought we liked each other now." He's got a full-on puppy-dog eyes and pout thing, and leans into me, ever so slightly.

I laugh. "I'm fine, and yes, we do." I run my fingers through my newly redyed purple hair. "But I have to focus on Grace. And Abby forgives me. She's all in. I'll see you tomorrow. Okay?"

"Okay." Phil reluctantly leaves, but there's an unresolved tension that remains.

⌘

The next morning, I call Shelia. "I feel terrible about the way I treated you," I say, all whiny like, then worry my complete 180 might look suspicious. "I was afraid to tell you before. Someone called the police. I was so scared; I didn't know what to do, but I should have come straight to you. I'm so sorry." I'm careful not to let my voice sound fake. It's why I call instead of going to her house. I'm afraid my body language might give me away. So, I'm pacing around my living room, fidgeting with anything not attached to something else. "I found out it was Philippe who called the police, and I need you on my side. He's out to get me, so if

284

there's anything I can do, I want to help."

The bit about Phil gets to her. She sounds pleased I came around, but still hesitant. "Tell me everything, and don't make anything up," she says.

And man, with the tone she uses, I see why people fall in line.

"Gretta said she wants to come back," I say. "But, he said no, he won't take her. They fought about someone he supposedly had an affair with, or wants to. I couldn't make out who."

Shelia is quiet, then says, "I want proof."

The funny thing is, I have it. I send her picture after picture of Phil and Gretta arguing, and Shelia is eating it up. I even send a short video where you can barely make out the name Shelia. We had fun staging this. It looks authentic because I shot them in my space between the hedges and their house. But this time, the window is cracked, so some of what they're saying can be heard. She'll know the fight was about her. Gretta even mentions something about running for PTSA president, and how good that would be for their son.

Shelia's quiet, and I wait to see if she believes it. "You've done well," she finally says. "There might be an important position for you in the near future."

"Thank you," I say, trying to sound appreciative. But I'm still thinking she may know our plan, and she's playing along. I stick with the plan because I know what's coming. It'll be worth it in the end. "Call me if you need something, anything," I say, before hanging up.

⌘

Grace's job when she's at Katie's is to be our eyes and ears on the ground. I'm torn whether to include her in this, but she wants to help. I feel it's something a good mom would do. I tell her, "Don't do anything you're not supposed to, or out of the ordinary. Just act normal. And, if things get crazy, call me and I'll come get you."

We're getting help from others too, people who aren't even in the school district. Gretta's brother is a lawyer. We want to do everything by the book so it's foolproof. When I told Abby, she wants to take a couple of days off and help. She's valuable because nobody knows her. But then I remember, Shelia met Abby once. I'm hoping she won't remember.

I talk with people on the letter list. The ones who pass our test, and want to help, give me leads to others they think may join our cause. We reach out to as many people as possible without causing suspicion; I think. It's difficult to get an accurate feel of who's on our side before giving away too much information. You'd think it'd be hard, but it doesn't take much for people to break. They want to stop the harassment. Even the orange-ziplock mom whispers to me that she wants in. A few people never break, and I worry they'll say something to our target. Word is getting around.

We'll implement our plan five days from now. Grace tells me Shelia knows something's going on, overhears her whispering to Coach, but doesn't hear exactly what she says. I'm thinking our plan is ruined, so I up my pretend loyalty to her by asking about the new position she mentioned. She needs to think I'm interested, and that I'm relying on her to get it, so I call. After I mention wanting the unknown position, I offer to do her errands. Maybe I'm going too far.

"Yes, I need you to bring some equipment back to the rental store for me," she says.

Easy enough. This was yesterday. I go to her house shortly after the call, and she loads my car up with band equipment. An image of the black-clothed young men hanging in the parking lot pops in my head. "You know where it is," she says, reminding me she'd seen me there. "And bring me the return receipt." I comply. I sign for the return and go straight to her house, receipt in hand. She looks pleased.

I'm still worried that she's on to us, so that night, I start our meeting by saying, "Phil, you should accidentally run into Shelia and flirt with her. She'd love the attention and we need a distraction to get her off our track." I love this idea. So does Gretta. Phil isn't so keen.

This suggestion might be a little for my sake, too. There's still some tension between me and Phil when we're alone. I don't know if it's just me or he feels it too, but I've been carrying around my glasses and pop them on now and then, just in case. I need to focus on getting my good-mother status back.

"I don't know," says Phil. He's hesitant, and mostly looks at me when he says this. "I'm not sure if I can. Every time I get close to that woman, my anger resurfaces." Then he elaborates with his story of his light bulb and water bottle rant. The light bulbs didn't work, or worked for only a day or two, and he had purchased several cases to help raise money for the school. He quickly went through bulb after bulb, then used an older Sylvania he had lying around. He didn't get around to throwing the rest of the faulty bulbs away because this was during the Shelia/Gretta era. He had other things on his mind. When I saw him, he used one of Shelia's bulbs and the entire episode came pouring back. I don't blame him for being upset.

The water bottle scam was recent. I remember Grace bringing home a flyer, but I wasn't in a position to donate. Phil heard about the donations from Gladys, and filled his car with cases of water and brought them to the school, but the school wouldn't take them. They didn't have the Dream Water label. When I saw him at the grocery store, he couldn't return the water he bought, and the shelves were empty of Dream Water. I understand why he acted so strangely.

At our meeting, Gretta said Shelia bought cheap products and labeled them as her own. She didn't care about quality, which explains the bulbs. I'm guessing her water bottles were simply out of the tap. Shelia must have something on the grocery store manager to have access to his shelf space.

"You can handle the flirting," says Gretta. "You can be very charming when you want to be."

"Take one for the team," I say. "God knows I am." Then I add, "You have to do it more than once. So she thinks it's the real thing and not just a happenstance, and do it when I'm around. I want to see."

He pretends to be angry and throws a wadded up napkin at me. Then he agrees. Everything is falling into place.

⌘

Our biggest asset is Beth. She discovers the motherlode while she's looking into the real reason Miss Clark was fired. We've become good friends in this process. She doesn't want to be there when it happens. She doesn't want to be connected with what we're doing. She's afraid she'll lose her job if she is. We all agree not to mention Beth if we're questioned.

This morning, Beth calls me with some bad news. Shelia has me connected to something bigger than the letter, without my knowledge, and I could be in a lot of trouble. Remember that "business that's about to be audited" text? It could come back to bite me.

Subject #57: Eddie - Session 41
Topic:

Me, Again.
(I'm sorry to break the rules, but...)

It happened! Yesterday at the PTSA meeting. That's why it's been six days since I'm here. We've been getting ready, and as you can see, I died my hair a chestnut brown for the occasion. I told Grace I chose this color because Shelia makes me nutty. Here's the play by play.

We plan to out Shelia at the PTSA meeting. I dye my hair because I want the board and parents to view me as an upstanding member of society. The pencil skirt, dark hose, and long sleeves are part of my uniform. I think I look the part.

I arrive early to get set up, we all do, and the whole while, my insides are shaking, but I think I'm holding it together pretty well. No one notices.

Phil's outside ready to detain Shelia by wooing her. Abby's

there too, acting as backup in case Shelia gets by Phil. Abby's plan is to offer services Coach can use for his business with the potential to make a lot of money. We never mentioned to Shelia what Abby did for a living when they met, and Abby's armed with lots of props, so it seems legit, and it's not odd Abby's talking to her instead of Coach. It's the way they have things set up. I keep looking back each time the door opens to see if either of them are engaged with our target, and happy when I see she hasn't arrived.

So I'm inside waiting for the meeting to start, going through my paperwork, and hoping I've got enough evidence that they'll believe me. The meeting can't officially start without the President, Shelia. I'm here early because what I want to discuss isn't on the agenda. The only time I have to make my case is before the meeting starts, and that's however long we can delay Shelia. It's a weird way of doing things, but she set it up this way herself, so she doesn't have to hear parents complain about things she doesn't care about. She often purposely makes herself late. It's something we're counting on.

The rules state that anything can be added to the agenda if it's presented to and approved by three of the five PTSA board members prior to the start of the meeting, and only if at least three members are seated. I only have a small window. It's important Shelia not be here until the bulk of my evidence is revealed. The rest of the board is here, but not seated. I'm wishing they would sit. The waiting is making me frantic.

Two of the PTSA board members know the plan, the treasurer and the parliamentarian. I'm glued to the front of the room to have dibs at the podium, so I gesture to Gretta to remind these board members to take their seat. But, we need all four board members seated to get one more approval, since we don't know which one is our best bet, the vice president or the secretary. They both seem loyal. If the two unknowns vote no, Shelia would be the tiebreaker.

It's weird, but I have to be clear that what I'm about to say is not part of the meeting. I have to say, word for word, that I'm a parent with concerns, voicing my opinion. The parliamentarian warned me, or my request won't be added to the agenda. The parliamentarian is the person who makes sure the bylaws are followed. I had to look that one up. She wrote the words verbatim and I plan to read them exactly as written.

There's a microphone at the podium, which is at the front of the room facing the board. Three board members finally sit, but while looking at my notes, a woman beats me to the podium. Fuck. I'm already making mistakes.

The woman asks to alter her child's bus route so he doesn't have to walk in the street around a blind curve into oncoming traffic, with no sidewalk. But she doesn't say the words about it not being part of the meeting. I want to run to her and slip her my cheat sheet, but we're running out of time. So, I wait, watching the clock. She's taking a long time. It's a simple request, a common sense one. The expandable folder I'm holding feels like it's actually growing in my arms, getting heavier as I wait.

They deny her request, which is ridiculous. When she turns, she looks humiliated for even asking. She sulks away, and I take the podium. My turn to face the firing squad. Placing my folder on the surface, I confront the seated board. It's going to be a tough crowd.

I start. "Hello, my name is Eddie Hest." Then, I regurgitate the proper words, then begin. "I'm calling for the immediate resignation of the PTSA President Shelia Davis." I get right to the point, and it draws attention. The room is silent with everyone focused on me. I'm wearing my glasses. They've become like a shield. The vice president begins to object, but the parliamentarian whispers something to quiet her. I hold up a stack of papers, feeling like I'm a lawyer in a high-profile class-action suit. "I have proof that Shelia Davis blackmailed several parents to falsely accuse Miss Clark of wrongdoing and get her fired. And Shelia Davis did this because Miss Clark..."

"WAIT!" A tremendous roar comes from the back of the room, interrupting me. It booms, even echoes, stopping me in my tracks. Shelia has broken through both our barricades, stringing Phil and Abby behind her. Her voice carries louder than mine and I'm on a microphone. She gives me a double-take because of my new do and my suit-dress. "It's lies! Don't listen to her! She's a drug addict!" Shelia holds up an envelope with the information about Grace's dad. I should know. I've seen it.

She rushes down the aisle and Gretta stands to block her way. Miss Clark stands as well. Then, everyone we've interviewed joins them. There's a sudden burst of elation, a camaraderie with the gathering of this army. I'm moved just by watching. They're blocking Shelia's way, but she's trying to push through.

Someone shouts to let me continue. The vice president and

the secretary look confused, but Shelia doesn't. She knows exactly what I'm going to say. Or maybe she only thinks she does.

When I look at Miss Clark, her eyes are pleading. She wants her name cleared. "Miss Clark did nothing wrong. The letters with accusations are false and were written by Shelia Davis herself. The only thing Miss Clark did was to put in a request directly to the principal for school supplies, which wasn't anything that wouldn't have been okay a couple of years ago, before Shelia Davis changed the rules. What Miss Clark failed to do is have the bidding process go through Shelia Davis." I'm using her full name because that's what I've seen in courtrooms on TV. I turn to see people who aren't standing are on the edge of their seats. There's electricity. I'm on a roll.

"I have a sworn affidavit stating Sheila Davis blackmailed the parliamentarian to change the PTSA bylaws without the approval or knowledge of the board or anyone else." Arjun gets up and takes Grace and Katie out of the room. I'm glad he's thinking. I should have arranged that. "The change declares that only the president of the PTSA needs to sign off on the bidding process and how money is spent. The principal can't even do it. Then Shelia Davis blackmailed the treasurer to keep quiet about not having any financial statements go through the proper channels. Shelia Davis created a false accusation to fire Miss Clark because she didn't want anyone knowing, or looking in to, what the bylaws actually are, and how they'd been changed." I turn again to look at the crowd. I am absolutely killing this. But wait, I'm not done.

"There's more, even the District School Board is unaware," I say.

"She's lying!" yells Shelia, and I turn to see several dads have made a human wall around her.

"Before changing the bylaws, Shelia Davis first changed PTSA procedure, making the PTSA president the only liaison between the PTSA and the School District Board, claiming information needs to come from only one source because of past contradictory requests that resulted in wasted money. The Board approved this with good intention. But now, every activity, whether it's purchasing school supply kits, the festival, teacher appreciation, even setting the school lunch menu, is awarded to the highest bidder, and the district's school board doesn't know."

There's a hush in the room, and I turn to see Shelia shrinking as if to hide behind the dads. She has a look of horror as I turn back to the board. "The highest bidder is twenty to fifty percent higher than the next highest bid. SCHOOL DREAMS is awarded one hundred percent of the contracts." I hear the room gasp. This is the bombshell Beth uncovered and made copies of before refiling everything. I wish she were here to see.

The vice president and the secretary wriggle in their chairs as if they're debating if they should stay loyal or abandon ship. I continue, "This company is a shell company. It was difficult to find out who owned it, but we did. This company is one hundred percent owned by Robert Davis, Shelia Davis's husband. And I don't think even he's aware of it." Here's when I hear murmuring behind me, which keeps me going. "It's possible this nepotism is a federal offense, but at a minimum, it's certainly an ethical conflict of interest. Your tax dollars are lining the Davises' pockets instead of going toward your child's education. She's been doing this for years. Do you remember the faulty light bulbs the fifth-graders sold to raise money for camp? And the expensive water bottle donations the school collected when the neighboring town had a water main break? They accepted only bottles from DREAM WATER for donation. And, the price was double of any other water. Both products were channeled through the Davises' company."

I continue without missing a beat. "Donations and fund-raising events are supposed to be safeguarded and used only for purposes related to the goals and objectives of the school." I'm pumped. She's fuming and pushes, but is unable break through the large dad chain.

"She's taking money too!" Shelia yells, and I pause and turn to face her. "Tattoo Dreams. Look it up," she says. Images of all the merchandise Shelia gave me, which litter my entire house, flash before my eyes. The little logo at the back says Tattoo Dreams. Then she yells, "She's using the school's money for personal benefit. Purchasing band equipment to use at her drug parties!"

It hits me. I see her at the party rental store. She has me sign an envelope from the County Clerk's office. I remember the name written above mine, Tattoo Dreams. Shelia put the company in my name, and is having the school support her son's hobby. She must see me at the front of the room putting two and two together, because then she yells, "Tell them you're lying. Take it all back."

And all I can think is that she's doing it again, trying to blackmail me, but now I see her as pathetic. I even feel sorry for her. And because I'm in front of an audience doing what a good mom would do, I keep going, not concerned with her threat. Once everything is out in the open, it'll be evident how I'm involved with Tattoo Dreams. I look at her directly in the eyes and shake my head, then begin to speak more quietly, making the audience listen more closely.

"There's more evidence of blackmail and abuse of power. I have affidavits. I'll start with mine, which details how Shelia Davis threatened me. The threat was recorded."

Gretta's the one who pressured me into contacting the lawyer after Phil mentioned it. I hesitated, not wanting to give them anything they might use against me. But it turns out she has a friend at the firm. It took about a week to get, and luckily, the threat was clear as day. I hold my phone up to the microphone, and the recording fills the room. Otherwise, it's dead silent.

My evidence is irrefutable. As the recording plays, I turn to see the reaction of those who didn't know our plan. All eyes are large, and most people are smiling. Several mouths are, what's the word? Agape? People record me and the reaction of others with their phone. When the evidence is finished playing, I continue, "This woman writes, updates, and passes her own bylaws. Shelia Davis is responsible for training, counseling, and providing information to parents and teachers. She oversees the activities of the school board and meets with the principal for status on current officers. She fills vacancies with people she's blackmailed, but only if they comply. If they don't, she ruins them. When she makes plans with the PTSA for the school year, anything that might raise a red flag, she takes care of herself instead of delegating, especially when it comes to the budget and treasury. She alone appoints or approves grade level reps and room reps. And why does she do it? Power and money. She alone funnels the taxpayers' money, your money, directly into her bank account."

I take another stack of paper from my folder. "I've got years of evidence on who ran each committee and where the trail of money went. The affidavits confirm and coincide with committee heads and those who were stripped from their post. Shelia Davis has too much power for one person. It has made it easy for her to skim from the top." Shelia gives me the stink eye, like she's planning some kind of revenge. But for now, the parents keep her well contained.

"I also demand Shelia Davis be forbidden to have any dealings with the Girls Soccer League, and that her husband resigns from his position as coach." I explain what prompted her threat to me. Then say, "I have an affidavit from the dad who found the girls abandoned on the soccer field and another from Doug Peterson, the Girls Soccer League chair, who she blackmailed in order to set up the teams unfairly so her daughter's team would win." I'm careful to only name key people and their position to make my case. I don't want it known how Shelia blackmailed them. Even though the documents will eventually be public record, I want to disrupt the lives of the people who helped me as little as possible.

It's weird that Shelia can dig up this much dirt on so many people in such a small community. But she's an instigator, a master at getting people to do things they're uncomfortable with, like Abby, but in a bad way. It's a wonder the suicide rate isn't higher than it is. Because, for most people, there's no way out.

I sum up my case by stating again what I want to happen, what the team wants to happen, so there is no question. "Shelia Davis needs to be relieved of all volunteer and appointed positions, and not be allowed to occupy them ever again."

"Noooo!" Shelia shouts, then collapses to the floor, but the dads help break her fall.

Everyone whistles and cheers. I hear someone shout to lock her up. The crowd is getting emotional, and so am I. Miss Clark smiles and I notice she's crying. *This* really affects me. I feel like I'm letting her out of a cage. I have fifty-seven affidavits, each a separate incident, each incident a live person that our plan will set free. And this doesn't take into account all the people Shelia got to that we don't know about. They'll be free as well.

I'm glad the dads are still surrounding Shelia. I hadn't thought about the reactions I'd get from the parents, and don't want this to become an actual lynching, so I try to bring some order. The only thing I can think of is to tell my story about why we should go easy on her.

I toss my notes aside and ad-lib, coming clean on what Shelia used to blackmail me with, specifically, Grace's dad. The room is quiet again. I know I said this was something Grace should decide, but I can't think of anything else that would so eloquently illustrate my point. I don't reveal what Shelia made me do, but I tell the room what it's been like for Grace to have a parent in jail, how I kept secrets from her and how she never had a father, how at times, she was an outcast for something her dad did. We both were.

After I tell my story, the only sound is the slightest movement of chairs, and a whimpering from Shelia, who is on her knees, with her face in her hands. I want to believe the people in this community understand, that Shelia understands. So I say, "We've been working with a lawyer and have all the evidence ready to submit to the School Board, or State Comptroller, if needed, if Shelia Davis doesn't adhere to our terms. It would trigger an immediate audit, and most likely a $500,000 fine, plus return of all the money she's skimmed from the school fund. Plus jail time." I pause, letting this sink in. For Shelia.

"It would be a huge media story," I say, then ask, "Do we want that for our community? Think about what that would do to our kids." But, I'm considering what's best for Katie. I don't want to say that. She may be able to hear from wherever Arjun took the girls. "Shelia needs to step down from everything, forever, and the school board can decide the best way to retrieve any money, if they want to. If Shelia doesn't comply, we'll give everything to the Comptroller." Phil, Gretta, Arjun, Abby, Beth, and I had all discussed it. We want to give Shelia a way out, for Katie's sake.

"That's blackmail!" Shelia shouts. She's still on her knees. I laugh, glad she sees the whole do unto others thing.

"I prefer to think of it as negotiation," I say. Then pause when I'm interrupted by the vice president, unsure if this is a good thing.

"Since the president is not seated, I declare myself acting president and we'll start the meeting. First order of business is to add an agenda to the top of our list. The removal of Shelia Davis as president."

Everyone cheers as I breathe a heavy sigh of relief. The rest of the board seconds, thirds, and fourths the motion, and Shelia is quickly voted out. "We'll set up a committee to weed out Shelia's hand in everything, starting with reverting all the bylaws she's changed, with the stipulation that everything is transparent and written. Also, the parents are to be aware and have a say in any new procedure," says the new acting president. The cheering erupts again.

"Ms. Hest, will you head up the new committee?" says the acting president, and I hear whoops from the crowd.

"Wow," I say. "Such an honor, but with my business and being a single parent, I won't be able to give you the time needed to right all these wrongs. I have to respectfully decline, but I'll assist in anything you need." It sounds like a good excuse, but the real reason is that I'm so emotionally drained, all I want to do is hide under my covers and forget any of this ever happened.

"I understand, but we can never let this happen again," says the new interim president. I'm thinking this woman may have been blackmailed by Shelia, as well. "I motion we ban Shelia Davis from campus until we figure out how to handle her. She will be allowed to pick up and drop off Katie, but she is not allowed to come inside or talk to anyone unless she's spoken to. We'll invite her in to see us when we are ready." There's more cheering.

"Shelia, please leave," says the new president, who steps into her position quite well. The cheers and clapping get louder as a group surrounds Shelia to escort her out. I'm still pumped just talking about it!

Once Shelia is outside, I gather my files and as I'm leaving the podium, I see Phil and Gretta in the back of the room. The way they stand. The way he touches her face, then brushes his palm down her arm to take her hand. I know their relationship isn't done. This may have brought them closer.

⌘

So, since yesterday's PTSA meeting, I'm getting phone calls from parents and teachers asking me to run for PTSA president, last night and this morning. They need to have a new election to fill the vacant post within thirty days. I'm told the VP stepping in is only interim. She doesn't want the job.

I invite Phil over around noon today. I don't have to wear my glasses anymore. The tension is gone. Ever since I saw the way he looked at Gretta. "I have no desire to be president," I tell him. "I wouldn't be good at it. You know who should run is Gretta. She knows what needs to be done, and because she was involved in exposing Shelia, everyone trusts her."

He's smiling, almost jumping up and down like a little kid. "She's already thinking about it. With Shelia out, she wants to move back. There isn't enough green space where she's living. Josh wants it too!"

Even though I saw this coming, I'm slightly disappointed. For me, not for Gretta.

"That's wonderful news," I say, and give him a hug. It's my goodbye hug. It wouldn't have worked out between us anyway, being neighbors and all. Now I'll be able to concentrate on Grace, and I'll have a new friend living right across the street. So, it's all good.

"So I bet life will be different for you with Shelia out of the picture," says Phil. His words are soft, and the way he looks at me reminds me of that first kiss. It's like he's saying goodbye to what might have been.

"I know," I tell him. It's all I can say. I see myself at the podium, being that good mom image I always wanted to be. But can I maintain it? It's hard to imagine a life without Shelia tormenting me, one where I'm not planning justice with my new friends. It seems kind of lonely.

Subject #57: Eddie - Session 42
Topic:

Beth

Whew! My mind is still all over the place. So, continuing from yesterday. When I'm home from the PTSA meeting, I call Beth to let her know Shelia is no longer head of anything. She says she's heard. I'm not surprised. Then I tell her about Tattoo Dreams, and how stupid I feel for not realizing what Shelia was doing.

"I know about that, too," she says. Then, "I felt weird mentioning it because I thought you knew. Shelia handed me paperwork for a sound equipment rental to file in her secret 'Shelia Only' box. I saw your name on it."

All this time she thought I was involved, and doesn't say anything. "You should have asked me," I say, imitating her tone. "You can ask me anything. Really."

"Okay. You too," she says. "I still don't want anyone to know

I was involved, but I can access any file to prove you're innocent."

"Great. Thanks," I say. "Let's meet for lunch, and this time, I'm not trying to get any info from you. Just lunch."

She agrees. Her voice sounds as if she's smiling.

⌘

Abby's left for London today. The thought that a doctor is involved keeps bothering me, so yesterday after the session, we confront Dr. Hawk about the drugs in the ceiling thing. He did tell Shelia he'd heard the kids hide drugs in the ceiling, but there were no plans with her to retrieve them. I believe him.

Anyway, Beth calls this morning and says, "Miss Clark is back at school and you'll never believe it. She dyed her hair purple!"

The thought of this makes me melt, even renders me speechless as I do my best to control my voice from becoming all emotional. She must have gone straight to the store from the PTSA meeting, bought the dye, and gave herself a new look last night. And this is from a woman who has kept the same look since the '70s, if she's even that old. I can just see her walking defiantly into the school, purple hair, head held high, without any hint of moisture glassing her eyes. It's a beautiful gesture and I am truly humbled. Instead of fucking up, I made someone's life better.

Beth tells me, "Last night after the meeting, Mr. Barneyak went through the stack of boxes in the storage room labeled SHELIA ONLY. DO NOT TOUCH."

So Shelia hid everything in plain sight. It's required that all paperwork be stored at the school. It's weird, it's the one rule she follows. I gather my composure. "Did you see anything more about me and Tattoo Dreams?" I ask.

"Yes, but don't worry," she says. "It's clear she set you up. The signatures don't match. I checked."

"What about the treasure chest?" I ask.

"It's back in Miss Clark's room," says Beth. "When I saw maintenance carrying it to the dumpster, I had them put it in storage instead."

I'm beginning to think that Beth is the real superhero in all of this.

⌘

After the call, I get back to sewing. I'm way behind, and I'm thinking about the fifty-seven wishes I made on the ladybugs. It's just now I realize I had fifty-seven affidavits *and* I'm Subject #57. Fifty-seven is my number. My wishes actually came true. I thought the Grace wish came true first, the one that she'd be okay with everything I piled on her, but it was actually mine that did. I just didn't see it. I wished for some guidance on what to do next. Remember?

I stop sewing. My mind is sort of on overload. That bug that clung to my sleeve was showing me what I needed to do. It's like the bug was me, and I was telling myself to go and move. Something about this advice feels right.

We've only lived here for like three and a half months, but I feel bitter about this place. I don't like the person I am here, and I don't like the mother I've become. This is where I found those words scribbled in green, "I hate mommy." I'll never forget the inexcusable things I did, and I want to put the memory away in a drawer, spread a hanky over it so I can't see it.

Grace needs to grow up somewhere without all this negative history, sort of like the childhood I had. (Minus my cousins.) It's always a risk when you move, and I've learned "Suburbia" doesn't encompass a single lifestyle. Each community is different, and remember, different is a good thing. You never know what it will be like until you live somewhere. The people in Rossville are fine, when Shelia isn't meddling in everyone's life. They just aren't my people. Also, it might be weird seeing Phil and Gretta together. Will that make me jealous? I don't want to be that person either. Watching them would remind me of my reflection in the window, and I want to be kind, inside and out, like Beth. Then, I'll be a good mother.

Subject #57: Eddie - Session 43
Topic:

Me
(More Accurately: My Superpower)

So, yesterday I said my mind was still on overload, but today things have slowed considerably now that Shelia isn't blackmailing me and Miss Clark is back at school, and I'm feeling kind of empty. I'm the topic for today, so I can find some restitution. For myself.

I've mentioned my superpower a couple of times, but never explained. It's why I've been struggling when this should have been easy. I feel silly now about the proclamation of even having a superpower. Anyway, here's the story.

Granny discovered my superpower at a family gathering when the cousins were being extra hard on me. She was looking out the window and could see something special come down from the heavens, like the transport beam in *Star Trek*. The beam landed on me and filled me with this power. I didn't even know it happened, and no one else saw it. It was like a miracle that she did.

So, what's the power? *I can be confronted with any horrible or unjust situation, and I have the power to choose, choose how I react.* That's it. She came outside and explained everything. Maybe she was only trying to teach me something. You know, not respond to evil by being evil. Some people may not think the power to do this is super, but they're wrong.

Something clearly was off with me and my power because before implementing our big plan, I chose how to react, but no one would categorize what I did as super.

Before acquiring my superpower, I'd get so tired of hearing "You're too sensitive" or "They're just playing with you." It's what my Aunt Donna would say, the Cs' mom. And teachers said it, too. But saying someone's too sensitive just makes it worse. After Granny tells me about my superpower, in my mind, I'm dodging bullets, my wrist deflecting them, sending them through the air like I'm Wonder Woman. Deflecting the unkind. Deflecting the bullies. Deflecting the urge to lower myself to their level. Pew. Pew. Pew. Clearly a power. Right?

Simply knowing I had it made the cousins' jests less effective, so I knew their comments weren't real. My powers gave me confidence to do what I wanted in life, made me unafraid to be different. Although I started using them right away, this courage didn't kick in immediately for everything. It was more like a gradual mastering.

Granny used to whisper in my ear, "Dare to be different."

She'd be proud of me in that respect. I know I'm different, especially in my family. But it took some practice. I had to see what felt right for me. And the easiest way to do this was through my appearance. It's something I can immediately change and everyone can see. Mom thinks I started the whole multicolored-hair/tattoo trend, which I began playing with when I was in high school. She never mentions the multiple piercings. And I did start this trend, at least in our neighborhood.

But, Psycho Soccer Mom was shooting bullets at me so fast, I couldn't keep up. It's like she's my kryptonite. I was so overwhelmed, I forgot I had the power to choose, to say no.

Anyway, that's me. Now you know everything. Well, maybe.

Subject #57: Eddie - Session 44
Topic:

Grace
(and Me, and Mom, and Granny)

It's been two weeks since I've been here and during that time I've been trying to make some sense out of everything that's happened. I don't know, maybe this whole monologuing thing to myself is working because I find myself doing it at home, too. Regarding my superpower, what it doesn't do, I've recently figured, is enable me to choose wisely. That's up to me, and comes from experience.

Anyway, after thinking about it, my mother was a good mother after all. She was always there for me and loved me no matter what I did, which I'm sure was hard. Maybe that's all that's required to be a good mom—be there, love, and support.

But after considering, there's more to it than that. Unconditional love and support goes without saying. I have to be proactive to be a good mom.

Here it is, in order. First, keep Grace safe. But, be rational about it. Safe without forgetting what's right and wrong. Second, keep her healthy: proper food, shelter, take her to the doctor if she's sick, things like that. Third, teach her how to take care of herself, which evidently I've been doing pretty well without realizing. And that's it. It only takes three things to be a good mother. I need to be careful on that first one. That's the one that seems to bite me.

So the Friday after the PTSA meeting is when the maybe happens, the one I mentioned at the end of last session. I'm sewing, when it dawns on me. After years of trying to get away, I realize the safest place for Grace to be is home. When Grace gets back from school, I ask, "How would you feel about leaving your current school and Katie?" She gets the happiest look on her face, one I haven't seen in a long while.

"The people here are kind of weird," she says, and like I said earlier, she transitions well. But then, she isn't moving to another new place. I'll be taking her to someplace familiar; she's going home. We both are.

We get in the car, but don't quite make it to Mom's. Instead, we drive around the side streets searching for a for sale sign. Grace loves the idea of living close to her grandmother. She remembers living here and her friends from kindergarten. She loves the playground at the elementary school. We sometimes go there when visiting Mom. It's my old playground, too. It still has the tether ball pole where me and Abby became blood sisters for life.

As we drive, it gets more depressing. I'm not seeing anything for sale. People tend to move in the summer, and now that we're a couple months into the school year, nothing's available. I give up, at least for today, and we head toward Mom's.

I'm almost to her house when Grace yells, "Stop!" It's a *Miracle on 34th Street* moment. There's a house for sale across the street, two houses down from Mom's. It's the Delaneys' house, and I sort of remember Mom mentioning they were moving to Arizona. I used to babysit their two kids.

When we knock on the door, I notice the address: 5757. Mrs. Delaney remembers me, and shows us around. Their furniture has been moved, so the house is empty, and they've done a lot of updating. It looks nothing like Mom's house, even though they were probably built around the same time. Grace likes it. So do I. It's a little bigger than our current house, and would be a sideways move financially. It's farther from the city, so we'd get something nicer for our money.

After leaving the Delaneys', I tell Grace it's up to her whether we stay where we are or move. I'm not sure if her friendship with Katie is enough to keep her there, but I don't want to assume anything. I've made some poor choices. Her opinion is worth considering.

"I want to move here," she says. It does and doesn't surprise me. Her grandmom's here. She understands how important family is. The ones who treat you well, anyway. Grace's current school was probably tougher on her than I know, emotionally, not academically. We go back to the Delaneys' and tell them we'll take it.

Next, we go visit Mom. I let Grace tell her the news. Grace is so excited that I feel bad about the last move. Mom hugs Grace. I can tell she's happy we're going to be neighbors. While Grace tells her about the new house, I get a call from the Delaneys' realtor.

⌘

I manage the financing, especially because I'll get more than what I paid for the old house. With Shelia out of the picture, it's already a better place to live. Word gets out fast. But, it's not a better place for us. We belong here.

When we move into the new house, there's a brand-new bicycle in the living room with a big pink bow. The Delaneys. They let us move in for free until the final paperwork goes through.

My move was easy. I hadn't unpacked a lot of boxes when we moved to Rossville. Maybe I knew what was coming. I got the guys from Dylan's frat house to help, plus Arjun and Phil. People will do a lot for you if you give them pizza and beer. All I do is rent the U-Haul. Beth helps me and Grace unpack. She's great at organizing the kitchen, and we've become good friends. She'll never replace Abby, but she's become just as important. I'm hoping some of her kindness rubs off on me.

Once the pizza and beer are gone, everyone leaves except Arjun and Phil. Grace is in her new room, and Arjun walks around the house, calculating the space. I'm alone with Phil for the first time since his visit right after the PTSA meeting. It feels like a lifetime ago because so much has happened, when it's only been about a month. He adjusts boxes and furniture, that don't need adjusting, so it seems there's something he wants to say and doesn't know how.

"So," I say. "Have Gretta and Josh moved back in with you yet?" He stops his fidgeting and flashes me a quizzical look.

"What? Oh God, no. She's not moving in with me; she's getting her own place. I think she's found one. Is that what you thought?" His face flushes, and he has this smile, like something suddenly makes sense.

"Well, ya," I say. "You said she was moving back. What else should I think?" I wonder if I was hasty in my decision to flee, then remember why I did.

"We're not getting back together," he says it as a finite statement, and I can't help but think about that first kiss. Our only kiss. It's good we're not neighbors.

Arjun comes back to the room. "This house is nicely laid out for the amount of square footage. It feels like you have extra space." He's right. The garage is finished out nicely, unlike the old house. It's like an extra room, and it's heated. Who heats their garage? I think it was Mr. Delaney's man cave. Now, it's my workroom. I expect my business to be slow until I can tap into this new area. It's fine. It will give me time to reflect on what it means to be a good mom, plus setting a good example by being kind to others.

By the end of move-in day, empty boxes are all over the lawn. I'm outside saying goodbye to Arjun and Phil, and I'm tired. Arjun drives away, but Phil dawdles.

"Why aren't you wearing your glasses?" he says. "I like them. They're sexy." He touches my arm. His message is strong. My mother was wrong; the glasses don't work, and I'm a little flustered. But, the moment is interrupted by an approaching neighbor. "See you soon," he says, and touches my face gently before getting into his car.

The neighbor walks closer as Phil drives away, and I turn to the boxes on the lawn, thinking I'm going to get yelled at for the mess, something like Phil's reaction, no, Tracksuit Man's reaction before we knew each other. "I better get these up," I say before he can comment. "Don't want the homeowners' association to get upset with me." Maybe he's the neighborhood's Gladys.

"No worries," he says. "We don't control how people live."

He smiles and I know instantly Grace and I made a good choice.

⌘

Right away, we're deeply involved in our new lives. Grace is settled in school and has rekindled her kindergarten friendships. Some friends even live in the neighborhood. It also turns out that there's a lot of work here for me. I'd forgotten this was why I got my business started so quickly. I'm so busy, I don't have time to dye my hair back to purple or another color that matches my mood. And right now, I'm not sure what that color would be. When I'm busy working, Grace hops on her bike and rides to her grandmom's. It feels like we've lived here for longer than a week.

A few days after the move, Arjun tells me he isn't happy at the communal frat house. There's too much noise and not enough privacy. I flashback to his assessing my space when he helped me move in. "Why didn't you say something sooner?" I ask. I love the idea for him to move in with us. It will help pay the bills, and I can use the extra money to buy Grace a new bed and proper furniture for the rest of the house. He's the closest thing to a father Grace has ever had. Mom likes him too. I'm happy, but then I think about the last ladybug wish I made for Arjun, so I know he won't stay with us for long. My ladybug wishes seem to come true.

⌘

Mom has the entire family over for Thanksgiving dinner, and I begin the short walk. Her sister Donna and Uncle Bob have moved to Florida, so it's only the Cousins and their families. Grace is already there, and being the eldest grandchild, happily babysits the younger ones. Arjun will come when he gets home from work. He's probably the only one at his office working on Thanksgiving. Walking these sidewalks feels safe, like the safety of my childhood, and I think, *this* is what it feels like to be a good mom.

As I walk, I realize I was wrong when I said I have two

secrets. I had three. Grace's dad. I'm relieved that isn't a secret anymore. It feels so good to be free of it, I consider letting the other two loose on the family, sort of a gift to myself.

When I get to Mom's, she's bragging about my beautiful house, and how close we are. Everyone knows I have a new man living with me. They ask me about the house, but they're more interested in the enigma called Arjun. When he arrives, Tiffany and Stephanie don't hide their shock. They think he's gorgeous, and he is. They think we're a couple, and Arjun, Grace, or I don't tell them any different. When they ask Arjun about his work, they're impressed. There isn't anything they can tease me about now. Except...

Now is as good of time as any. So while everyone is sitting in the living room with a paper plate on their lap, I raise my hands and get their attention. "I have a confession to make," I say. Maybe it's this whole talking things out in the open thing that gives me the confidence to confront them, kindly confront them. I've learned to behave myself. I wink at Grace, put my plate down, and stand. "Well, actually two."

I tell them what my name means, and then about my superpower. The whole thing comes across as some kind of skit, entertaining. I'm in the spotlight, which is where I like to be. Right? Where I never was with my family as a child. That's fine if they're laughing. For me, it's a cleansing. They think the name thing is funny, but when they laugh and start to tease, my hot guy gives them a disapproving look and they stop. Here's where I realize I'd been behaving like my cousins by doling out unkind nicknames based on first my impression. That will stop. We all know there's nothing in a name; take Tracksuit Man for example. The good thing is, since I brought the name thing up, I control it.

When I tell them about my superpower, they think it's a pretty cool way of looking at life. And it is. That comes from Granny. She looked at things in a way that benefited her. I tell them how I used my power to make the choice to move near my mommy. I give Mom a kiss. She blushes; she likes I call her that. I never do. I should. The word *mommy* is much more emotional than *mom*. Maybe that's why seeing it in green in the scrapbook was so painful. (By the way, Katie wrote it.) After my standup, they don't think I'm uncool anymore, but consider me spiritual. For the first time, they ask me about my tattoos and what they mean.

⌘

Arjun pulls me aside and presents me with a box he brought with him when he came to Mom's. The Cousins discreetly watch us. Even before I open the box, I know what it is. His necklace. He whispers, "We aren't a couple, and at some point we will find an appropriate mate, but you are my soulmate, or more accurately, my soul-friend."

When he does this, I'm not sure how to respond. Giving this particular necklace to someone is a huge deal. "Is this a show for my family?" I ask. He knows the background there.

"No," he says. "It's tradition to give it with the family around.

I want you to accept it and keep it forever. I don't plan on getting married again."

"I know you don't consider me in that way. Are you sure you want to be bound to me?" I ask. "I'm pretty much a hot mess."

"No, Eddie, you are perfect. You've helped me see that it's okay to be myself, and for that, I am forever grateful." Then he says, "I want to go home." Darn that ladybug. He must see I'm speechless, so he says, "Don't worry. I don't plan on leaving for several months."

Knowing he is breaking all the rules of his culture by giving me this necklace (I'm not his wife), I see in his eyes he wants to hold on to what we have together, but he also wants to go home, back to his family, back to his culture. "How about I hold on to it for you. If ever you want it back, just let me know," I say, holding back tears.

I wonder if me moving near my mom gives him the idea. I'm both happy and sad at this news. I put his necklace on and glance at Tiffany and Stephanie. They're smiling. And while I'm sure they have no clue to the significance of the necklace, they know it's special.

I give Arjun a hug, then say "I'll be right back." I run home to grab something.

⌘

When I return, Tiffany and Stephanie have surrounded Arjun and are grilling him. I take him aside, mid-sentence, and offer him a gift. He'll recognize the box too, and stands completely still as I take Grandmom's necklace from the velvet and slide it over his head. It doesn't carry the significance the necklace he gave to me has, but to me, Grandmom's necklace is just as special. Tears form as he takes the two dangling pearl drops and holds them to his heart, then tucks them under his shirt. We hug again. And as I turn back to the family, Grace has come inside and sees the whole thing. Even though it's slated to be hers, she'll be happy with the necklace's new owner. It's still in our family. Tiffany and Stephanie are watching. Mom just stands and smiles. I know they all recognize what Arjun has laid against his skin.

"I'm happy for you," I say. "You *should* see your family. And I'll be fine. Beth can move in. She needs a nicer place to live, and it will help both of us money wise."

He says, "That's a great idea."

I've just told my family the two secrets I've been hiding, but now I have two more. The first, Arjun isn't my boyfriend, and will soon move away. But, maybe secrets are a part of life, and they're important because you share them with someone special.

⌘

"I can't believe you've done so well for yourself," whispers Stephanie, meaning Arjun. It's a snitty remark that comes when everyone's getting ready to leave, as if whatever man's at my side determines my success. But the remark doesn't bother me. I don't have to tell them Arjun is gay. His sex life isn't their business. But, him not being my boyfriend brings me to my second new secret. Phil.

I'm facing the people who had made me feel bad about myself for so many years, but they've also helped make me the person I am today. Mom's in this group, although she didn't make me feel bad, it's just I never understood her. But I'm trying. She wasn't the mom I thought she should be. But maybe she was the mom I needed.

Anyway, after Stephanie's remark, I'm thinking of Phil and his comment about my glasses. Using them as a protective shield clearly didn't work. But then, maybe I misunderstood what Mom's little saying actually meant. Maybe the glasses were a good thing. You know, girls wear them so they're not distracted from what's important, so they can focus on things like getting a good education or being a good mom. That's pretty deep coming from my mother. So, my advice to every girl is, put on your glasses. Anyway, I'm pretty sure I've become that good mom image I've always wanted to be. I don't need glasses right now.

⌘

So I'm declaring this to be my last session, and it feels like it's been a long one. I didn't make it the full year, but I'll still take that survey. Since I've moved, the lab is just too far away. And anyway, more importantly, *I've* moved on. I realize I have the power to choose what *I* do, but not what anyone else does. Hearing me say everything out loud has been helpful.

I'm coming out of these sessions a better person, and if I'm rational about things, I'll make good choices. Then, I'll be a good mom. No wait. I already am.

⌘

And by the way, since I'm a good mom, I think I deserve a little fun. Right? The fun I've chosen wears a tracksuit, well sometimes. I'm gonna keep the relationship with Arjun a secret, at least until he leaves, but secret number two? I don't care who knows about it.

Stop Recording.

CATHERINE CASTORO

<u>ACKNOWLEDGMENTS</u>

A big THANK YOU to...

My friends and family, whose understanding, encouragement, and support helped me realize my dream of publishing my first novel.

South Austin Writers Critique Group: Gogi Hale, Amélie Corner, Chris Kerns, Britta Jensen, Flor Salcedo, Charlie Reed, Gail Guernsey, Mary Etheredge, Ursula Pike, Patsy Stierna, Sandra Vasquez, Karen Bateman Walters, and others. Austin Christian Writers: Zack Russell and Elisabeth Wheatley. Writers' League of Texas, Richard Santos. University of Oxford Department for Continuing Education: Jenn Dunn, Amal Chatterjee, Elizabeth Garner. Jericho Writers. My Editors: Caroline Hulse, Kate Rizzo, Sandra Ogle. Beta Readers: Maureen Turner Carey, Sherry Fields, Ann Strand, Shelley Friend, Sindhu Nellibandla, Melanie Kinslow, Kaye Dunn. Austin Indie Author Support Group. Terrie Dreyfus and Doug Ciskowski for audiobook coaching.

And especially: Mike Castoro, Michael Castoro, Sadie Castoro, and Furgus.

And mostly, thank you reader, for giving me a chance.

326

TOPICS FOR READING GROUP DISCUSSION:
(SPOILER ALERT!)

1. Eddie tells her story while in therapy sessions. Why do you think the author chose to do this?

2. Eddie's grandmom tells her to "Dare to be Different." Does this affect the way she lives her life? Does it help or hinder her? Why?

3. Eddie gives nicknames to people she doesn't get along with. Why do you think she does this? Why doesn't she give one to Beth?

4. When Phil comes over the first time to apologize, Eddie notices he's wearing jeans. Why is this important?

5. Do you think Eddie's view of herself as an outsider is self imposed? Why?

6. How is Eddie's relationship with her daughter different from her relationship with her mother? Her gran? Why?

7. When Eddie dyes her hair brown and wears a conservative skirt and blouse, she calls it a uniform. Do you think her regular everyday style is a uniform as well? Do you think she thinks it is? Why?

8. Eddie's grandmom tells her she has a superpower, the power to choose. Is this helpful? Why do you think?

9. Eddie thinks there are three things needed to be a good mom, plus unconditional love. Do you agree? Why?

10. Is Eddie's battle actually with suburbia or herself? Discuss.

11. What are your favorite Eddie moments? Your favorite takeaways from the book?

12. What messages do you think the author was trying to convey?

<u>AUTHOR'S NOTE</u>

I appreciate you giving an unknown author's work a chance. Indie authors face many challenges in promoting their books without the support of a major publisher.

If you love books, and have ever lived in a place where the neighbors are a little crazy, then you are an honorary member of The Eddie Hest Ground Team. As a member, I ask if you would help spread the word about *Eddie Hest vs. Suburbia*. Tell your friends and please leave a review on Amazon and Goodreads. Additionally, you can make a request for the book at your library, either in hard copy, ebook, or audiobook. I'm extending a warm welcome to you to join Team Eddie and help spread the word by writing a review. To make the review process as easy as possible, scan the QR code below to be directed to a link to the review site. A few words would be greatly appreciated!

I'd like keep in touch and ask that you subscribe to my mailing list. You'll receive members-only promotions and freebies, updates on events, and information on upcoming novels, but not too often. We all get way too many emails. Scan the same QR code on the previous page to join the mailing list, and thank you, dear reader! You are truly valued and cherished!

All the best!

Catherine Castoro

CATHERINE CASTORO

ABOUT THE AUTHOR

Catherine Castoro is the author of three
children's books under the pen name
Catie Cat. She enjoys hiking, yoga, painting,
music, traveling, and gardening. Born in the
suburbs of Detroit, she has two grown
children and lives with her husband and
Lakeland Terrier in Austin, Texas.
Eddie Hest vs. Suburbia
is her debut novel.

Visit Catherine at catherinecastoro.com